Also available from

Kasey Michaels

and HQN Books

And coming in April 2009

**A Sunshine Girls Romantic Caper
*The Beckets of Romney Marsh

Kasey Michaels

Mischief becomes her

HQN™

ISBN-13: 978-0-373-77318-3
ISBN-10:   0-373-77318-8

MISCHIEF BECOMES HER

www.HQNBooks.com

Printed in U.S.A.

Dear Reader,

When you're the baby of the family, Daddy's Little Princess, you might grow up with certain assumptions. For Jessica Sunshine, one of those beliefs is that Daddy can do no wrong. Her older sisters, Jolie and Jade, most definitely mourned their father's unexpected death, but Jessica was devastated on so many levels. Illusions left over from childhood were shattered cruelly when she learned that Teddy Sunshine wasn't only gone, but was accused of murdering a Philadelphia mayoral candidate's wife before taking his own life.

Jessica, now a cable news journalist, joins her sisters in their search for the truth—for surely what the world believes of Teddy Sunshine cannot be the truth. She enlists the reluctant aid of police lieutenant Matt Denby as she goes on a crusade to solve old crimes and new, never doubting her father's innocence.

What Jolie Sunshine learned in *Dial M for Mischief* Jessica adds to in *Mischief Becomes Her*, paving the way for Jade Sunshine to fit in the last, potentially damning pieces in *Mischief 24/7*. Only then can they travel to England in the next novel, to help the men they love discover the last lingering secret of the Becket family of Romney Marsh—a priceless but cursed emerald known as The Empress.

But for now, sit back and watch as Jessica Sunshine takes crime-solving to a whole new level, daring any mischief, breaking rules and making up her own as she goes along, while finding more startling pieces to the complicated puzzle that surrounds Teddy's death.

Because Jessica is Daddy's Little Princess, she's a woman on a mission, and nobody had better get in her way! Did you hear that, Matt?

Enjoy!

Kasey Michaels

Mischief becomes her

To Kathy Fry and Joann Gartner
Thanks for keeping the family fed!

CHAPTER ONE

"JESS? HEADS UP there, kiddo. We're back to you in five…" Kevin Mulhally held up his right hand and went silent for the rest of the count. *Four, three, two, one…*

Jessica Sunshine, her professional stone face in place, waited a single heartbeat after the producer pointed a finger at her and then smiled into the camera as if delighted to see her cable TV audience.

"And welcome back," she said smoothly, pushing a lock of blond hair behind her ear. "Again, tonight's special live segment of *The Sunshine Report* is devoted to this reporter's personal tragedy—the loss of my father, retired police detective Theodore Sunshine, and the accusation that he murdered the wife of front-running Philadelphia mayoral candidate Joshua Brainard before taking his own life. And I'm here to tell you, folks, that accusation's a bunch of horse hockey pucks."

Jessica ignored the audible intake of breath from her sister Jolie, seated in the only other chair on the small carpeted dais that looked good on TV but was really threadbare in spots and still held a stain caused by Chickpea the Clown when he'd lost his three-martini lunch during his interview with her last month. Confront a guy in white-face with photographs of him buying a nickel bag behind the Dumpster outside the studio while filming a week's worth of his popular kiddie show and you just don't know what will happen.

"That sound you just heard," Jessica continued, "was that of my big sister, Hollywood star and general all-round good person, Jolie Sunshine, being horrified by her baby sister yet again, showing that those birth-order studies are true—the baby of the family is often the most prone to making waves. I don't know why they're shocked, either striving middle child Jolie or our perfect firstborn sister, Jade. I mean, really folks, you're not shocked, right? And you've only known me for two years. They've known me forever. Jolie," she said, swiveling her chair to face her sister, certain the camera would follow her, "do you disagree with anything I said?"

Jolie Sunshine—slim, tall, brunette and looking coolly beautiful and at ease in front of the camera—tipped her head to one side. "You mean, am I shocked? Hardly. Not when I spent several years answering the phone only to be asked if the mouth was at home."

Jessica laughed as she tossed back her hair once

more. Jessica's greatest on-air assets were her spectacular good looks—a face and body that could have helped her if, like Jolie, she had set her sights on Hollywood. Luckily, as she pursued a career in television journalism, she also brought along a sharp-as-tacks brain and more guts than most of the men in her professional orbit.

She just had never embraced the politics of news reporting, and didn't suffer fools gladly, which was why she was only tonight coming off a two-week on-air suspension for asking the wrong question of one of the targets of her always penetrating interviews. In fact, if she hadn't been able to deliver Jolie for her show, that suspension might have become permanent.

But, to Jessica, that was only a piddling little technicality, and she wasn't about to change the way she worked… Or did her bosses really think she should have been happy being the weekend weather girl she'd been before she got her own show? With a last name like Sunshine, that gig had been pretty much a joke, anyway.

"The mouth? Ouch! Haven't heard that one in a while. Gee, thanks, sis. Now I suppose I'm going to have to live that nickname down all over again." As quickly as she had laughed, Jessica sobered. "Okay, that was fun, a bit of tension-easing, I guess you'd say. But let's get back to the reason you're here tonight, Jolie, the reason we're both here. Do you mind if I give a quick recap for anyone who might just be joining us?"

Jolie spread her hands in the graceful, eloquent way that kept every eye riveted on her when she was up on the screen at the local multiplex. "Go for it."

Jessica turned once more to look intently into the camera, her huge brown eyes reaching beyond the lens to make everyone munching corn chips while watching at home sat up and paid attention, knowing she was speaking directly to them.

She took a steadying breath as she collected her thoughts, and then went for it.

"When Teddy died, we all were devastated. But our grief turned to anger when he was denied the departmental funeral he so deserved, when his name was connected to the murder of Melodie Brainard. You see, before he was injured on the job and retired to head up the Sunshine Detective Agency with our sister Jade, Teddy had been one of Philadelphia's finest for close to thirty years. He'd earned his detective's shield and worked the homicide table, and had one of the highest clearance rates in the department—meaning, he took a lot of killers off the streets. He was good at what he did. He was damn good."

"Steady, Jess," Jolie whispered, and Jessica took hold of her sister's hand as the camera panned back to show the gesture. Good television; this was good television. Cable television, where a reporter could bend the rules when her name headlined the show. The part of Jessica that operated for the public knew that. The rest of her could have a good cry later, once she was alone.

For now, she'd play the camera.

"Okay, that's the recap. Now on to what we're here about tonight. Teddy was so good, so dedicated to bringing criminals to justice, that he continued to investigate cold cases even after he left the force, all of them about a dozen years old, cases he had worked on and had not solved. Those cases, those victims, ate at him, haunted him, and he longed to give them justice. Isn't that right, Jolie?"

"Our father always believed he stood for the victims, yes. And for their families, who wanted closure. Deserved closure."

"Right. He was working on four cold cases in the weeks before he died. We believe what Teddy learned about one of those cases is the reason he was murdered. Yes, murdered, with that murder made to look like a suicide. Tonight, I'm happy to report that Jolie Sunshine and her fiancé, Samuel Becket, have brought one of those cold cases to a conclusion. We'll talk more about what has been called the case of the Vanishing Bride in our next segment, but for now I want to tell you about the other three cases we're currently working."

She squeezed Jolie's hand. "Yes, that's what I

said. The cases *we're* working. Jade, Jolie and I are picking up the pieces Teddy left behind, and we *will* solve these cases. We *will* find answers. We will clear our father's name. But we need your help. We've prepared a quick summary listing of the cases we're working on, and I ask that you also pay attention to the phone number that's been scrolling along the bottom of the screen the whole time I've been sitting here bending your ears. Kevin? Are the cases up now? Good man, thank you."

Jessica looked at a monitor to the left of the dais to check the order of the cases on the screen.

"Ah, I like the way you handled that graphic, Kevin, thank you. See the line through the Vanishing Bride case, folks? That's our solved case Jolie will tell you about shortly. It's quite a story! Next up is the Fishtown Strangler. I'm working that one," she said, allowing some pride into her voice. "Six women were raped and strangled in the Fishtown area of Philadelphia twelve years ago and the case remains open. No big surprise there, as the victims were all ladies of the evening, shall we say, and public interest in such cases dies in a hurry. It shouldn't. Murder is murder."

"No humans involved," Jolie interjected quietly. "Isn't that what you heard such cases are considered by so many, and how the victims are relegated to persons of no worth? I hate that. Everything about us that is human should hate that."

Jessica wanted to hug her sister. "That's why I'm so determined to solve this case, Jolie. *Everyone* counts. Next up is a very sad case, that of the senseless shooting death of a well-known Scholar Athlete, Terrell Johnson. Terrell's body was found on an inner-city Philadelphia basketball court, a bullet in his head. Again, no suspects. And, finally, a story that captured not only the heart of Philadelphia but of the entire country, the case of the Baby in the Dumpster. On your screen now is a forensic artist's computer generated projection of what that precious boy would have looked like today had his life not been taken, his little body tossed into a Dumpster like someone's unwanted garbage. God, that one gets to me. They all get to me."

Jessica's eyes were moist as she looked at the computer image and she didn't bother hiding her emotional response when the red light reappeared on the camera drawn up close to her. "We're not superheroes, my sisters and me. We're not vigilantes, and we're not crusaders. What we are, my friends, is hurting, what we will continue to be until Teddy's name is cleared is mad as hell. And what we're not going to do is quit. Right, Jolie?"

"Right, Jessica," Jolie said, looking into the camera. "Our father is a victim, and like him, we're determined to stand for the victim."

"Good one, Jolie. So, my friends, my loyal viewers,

again I'm asking for your help. Something in one of these cases led to Teddy Sunshine's murder. He scraped a nerve somewhere and paid with his life. We're asking you to contact us through that phone number still crawling by at the bottom of the screen. You can remain anonymous if you wish. Just call us and, as the saying goes, leave a message at the beep. One of the Sunshine Girls—Jolie, Jade or myself—will personally return your call, I promise."

She paused, closed her eyes for a count of three, and then looked once more into the camera. She thought she could feel her skin drawing tight across her cheekbones as she spoke from the depths of her soul. "And you. You out there, the person who framed Teddy and then murdered him to protect your own crime. Don't rest, don't sleep. Don't relax for a moment. Because we're coming for you. You can depend on it."

Jessica mentally counted to three yet again, her gaze intent on the camera lens, before ending quickly as she slowly turned her head away from the camera in her signature go-to-break move. "We'll be back in two minutes for more of my exclusive interview with Jolie Sunshine."

Jessica kept her profile to the camera until Ben called out, "And we're clear! Great, Jess, just terrific."

"Sure, he thinks so," Jolie said, sighing. "He's thinking great TV. I'm thinking—and I know everyone else is thinking—why not just paint huge red-and-white targets on our backs? Cripes, Jess, working on the assumption, of course, that we're right about this, that you just invited Teddy's killer to come gunning for us, like we're looking for some shoot-out in the O.K. Corral, or something. You didn't tell me you were going to get so personal. You certainly didn't tell me you were setting up some sort of hot line so that anyone who wants to can kill time calling us to…well, I don't know what sort of calls we're going to get, but I'm not very hopeful any of them will mean anything. And with me leaving for the Coast with Sam tonight, and then for Ireland in two weeks? We'll be filming on-site for at least two months. I won't even be here to help."

"Relax, big sister, nobody's going to come *gunning* for us," Jessica assured her. "That only happens in bad movies. Besides, now that we've declared ourselves, if any of us shows up dead, the police will know we were onto something."

"Gosh, and that would prove we were right, wouldn't it? How brilliant. Why didn't I think of that?" Jolie said, rolling her eyes. *"Are you nuts?"*

Jessica tilted up her chin as Marge the makeup artist patted some color onto her cheeks. "I think the jury's still out on that one. When are you and Sam taking off? Do you have time for a quick dinner with Matt and me once this is over? I'm really jazzed, and being jazzed always makes me hungry."

"Breathing makes you hungry," groused the woman on a perpetual diet for the cameras. "And no, we're going straight from here to the airport. Sam's having a basket of something delivered to the plane from one of his favorite restaurants. Probably something delicious and fattening, as he's always pushing at me to eat. I have a publicity interview tomorrow night I can't get out of, unfortunately. And don't change the subject. Do you really think going public like this is going to help?"

"One minute, Jess," Kevin warned her. "But first tell me something, okay? I get the old cases, those cold cases your dad was working on when he died. But how does Melodie Brainard fit in here? You know, the one they said your dad strangled?"

"And there's the problem. She doesn't fit," Jolie told him quietly as Jessica pursed her lips for a quick reapplication of lip gloss. "Does she, Jess?"

"Sure, she does. And we'll figure out how one of these days. Don't ask too many questions, Kevin," Jessica told him with a bravado she didn't feel. "Just be glad I could pull Joshua Brainard's name into the telecast, okay? We're going to get a lot of follow-up with this one—sex, murder, politics, the big three. Cable *and* network, at least in the tri-state area. So don't look gift horses in the snout. Ready, Jolie?

Now, what was the name of your new movie, again? What's a sister for, if she can't give her sister a plug? I mean, that is how I got you to do this interview in the first place."

"In a minute. Uh, Jess? Did you happen to look over there, to where Matt's standing?" Jolie asked quietly, her hand held over the small mike clipped to her blouse. "No, don't look. Lord, his face is red. I think he's about to explode."

Jessica kept her back firmly turned to Philadelphia homicide detective Lieutenant Matthew Denby, who had volunteered to help them with Teddy's cold cases and who had, against her wishes, put himself in the role of her partner and protector. "Good. Then maybe he'll go away, stop dogging my every footstep and second-guessing my every idea."

"Jess, your mike's live," Jolie whispered, shaking her head. "He heard you."

"Oops," Jessica said, grinning, as she'd known darn well Matt would hear her. "Did I also mention that he has a lousy attitude about the media, even for a cop, that he has absolutely no sense of humor, and that he's old as dirt and is going to have a coronary any day now if the empty fast-food bags in his Jeep are all his?"

"No, you hadn't mentioned any of that," Jolie said dully, removing her hand from her mike. "Where's Sam? Man, all of a sudden our plane can't take off soon enough…"

"SORRY, BUT I HAD TO GO outside to take that call. So," Sam Becket whispered, rejoining Matt in a dark corner of the large studio as the interview went on thirty feet away, "what did I miss?"

"Trust me, you don't want to know," Matt told him, not taking his gaze, his fairly hot gaze, off Jessica's back. "But if I kill her, there's not a jury in this world that would convict me."

"Uh-oh. Don't tell me she brought your name into this. She promised not to get you in trouble."

"Oh no, she didn't do that. As far as the department is concerned, I'm still on vacation, and nobody knows I'm helping you guys. I liked Teddy, I really did. I respected him, both as a cop and as a man. But, damn, how did he let Jessica grow up to be so…so…"

"Independent…impulsive…smart-mouthed… *gorgeous?*" Sam offered, grinning.

"Yeah, that. All of it," Matt admitted, shoving his hands into the pockets of his khaki slacks. "I thought I was getting used to her after these last few days, but she just topped herself. She set up a hot line for tips on the cold cases. Right after she dared the killer to try to stop them from uncovering his or her identity. And you know what, Sam?" he asked, turning to look at Jolie's fiancé and his new friend. "She has no freaking idea what a disaster she just unleashed on all of us. None. Or, worse, she does, and she doesn't care."

"My vote is for the latter," Sam told him, sighing

as he looked toward Jolie. "I'm glad I offered my house to the girls for the duration. If you want, you're welcome to stay there, too, and save yourself running back and forth every time Jess decides it's time to dress up like a hooker and do a little investigating on some seedy street corner at midnight."

Matt actually felt embarrassed color run up into his cheeks. He didn't want to know if that embarrassment was for Jessica, who already had pulled that potentially dangerous stunt, or for himself, as he was pretty sure he'd see the way she'd looked in her short skirt and plunging blouse in his dreams for a long time.

"She promised not to do that again. Although I have to tell you, she makes a damn good-looking hooker. The funny thing is, we actually got a call from one of the working girls she met that night. We've now got another address on Tarin White, the second-to-last victim. I hate telling Jess, though, because she's going to gloat."

"Count on it. Look, Matt, I've got the perimeter walls, the Bear Man and his wrestling pals at the gate, and a top-of-the-line security system. I'll be with Jolie in Hollywood for two weeks, not that there isn't plenty of room for everyone. We've been lucky so far, but if the girls are right and they could be flushing someone out of the woodwork, I'd rather Jessica and Jade, at the very least, are taking the proper precautions. Besides, Court will be there."

"You know, for a moment there, watching the

phone number crawl across the screen the way it is now, I thought about your cousin. I may have to keep *him* from strangling Jessica."

"Why?" Sam looked toward the closest monitor. "What number did Jess— Holy crap. That's Jade's cell number, isn't it?"

"Yup," Matt said, sort of rocking on his heels now, because it was good to know that he wasn't over-reacting, that Jessica Sunshine truly was a pain in the neck—and parts south.

"This is going out live, right?" Sam said, shaking his head. "No way to stop it? I'd better call Court in case he's not watching, give him and Jade both a heads up. I'll be right back."

Matt watched Sam Becket head for the hallway once more, already pulling his cell phone from his jacket pocket. As of a few days ago, he'd never met Sam or his cousin Court Becket, had never met Jade or Jolie or Jessica. He wouldn't know any of them now, if someone hadn't tried to burn down Teddy Sunshine's house.

He'd been on his way to offer his condolences to the daughters on Teddy's death when the call came in about the fire, about Jade being caught in it. That in itself might have been enough to set his homicide-detective senses tingling, the arson. But he still had to ask himself how much was his concern for truth, justice and the American way, and how much of his interest had to do with his sharp, physical reaction when he first saw Jessica Sunshine.

She was too young for him.

She was a pain in the ass. A major pain in his ass.

God, she was beautiful. Too beautiful for him. And so obviously hurting.

So, instead of walking away, he'd put in for some vacation time and joined the Sunshine girls and the Becket cousins in this stupid, harebrained, potentially dangerous crusade to solve Teddy's old cases and discover who murdered Melodie Brainard—all while privately hoping to hell that Teddy hadn't really done the crime, and then eaten his police revolver.

At least some of the reason for his involvement was logical, damn it. He'd been the primary on the Brainard murder, until someone got to the brass upstairs and pulled him off it. That had pissed Matt off, definitely. The unholy rush to declare the dead Teddy Sunshine Melodie Brainard's murderer had also pissed him off. Teddy had been one of them for a lot of years; he'd deserved better.

If the department called the murder and suicide closed cases, there was little Matt could do to keep the cases active. Not on duty, anyway, not if he didn't want to end up on foot patrol down at the docks. Working the cases on his own, on his own time, had been the reasonable answer. Pairing up with others with the same mind-set had bordered on logical, except for the fact that he was dealing with rank amateurs.

Amateurs, he reminded himself, who had already cracked the case of the Vanishing Bride, although Teddy had done most of the legwork before his death.

Now Jolie and Sam, lovers years ago and lovers again, were on their way out of town, leaving Jade and Court and Matt and Jessica behind to work the cold cases from Sam's mansion: Command Central.

Maybe he should move in for the duration, Matt thought, looking across the studio to see that they'd gone to commercial yet again, and Jolie and Jessica seemed to be locked in a fierce battle of whispers. Something was up, or Jessica wouldn't have covered her mike.

The three sisters loved one another, that was clear. But, cripes, could they fight. Teddy had raised three strong-minded daughters. Jolie had, Matt had learned, gone to Hollywood after giving Sam's ring back to him, to prove she could make it in the movies. And she had done it, become a star. Jade had stuck with Teddy at the Sunshine Detective Agency, even after her marriage to Court and even after being shot at, so that Court had handed her an ultimatum: the job or the marriage.

They'd been divorced for over a year.

Yes, strong women. Stubborn, headstrong women. And maybe Jessica was the strongest of them all, because she had battled her way from local weather girl to having her own weekly show on cable, living the life of an investigative reporter, actually being taken seriously in such a male-dominated arena.

Matt hated reporters. That came with the territory: cops and reporters were natural-born enemies.

Bringing him back, yet again, to why he was standing here, watching Jessica throw another firecracker onto the fire, and not walking away, saving himself and maybe his job.

"Well, that was fun," Sam said, standing next to Matt once more, even though Matt hadn't heard him approach. "I didn't tell them anything they didn't already know. So far, Jade's fielded six calls for Jessica and twice that for Jolie. Now everything is going to voice mail."

"And nothing substantial in any of the calls, right?"

"That depends on whether or not Jess or Jolie might be interested in three proposals of marriage, an invitation to perform at Grandpa Somebody-or-other's ninetieth birthday party, and one fairly obscene proposition that Jade is thinking of forwarding on to the police."

"And the nuts have barely begun to drop from the trees," Matt said, caught between a grin and outright disgust.

"To tell you the truth, I think Jade sounded a little upset that no one wanted to talk to her."

"And everyone tells me she's the logical one."
Matt looked toward the set to see that both women
were unpinning their lapel mikes. "Looks like it's
over. You two have time for dinner?"

"Thanks, but no," Sam told him as Jolie walked
toward him, his attention clearly shifting to the
woman who appeared to be looking at him as if he
was her only safe port in a storm. She was waylaid
by a few of the crew, asked to sign autographs, and
complied with her patented Jolie Sunshine smile.
"We really want to get in the air. You going to move
in? Really, I think it would be a good idea."

"Yeah, I think I will, thanks," Matt said as he
watched Jessica thanking her crew, even going up on
tiptoe to kiss the guy named Kevin. "And here comes
Trouble, smiling like she did something good, and
probably expecting a pat on the head. Must be a
blonde thing, huh?"

"Jess isn't blond, not naturally. Remember, I knew
her five years ago. Forgive the obvious stereotype, but
under that pretty remarkable hair color beats the no-
nonsense brain of a brunette. The body, however, Jolie
tells me, is completely genuine, just in case you might
have been wondering about that. Because I've seen the
way you look at her, Matt, when she's not aware of it.
Forewarned is forearmed, as the saying goes. Jessica's
steel wrapped in velvet, as ambitious as Jolie, as tough-
minded as Jade, and as persistent as Teddy."

"Warning taken. But you left out the mother."

"She left herself out, running off when Jessica was not even into her teens, I think. Jade still hasn't been able to reach her or her husband—who is also Teddy's brother, if you're at all interested in bad soap operas. They live in Hawaii, or did the last time she was in contact with either of them. They probably don't even know Teddy's dead."

"Jess told me that much, yes. She also considers them both suspects, probably because she'd rather hate her mother than admit to the hurt she felt when the woman deserted them. I've put out a few feelers, but nothing's come back to me yet."

"Nothing's come back to you on what?" Jessica asked, wiping at her cheeks with a bunch of balled-up tissues and then frowning at the color she'd wiped from her skin. "God, Madge was heavy on the blusher tonight. Never mind. If you had anything good, you would have told me already. So, what did you think? Great show, right?"

"Right. Fantastic." Matt motioned toward Jolie. "How about you say goodbye now and we get back to Sam's place so Jade can strangle you?"

Jessica's sherry-brown eyes twinkled with amusement. "She's already getting calls, isn't she? I was going to put up a special number, but there wasn't time to arrange for one, and the producer refused to put up my cell number as a matter of station policy.

Jade's was the first other number I could remember. I know, I know, I've called out the whack-jobs. But all we need is one real call, one good lead, and it will all be worth it. Jade will see that." She looked at Sam. "Won't she?"

"Let me answer that," Matt said, and Jessica turned to look at him once more. "In the middle of the Fishtown Strangler case, the special Mayoral Task Force Commission, or whatever they called that bunch of politicos out for personal publicity, had the bright idea of putting out a public hot line. They even offered a pretty hefty reward for information leading to an arrest and conviction. I brought you copies of the file, Jess, the pertinent parts. What I didn't bring you were the transcriptions of the calls to that hot line, because I would have had to rent a truck to carry them. From what Sam tells me, Jade's only gotten crank calls so far, but there will be other calls. People confessing to being our guy, dozens of them. And they all have to be checked out. You just opened the door for any sad, pathetic loser out there, and since we can't tell who's lying, who's nuts and who might even be suicidal, God help us, we now have to check them all out. Still happy?"

"Not so much, no," Jessica admitted, shrugging. "But all we need is one good lead."

"Keep saying that, and maybe we will get lucky. But I wouldn't bet your economy-sized bottle of hair color on it."

Jessica whirled about to face Sam, who already had his hands raised protectively. "And they say women gossip. Jeez. Jolie! Come hit your big-mouthed beloved, will you?"

Jolie signed one last autograph and then walked over to join her sister, although she aligned herself with Sam, slipping her arm about his waist. "What am I missing?"

"Our plane would be the obvious answer, if it wasn't Court's plane and waiting for us," Sam said, pressing a kiss against Jolie's temple. He then wiped his hand across his mouth. "You taste like makeup."

"I know. But I'd rather not take the time to wipe all of this off and reapply for the cameras that are bound to be waiting for us at the airport. Right, Jessica Marie?" she ended, glaring at her sister.

"So I told my audience you and Sam are flying out to the Coast tonight by private jet. Big deal. It's publicity, right? Publicity is a good thing."

"After watching the paparazzi hound me at Teddy's funeral, how can you say anything so…oh, never mind. You're just clueless, aren't you?" Jolie narrowed her eyes. "Or you've got some other reason, like maybe you *want* the press at the airport?"

Jessica rolled her eyes. "Don't be silly, Jolie. I told you, I goofed up. There was no ulterior motive. Although, if you get a chance to slip in somewhere to the national press that you just appeared exclusively on *The Sunshine Report,* I wouldn't complain."

"You're a barracuda in pinup girl's clothing," Jolie accused her, and then sighed. "All right, all right. I'll give you a plug. But then you owe me. Big time."

"Absolutely. And I'll pay up, anytime you ask."

Matt, maybe because he was tired, maybe because association with the Sunshine sisters was affecting his sanity, suddenly saw a glimmer of humor in the entire mess. "Sam? You belong to any fantasy sports teams?"

Sam frowned. "Yeah. But what does that have to do with—"

"I don't know. This just seems like the female version. We trade Donovan McNabb for Brett Farve, and they trade insults and favors. I think I like the male version better. Come on, Jessica. Time you went back to Sam's house and faced your sister and her ex. I think they want to talk to you."

"I'll bet they do," Jessica said, looking a bit nervous for the first time in Matt's memory. "Will you come in with me? That way they won't kill me, not in front of a witness."

"Matt's going to move in while I'm gone," Sam said, earning himself a quick hug from Jolie, who seemed to think this was a good idea.

"He is?" Jessica looked at Matt. "You are?" Her eyes narrowed. "Why? Because if you think I need a babysitter, let me remind you that the two of us pairing up was never my idea in the first place. You just slow me down."

"I'm also old, have no sense of humor, and I'm bucking for a coronary. Yes, I heard. But flattery will get you nowhere," Matt said, taking her arm at the elbow. "Come on, let's go. We have to stop by my place so I can pack a few things."

"Your place?" Jessica turned to look at her sister, pulling a face of mock horror. "Are you going to invite me up to see your etchings? That's what dirty old men used to say back in the last century, isn't it, to lure innocent young things to their lairs? What do you think, sis? Should I go with him?"

"I'd say no, but that's just because I like him," Jolie said, winking at Matt. "Go, Jessica. And behave."

Jessica kissed her sister goodbye. "And what fun would that be?" she whispered, but Matt overheard her.

He fished in his pocket for the keys to his ragtop Jeep, shook hands with Sam once they'd reached the parking lot and left Jessica to open her own car door.

Because they might be reluctant partners, but tonight was not a date. You open the car door for a date, but not for a partner.

Now to figure out who the gesture had been meant to convince, Jessica, or himself…

CHAPTER TWO

JESSICA WAS a bundle of nerves, not that she'd let Matt know that, or anyone else in the entire world, for that matter. She liked being thought of as carefree, faintly flaky, a little foolish, funny whenever possible and ballsy as all hell. It was her persona, her protection, the armor she had donned as a child, third in line to her mother's always fickle affection and her rarely home father's notice; behind Jade, who was so damn perfect, and Jolie, who was so damn talented.

Because, if being number two made you try harder, being number three turned your life into a contest to be an individual; to achieve, to stand out—to be important.

The persona, the facade, whatever a shrink would call her act, also worked well once she'd gotten on air. She could smile and be nice and ask silly questions, put the person she was interviewing at his or her ease, and then go for the jugular with a penetrating question the person never saw coming until it smacked them in the chops like a wet flounder.

Because Jessica knew that it wasn't enough to be

pretty or funny or congenial or even sneaky. You also had to do your homework.

She had done her homework on Matthew Denby since the day he'd popped into her line of sight and into her way. He was the son of a cop, the grandson of a cop, and she wondered if he really had wanted to be a cop, or if he just figured he was following tradition by going into the family "business." Not that she'd ask him, because he hadn't volunteered anything about himself. But the question was on her list.

She wanted to know about his wife, who had died in a hit-and-run car crash six months after they'd gotten married. Mary Denby had been nineteen, and he'd been twenty, and in his second year of college. He'd graduated from the Police Academy the following summer. Had his wife's death prompted him to leave college and sign up for the force? Had he wanted to go after whoever had plowed into his wife's car and then left her to die in the crumpled wreck?

Jessica hadn't been able to find anything about an arrest ever being made in the nearly twenty-year-old case. Maybe it was a cop thing in general, or a quirk possessed by both Matt and her father, but she was willing to bet the case still ate at Matt, as Teddy's cold cases had eaten at him.

Another question she couldn't ask the guy, right now so pointedly pretending that she wasn't sitting in the passenger seat of his Jeep.

"Still mad?" she asked him as he pulled out from a light and shifted into second gear.

"I'm not mad," Matt said, still not looking at her. "Who said I was mad?"

"Your transmission, for one. You're going to strip the gears if you keep shifting like you're beating me with the gearshift."

He sliced a look at her as he jammed the car into third gear and then quickly to fourth, his features etched sharply in the light from the headlights of an approaching car. "You know, Jess, at first I thought you couldn't help it. But now I know better. You actually *work* at being a pain in the ass."

"So, how am I doing?" she asked, grinning at him, even as her heart skipped a beat. Company she might need while she worked on Teddy's cold cases. Analysis she didn't need, not from Matt, anyway.

"Head of the class," Matt grumbled, and then a small smile played around the corners of his mouth. "You really are a piece of work."

She decided it would be easier to take that remark as a compliment. "Thank you. I do get results, you know."

"Yeah, I know," he said, turning onto a small apartment complex in south Philadelphia whose best feature was that its brick walls were almost graffiti-free. "Believe me, I wouldn't tell you this if I could find a way around it, but the other night, when you hit the street corner with your hooker routine?"

Jessica struggled to undo her seat belt as Matt pulled into a parking space. "No! Someone made contact? Honest? Why didn't you tell me sooner? Who was it? Charmaine? Toots?"

"It was Carolyn Loretta Watts, alias Mama Bunny, aka Big Dipper, as a matter of fact," Matt said, rubbing at the back of his neck. "You gave her your card, I gave her mine, and she used mine as a get-out-of-jail-free card last night when she was picked up for solicitation."

"Oh, wow. This is all so…so TV cop show," Jessica said, quickly opening her door to follow Matt as he headed for one of the rusted steel doors of the nearest apartment building. "What information did she trade?"

Matt held open the door and let her move past him into a dark cement-block hallway that smelled vaguely, and rather appetizingly, of fried chicken. "Up the steps, third floor," he said, glaring at a kid of about seventeen or eighteen who was coming down the hallway and had stopped to ogle Jessica. "Keep moving, Ernesto. You can't afford her."

"And you can, *amigo?*" Ernesto shot back at him, his dark eyes running up and down Jessica's figure. "Didn't know being a pig paid that good."

"Yeah," Matt said, motioning for the youth to move on. "Big bucks, and they still let me carry concealed."

"Okay, okay, I get you. I'm moving. I gotta go

collect my five bucks now. Razi bet me a fin you were gay. But you're just dumb, right? Bringing a girl to this dump? Where's your *class,* man?"

"Friend of yours?" Jessica asked as the metal door clanged shut behind Ernesto.

"Believe it or not, yeah. He's a good kid. That act was strictly for you. He just pulled down a full ride to Penn State, main campus."

"Hey, that's terrific. Football, basketball?"

"Academic scholarship, Jessica. He's going to major in logistics." They'd reached the third floor, and Matt inserted a key into the second door on the left. "Don't fall for stereotypes."

"I'm sorry, I did do that, didn't I?" Jessica walked into Matt's apartment and waited for him to switch on a light. "Homey. If you just moved in last week," she said, looking around at the sparse furnishings, the bare walls. "How long have you lived here, Matt?"

"I don't know. Five, six years," he said, switching on two more lights and heading to a small alcove that contained a galley kitchen. He pulled open the refrigerator, spilling more light into the room. "Would you like a soda or something? Beer?"

Jessica was looking at the contents of a tall bookcase, tilting her head and squinting at the titles of what looked to be a lot of really boring books. "Huh? Oh, no. No, thanks. You go ahead. Let's get back to the information you got from our new friend."

Matt returned to the living room, popping the top on a can of soda. "She gave me an address for one of our Fishtown Strangler victims. Tarin White. Not the same one we had, a different one. She said she never knew White, but it seems they shopped at the same corner grocery store and she got the address that way."

"That was nice of Mama Bunny to help us out like that."

"Dream on, Jess. Bunny was working the angles, stashing away information she might be able to trade one day. If she hadn't gotten picked up, we wouldn't know what we know now. I'm going to go throw some stuff in a bag. The TV remote is over there on the arm of the chair."

"Okay, thanks," Jessica said, itching to follow him, see if his bedroom was as spartan as his living room. After the remark Ernesto had made, she believed it probably was.

She walked around the room once more, still searching for something, anything, that would tell her that, yes, someone actually lived here. But there was nothing, unless she counted several copies of a sports magazine each with a name and address sticker on them that matched Matt's name and this address.

With a quick look over her shoulder, toward the door in the far wall, she opened the top drawer of what looked to be one of those oaken desks her elementary teachers sat behind years ago. She took a quick inventory: checkbook, a few bills, a Phillies schedule on the back of a complimentary calendar, a roll of stamps.

She dared to open another drawer. It was empty. So was the next drawer. She finally struck pay dirt in the bottom drawer with a small, leather-clad album stamped in gold: Our Wedding.

She closed the drawer.

"Matt?" she called out. "Can I help? You don't want everything to get all wrinkled."

"No, that's okay," he called back to her. "I'll only be another couple of minutes."

Another couple of minutes. Did she dare? What if he caught her? She'd hate it if he caught her. Besides, she had no reason to invade his privacy, except for her raging curiosity…

She backed up, keeping her eyes on the doorway, and bent her knees until her fingers collided with the pull on the bottom drawer. Slowly, she eased it open, her heart pounding, her breathing quick and shallow as she squatted lower, her fingers searching in the bottom of the drawer until she could fit them beneath the cover and lift it.

She dared to shift her gaze from the doorway to the first page of the album.

Oh, God.

Jessica let the cover fall back into place and quickly shut the drawer. Babies. She'd caught a glimpse of two babies—two young, eager faces with a lifetime ahead of them. His wife had been a redhead, a little chubby in her short white dress—lingering baby fat possibly, as she'd been only nineteen. And Matt had been so young, so skinny, wearing a suit too short at the wrists and ankles and a shirt collar two sizes too large.

She shouldn't have looked. Now she'd imagine that carefree smile when she looked into his dour face, and want to see him look so happy again.

Not that she cared. Because she didn't care. Matthew Denby was a big pain in her neck, that was what he was. Years too old for her. They had nothing in common. He didn't even *like* her. And he really didn't look as much like Harrison Ford as Jolie, who always liked to compare people to movie stars, had suggested.

Jessica wanted out of this apartment. Now. Sooner, if possible.

"Matt?" She walked toward the bedroom. "How long can it take to pack a couple pairs of slacks and a few— Oops, sorry!"

Matt had been in the middle of pulling up a pair of well-fitting jeans, his upper body bare, the muscles in his arms and shoulders flexing as he tugged on the faded denim. He didn't flinch, didn't turn his back to her, but merely zipped himself up and closed the button. "See anything interesting?" he asked her, reaching for a navy T-shirt that lay on the bed.

"Hardly," she said, sniffing, when the opposite

was true. He was in really good shape for a guy pushing hard at forty. She liked the sprinkling of brown hair on his chest, the six-pack that was not as tight as a twenty-year-old's, but damn close. He looked touchable, less sculptured. As if his body was more lived in and comfortable. "You look good, though, for an old guy. You work out?"

"It's either that or chase the bad guys using my walker. Now, what are you doing?"

He pulled the shirt over his head, leaving his sandy hair flopped down onto his forehead until he ran his hand through its thickness, pushing it back. The shirt was thin, worn and must have shrunk in the wash, because it barely hit the waistband of his jeans. Was this the first time she'd seen him without a jacket? Yes, she was pretty sure it was. He was a whole different person now. Man, not cop.

What had he asked her? What was she doing? Other than staring at him, did he mean?

"Packing for you," Jessica said, recovering quickly as she walked over to the open closet door. "At the rate you're moving, we'll be here all night." She reached up to the row of shirts and slacks, three sports coats that looked as if he wore them hard and sent them to the dry cleaner rarely. "Not exactly a clotheshorse, are you?"

She felt his hands come down on her shoulders, and she let him turn her around to face him. "Jessica—

out. I can do without your help, and your comments, okay? Why don't you go look at my wedding album again. You couldn't have seen all of it with that one quick peek."

Jessica's entire body went cold, right before heat began spilling into her cheeks. "I didn't... I would never... How did you know?"

He turned her toward the dresser that was set at an angle in the corner of the small room, and the large mirror above it. From where she was standing, the reflection she saw was that of the desk in the living room.

"Oh. Well, that stinks, doesn't it?" she said quietly.

"Her name was Mary," Matt told her. "We were high-school sweethearts. Matt and Mary, Mary and Matt. Inseparable. I loved her as much as a stupid young fool could love anyone. Now I have to look at those pictures to remember what color her eyes were. Go away, Jess. In another week or so we'll be done with this and probably never see each other again. In the meantime, let's keep personalities out of this. We don't have to be friends to be partners, and we sure as hell don't have to share our life stories."

He still had his hands on her shoulders. Did he know that, was he aware that he was still touching her, that he was even moving his thumbs slightly over her collarbones? Did he realize that she wasn't breathing, seemed to have forgotten how to manage that automatic in and out of breath?

"You're right, Matt," Jessica said at last, after managing to inhale just as little shiny stars had begun to blink in front of her eyes. "And it…it wasn't personal. What I did? I'm just nosy. Maybe it comes with doing what I do. I'm sorry. Really sorry. I had no right to invade your…your space."

Matt tipped his head to one side. "Who am I hearing here, Jess? The real you or the professional you? I hate to admit this, but I can't tell. Are you being honest, or just saying what you think I want to hear while you loosen me up to spill my guts for you?" He put a finger against her lips for a moment. "And before you answer, remember—partners play fair with each other."

"You don't want to be my partner," Jessica reminded him, dodging the question, mostly because she wasn't so sure which of the possibilities he'd mentioned was the correct answer. That said a lot about her and the life she'd been leading, didn't it? She tried not to flinch at this nugget of personal insight that had picked a damn awkward time to lodge in her brain.

"I won't disagree with that. Although you're a lot prettier than Eddie Frantz and you don't smell like cheap cigars."

Jessica tried to laugh. "It's nice to know I've got

something working in my favor. So Eddie Frantz is your partner? Your real partner?"

"He was, until he retired six months ago. Now I work solo, thanks to budget cuts," Matt said, at last taking his hands off her shoulders, but only to reach past her to pull a shirt from its hanger.

"No, don't do that." She acted before she thought, another failing she might want to work on one of these days, putting her hand on his. "Just carry the stuff out on the hangers and save yourself the folding and unfolding—and the wrinkles. Go sit down on the bed. Let me do it."

He didn't move, and Jessica realized that she was now pretty much trapped half inside the postage-stamp-size closet, the two of them still too close for comfort. His space, invaded. Her space, invaded. The two of them sharing the same suddenly too-intimate space.

He didn't say anything, just kept looking at her, which forced her into speech. "We, um, we could *try* to be friends, Matt. Couldn't we? You know, like you said…for a couple of weeks?"

"I'm too old to be friends with a woman, Jess," he said, and he seemed to concentrate his gaze on her mouth.

She stuck out her tongue a fraction and licked her lips. She couldn't help herself, it was a natural reaction.

Jessica tumbled into speech. "Okay. You don't have to hit me over the head with our age difference. Not that it's so bad, you know. What? A dozen years? All right, so it's a difference. I agree it's a difference. But if two people find each other…you know…physically attractive, I don't see how… Wait a minute. You do find me attractive, don't you, Matt? Oh, cripes, you don't, do you? And here I am, opening my big mouth like some idiot teenager and—"

"Shut up," Matt said, his tone turning the command into a strange sort of endearment. "This once, Jess, just shut up, okay?"

His gaze was definitely on her mouth.

"Okay," Jessica breathed quietly.

The shirt and hanger hit the floor, unnoticed.

His hands came down on her shoulders once more, and hers found the sides of his trim waist, easily sliding beneath the too-short T-shirt to encounter his skin, to feel the ripple of reaction that seemed to run through his muscles.

He touched her lips with his. Lightly, briefly, barely making contact, so that involuntarily she moved closer, lifting herself to him, eager for another touch, another swift taste.

He slanted his head a bit more, brought his mouth to hers again, again only lightly brushing hers, but this time his teeth tugged on her bottom lip before he retreated once more. Yum…

Jessica felt a shiver run completely through her. Anticipation formed a knot in her belly. She wasn't used to this. The few men in her life had all seemed very much concerned with *taking*. That Matt had yet to move to fondle her breasts amazed her. She had always been pragmatic about her attractions, what drew men to her. Her semi-fame and her frankly lush body. Mostly *the girls,* as Jade mockingly called her baby sister's full breasts.

Suddenly the girls seemed to feel neglected. Jessica felt her nipples tightening, puckering. If her breasts could talk—and the way most men concentrated on them when they were supposed to be talking to Jessica's face, there were times she'd wished they could—they'd be yelling, "Hey, you—sport— we're right here. Don't pretend you haven't noticed. A little attention, okay?"

Again the advance. The gentle touch of mouth to mouth. Again the retreat. Jessica's need to hold on, to cling, doubled and then redoubled. What was he doing? He was driving her crazy, *that* was what he was doing.

Why was he doing this to her? Or *not* doing this to her…

Matt made no secret of the fact he wasn't crazy about her career choice. That was already a given.

As for his opinion of her body? If her body, possessing it, wasn't his top priority at the moment, then why was he kissing her?

Because that was the unspoken deal, wasn't it?

Not that they'd more than hinted at what the ground rules were to be. *Temporary partnership.*

They both knew what that meant, right? She was a grown-up…or at least had learned how to pretend to be one.

Jessica didn't know she could have so many thoughts in such a short time, but by the fourth time Matt teased her with his gentle kisses she was ready for him. She tried to put her arms all the way around him, slide fully into his embrace.

But, as if he knew what she planned, he smoothly shifted his hands to her waist, keeping their bodies apart. Concentrating all her feeling to what he was doing to her mouth. Her suddenly very sexual, aroused mouth, the mouth that seemed to have a hot line of sensitivity it could magically share with the sudden sweet ache between her thighs. Who knew?

Sighing with her need, she opened that mouth to him.

When his tongue touched hers, skyrockets exploded behind her eyes, and if he had not shifted his hands to grip her waist, she might have fallen, for her knees had turned boneless.

And then she did know. *Anticipation.* Half the thrill of the game, wasn't it? She hadn't realized.

Boy, give a guy a few years and some experience on her, and there was a lot she didn't know.

Like, Matt gave as much as he took. And he took

his time about it. No fumbling, no ridiculously over-done heavy breathing, no quick rush to the bed. Choosing the marathon over the sprint.

Every part of her body wanted his attention, longed for it. *Anticipated.* The more he denied, the more she craved. Her breasts seemed to be tingling with the need to be touched. The tightness between her thighs demanded to be stroked, soothed, explored.

Still, Matt only kissed her. Now long, drugging, deeply intimate kisses. Sensation building on sensation. Want colliding with need.

It had never taken less to make her more ready.

"Matt," she breathed at last, when he began trailing his lips down over her cheek, along the side of her neck. He might not be moving fast, but she knew, they both had to know, where they were going. "Do…do you…do you have anything?"

He swore into the soft junction of her neck and shoulder. He lifted his head and took two slow steps backward, away from her. "Saved by my lousy sex life," he said, his smile embarrassed, his clenched fists betraying his frustration. "Unless you…"

Jessica shook her head. "I'm not as modern as people maybe think I should be. No, I've got nothing." She put her crossed hands to her chest and tried to steady her breathing. "So…um…so I guess that's that?"

The look he gave her with those sexy gray-blue

eyes nearly sent her to her knees. If she was in hell, she wasn't there alone. Nice to know, she guessed, but definitely not comforting.

"Yeah, I guess so." He bent down and picked up his fallen shirt and hanger. "I know a great hot-dog stand a couple of blocks from here. Are you hungry?"

She blinked at him. "So that's it? That's all you've got to say? Do I want a hot dog?"

He rubbed at the back of his neck, a gesture she already recognized as an unconscious habit, and then nodded. "I think that covers it, yeah. Unless you're into postmortems?"

"We've got nothing to post a mortem about," Jessica pointed out tersely, and then winced at how silly that sounded. "Do you think maybe we've both just had a lucky escape?"

"Ask me that in an hour or so, after my base animal instincts have had time for a figurative cold shower."

Jessica giggled, a release of tension she sorely needed at the moment. "Good thinking. And by then I can maybe come up with some good excuse, too. Like, I was seduced by the beauty of my surroundings."

"You'll have to do better than that," Matt said, lifting a bunch of hangers from the closet and dumping shirts and jeans on the bed before opening the top drawer of the dresser and pulling out socks and underwear.

Jessica grabbed the hangers and slung the clothes

over her shoulder. Suddenly she wanted out of this bedroom, out of this entire apartment. "No, *you* have to do better than this. Why on earth do you live here? And live this way?"

"What? I have a bed, a TV, a comfortable chair, a kitchen and a big break on my rent because I'm a cop and people like having cops around—except when they don't. I don't need anything else." He closed the suitcase and zipped it shut. "There. My laptop is in the Jeep. Now all I need is Mortimer, and we're ready to roll."

"Mortimer? You have a pet? It's nice to know you have some possession you actually care for, I guess. What kind of pet?"

"The kind you salute as you give him a Viking funeral in the toilet if he goes belly-up. But Mortimer's showing some real staying power, so I don't want to leave him to fend for himself."

"No, of course not," Jessica said, following him out of the bedroom and into the kitchen once they'd deposited suitcase and clothing on the couch. Sure enough, there was Mortimer, a small black fish with fancy long fins and really hideous bulging eyes. "Why do you keep him in the kitchen?"

"I didn't think the view was any better in the living room?" Matt responded, reaching into a drawer and pulling out a roll of plastic wrap. He ripped off a length and secured it over the top of the round fish bowl and then added a rubber band for extra security. "There you go, he's all yours."

"Gee, you shouldn't have," Jessica said as she automatically held out her hands to take the bowl. "I try not to accept gifts on first dates."

Matt removed a box of fish flakes from the single cabinet in the kitchen and tucked it into a pocket in his jeans. He opened another drawer, reached inside, and came out with a small fish net on a wire stick, which he aimed at her like it was a sword or something. "We're not dating."

"No? We're doing something," Jessica pointed out as she followed him back into the living room. "Or at least we were almost doing something."

"That wouldn't be dating," Matt told her as he disappeared into the bedroom for a moment, then came back into the living room, still strapping on his shoulder holster—and a very sexy look it was on him, that gun and holster, even though she wondered what admitting such a thing said about her. "That would be something with a nastier name. Damn, I forgot my jacket."

"Ah, don't ruin it. You're already wearing a shirt," Jessica reminded him, blinking rapidly, because she'd much rather deal with euphemisms, even if Matt was right. "Oh, now that just blows the hip and casual *Miami Vice*–remake look all to hell," she added as he headed toward her, one of his ugly brown tweed sports coats hiding the holster. "We have to go shopping."

He flipped down the collar of the jacket, which had caught half up, half down, and glared at her from beneath his eyebrows and his permanently creased forehead that either made him a thinker or a worrier or both. "I told you, we're not dating. You don't get to tell me what to wear."

"I have to be seen in public with you," Jessica reminded him, still holding tight to Mortimer's bowl. "You look like you shop at the thrift store—in their bargain bin. Think of my image."

"You have an image?" Matt teased as he picked up his clothes and the suitcase and nodded his head toward the door. "Never mind, of course you do. But there's nothing different in my clothes tonight. I just got rid of the shirt and tie, that's all."

"You did. You exchanged the shirt and tie for a cleaning rag disguised as a T-shirt. You're not a teenager anymore, you know. It's time to dress like an adult. Not that those sports coats you wear don't all look as if they were hand-me-downs from your highschool English teacher."

"Don't talk anymore. Move," Matt warned her, his index finger curled around the half-dozen or so hangers and slinging the shirts and slacks over his shoulder the way Harrison Ford might have slung a topcoat over his—not the same props, but definitely the same reaction in female hearts all over the world.

Damn Jolie for making her think Matt looked like Harrison Ford. He was cuter than Harrison Ford!

She waited in the hallway as Matt locked the door to his apartment and then she followed him down the stairs, all three flights, all with Mortimer sloshing around in his bowl and, she was pretty sure, giving her dirty looks with those big, bulging eyes.

"Ernesto," Matt said as they hit the foyer to see the kid lounging against the row of mailboxes, enjoying a taco. "Honest opinion here. Do I need new clothes?"

Ernesto shrugged. "You look like a cop, *amigo*. Those shoes? All cop. That jacket? All cop, and maybe some of some aged *abuelo,* a little bit. You can't help yourself, you're cop to the pigskin, if you know what I'm talking about. The shirt's bitchin', though, and the jeans aren't bad. She giving you grief?"

"She is," Matt said, looking at Jessica, who was still exchanging glares with Mortimer and wondering what the hell had happened to her upstairs that she'd ever considered going to bed with the biggest pain in the neck this side of the Mississippi. "I think she thinks I make her look bad."

"Man, nothing could make that one look bad. Except maybe for that thing. That is one very ugly fish. You bailing?"

"Only for about a week or so," Matt said. "Can you stay out of trouble that long?"

"Me? I'm never in trouble, *amigo,* you know that.

I'm one of the good guys. Look, see me taking this ugly fish from your girlfriend? How's that for being straight-up? Look, I'm carrying your ugly fish to your ugly car. Am I good or what?"

"Tell him he's good, Matt," Jessica joked. "Then maybe he'll shut up. Right, Ernesto?"

"Shut up? Oooh, I like this one. She talks just like you."

"No, she talks just like you—too damn much. You still have my cell number?"

Ernesto handed Mortimer to Jessica once she'd strapped on her seat belt and then pressed a fingertip to the side of his head. "I carry it right here. But I won't need you. Everything's just like you always call it—cool." He grinned at Jessica. "He's really old, you know. Maybe you want someone younger, *querida*. Someone without an ugly fish."

"Down, boy," Jessica said, but not meanly, and in a few moments the Jeep was moving out of the parking lot. She lifted the bowl from her lap so that maybe the water wouldn't slosh back and forth so much and Mortimer wouldn't get seasick. "Is Ernesto in some sort of trouble?"

"No, not right now, unless he's lying to me, which is always possible. Some people don't like to see other people doing well, you know? A good kid, no fooling around with drugs or gangs, and now a full scholarship and a way out of here for himself and his mother, not that I think she wants anything but money. There's always someone who isn't always happy about another person's success."

"I understand. That's what Jade thinks about Terrell Johnson, why he was shot. Somebody didn't like that he was getting out. His basketball scholarship, you know?"

"It's also possible the shooting was gang-related, although the grandmother swears Terrell didn't belong to a gang."

"You've read the file? Why? That's Jade's case. We're working the Fishtown Strangler."

"Cop curiosity," Matt said pulling into a small parking lot that fronted a chipped-paint wooden building that was little more than a shack. "I worked gangs for a couple of years, and I don't know if Terrell fits the criteria or not. I don't think he was ganged up, but he could have been a target. One or two?"

Jessica sniffed at the aroma of hot dogs that had already invaded the Jeep. "Two, definitely. With the works, including onions. I've got nothing else to lose tonight, right?"

"Onions it is," Matt said, and then he leaned across the space between the bucket seats and planted a quick, hard kiss on her mouth. "And if we both have them, we'll cancel each other out."

She would have asked him exactly what he meant by that last statement, but he was already gone, to stand in line at a window carved into the front of the shack. She watched as he exchanged high-fives and low-fives with a couple of kids, shook hands with an older man very properly dressed in a dark suit pressed to a shiny finish, and shot a look at three teenage boys who visibly shrank beneath his gaze.

Oh, yes, Ernesto was right. Matt Denby was a cop all the way to his skin and beyond. But he was also a man. More and more, quite an interesting man…

CHAPTER THREE

MATT THOUGHT and rethought his decision to be a guest in Sam Becket's suburban mansion a dozen times as he drove the Jeep along the Blue Route, and finally decided it was a good idea. Except when it was a bad idea.

Watching Jessica Sunshine eat hot dogs had been an even worse idea. Which, when he thought about that, made him feel like a randy teenager with a sick sense of humor, so he concentrated on why bunking in with his fellow "investigators" was a reasonable, if not a great, idea.

The house was huge, but Jade and Court would also be there, acting as chaperones even if they didn't know he'd cast them in that role. Then again, Sam may have thought he was casting Matt as referee when he'd made the suggestion, because Jade and her ex-husband seemed to run so hot and cold in their feelings for each other that a third party might have to step in at some point and send them both to neutral corners.

"What is it with Jade and Court, anyway?" Matt

asked Jessica as he turned onto the narrow macadam lane leading to Sam's gated acres. "I keep getting mixed signals."

Jessica popped a second breath mint into her mouth before she answered. "I don't see why," she said, grinning. "It's very simple. They love each other. When they're not hating each other, that is. It's all very made-for-TV-movie-ish, I think."

"Ask a woman…" Matt said, shaking his head. "I know that Jade continued to work for Teddy after she and Court got married."

"Right. Commuting between here and Court's house in Virginia. She spent about three days a week here, supposedly mostly working the account books and doing Internet and cold-call, in-person background searches for corporate personnel departments. Always saying she'd give it up when she felt Teddy didn't need her around anymore, which would have been never as far as my caretaking sister was concerned, and Jade and Court both knew that. But since Court travels a lot on his job, too, it seemed to work for them—fair being fair, what he could do she could do and all that modern-marriage crap. Right up until Jade lied to him, that is, said she never did anything even remotely dangerous, and then got shot at in a dark alley somewhere in Kensington."

"Yeah, I heard that part, too. What I guess I'm asking is—hell, I don't know what I'm asking."

"Sure you do," Jessica said, laughing. "You're wondering if there's some nifty reconciliation and happy ending in there somewhere for the two of them, which I think is really sweet of you."

"Oh, good, now I'm sweet. My evening is just getting better and better."

"But it is sweet. Jolie and I wonder the same thing. In the meantime, we both plan to do what you should do—stay out of their way. You don't want to get caught in the cross fire."

"I'll try to remember that. How's Mortimer?"

"Just sloshing around. If he starts doing the backstroke or the dead man's float, I'll let you know. Why? Do you think you should have punched a couple of air holes in the plastic wrap?"

"I didn't, not until you mentioned it. But we're here now," he said, braking as he turned the Jeep toward the closed gate to Sam's house. "And here comes Bear Man to check us out."

"I used to think Sam was a little too uptight and straight, you know? But he does things like hiring Bear Man as his gatekeeper, giving him a roof over his head and letting him think he's doing important work."

"Hello, Bear Man," Matt said as he rolled down the window and smiled at the one-time college football offensive lineman and teammate of Sam's, and more recently the former professional wrestler who had probably been tossed out of the ring over the top ropes one too many times. "How's it going?'"

"Hi back at you," Carroll Yablonski said cheerfully, flashing his too-white dentures at Matt as he looked past him to wave shyly at Jessica. Carroll's slightly scrambled brains hadn't been the only casualty of his years in the pro-wrestling ring. "Things are all quiet now since I was watching your show, Miss Jessica, and came out to tell the reporters that Miss Jolie and Sam were on their way to the airport. They blew out of here like they were shot from a cannon. Do you think they'll be back?"

"If they do come back," Matt told the man, "I know you'll handle them."

"I keep hoping I get to do that," Carroll said, and pressed his lips together, grimacing as he stepped back and flexed, all of his muscles bulging—the most impressive being the muscles in his neck. "Still got it!" he said proudly, and then went back to the gatehouse to press the button that opened the gates.

"No comment?" Matt asked as he drove through the opening and onto the long driveway lined with pavers.

Beside him, Jessica let out a pent-up breath and then giggled. "Oh, God, my eyes are watering. Isn't he adorable? Don't you just love him?"

"Love him? I wouldn't go that far," Matt said as he cut the engine in front of the entrance to the house. "He's sort of like a leprechaun on steroids, isn't he?"

Feeling pretty much in charity with the rest of the world even after what had been, all in all, a pretty frustrating day, Matt was still grinning as he and Jessica entered the foyer of the house and headed for the large living room.

It was a feeling that wasn't destined to last.

"You!"

Jessica stopped in her tracks, gave out a little yelp and then just as quickly jumped behind Matt, as if she could hide herself there. "Hi, Jade," she called out from behind him. "Court? You're holding her back?"

"Only reluctantly," Court Becket said as Matt pulled Jessica out from behind him and gave her a gentle shove toward her waiting sister.

Jessica took two steps and stopped.

Jade tried to yank her arm free from Court's grip, and then also stopped.

The sisters glared at each other from across a probably priceless Aubusson carpet as Rockne, Teddy's Irish setter, sat on his haunches between them, looking from one to the other and whimpering.

Matt found himself comparing the two women. Jade was tall and slim, regal. Jessica was shorter, definitely *fuller,* and about as regal as cotton candy on a stick. Jade was a brunette, Jessica was a…yeah, well, so they were alike a little, beneath the hair dye. But where Jade's was a sleek, sophisticated beauty, and Jolie was an ethereal beauty—where he'd come up with that word, he didn't know—Jessica was a wholesome beauty. The cheerleader type, the soccer mom, the cuddly one.

The one, Matt decided yet again, who could get away with murder simply with a playful tilt of her head, a sunny smile and a body that distracted any healthy male from employing anything remotely resembling common sense. Or, for that matter, thoughts of self-preservation.

Teddy Sunshine's girls. An altogether lethal group, singly and most definitely when pooling their talents, working together.

A lesser man would love to see two of them rolling around on that carpet in a catfight, Matt thought, biting his bottom lip as some inner male demon brought out the locker-room mentality his mother had always said was never far from the surface of any man's brain.

Jessica and Jade were still staring at each other, as if sizing each other up as to strengths and weaknesses and who might make the first move.

Court Becket caught Matt's eye and winked at him. "I know what you're thinking, but Jade's still pretty much on injured-reserve, so it wouldn't be a fair contest."

Matt dipped his head for a moment and then grinned. "Another fantasy shot to hell, huh?"

Jessica wheeled around to look at him, a question in her eyes. A confusion that, unfortunately, didn't last very long, as her eyelids sort of narrowed when her eyebrows shot up higher on her forehead and her nostrils thinned. "Oh, you're just *sick*. Both of you."

"I know," Matt said, grinning. "We're so ashamed. Aren't we, Court?"

"I'll have to get back to you on that," Court answered, removing his grip from Jade's arm as she looked at him as if she just realized he'd come into the room with dog crap stuck to the soles of his shoes. "Uh, that is, yes. Ashamed. Definitely. Look, Jade, Jessica is still waiting for you to tell her what an asinine thing she's done, remember? Asinine. That's what you called it. I remember. Asinine. Go…sic her!"

Jessica began to laugh, a release of tension everyone else seemed more than ready to share, and soon even Jade was smiling, although that didn't mean she didn't put a little extra force into the action when she tossed her cell phone toward Jessica, saying, "Here, listen for yourself."

Matt pointed toward the cleverly camouflaged bar at the far end of the big room and Court nodded his agreement. By the time he returned with two long-neck beers from the mini-fridge, Jessica was sitting on one of the large, curved antique couches bracketing a low round table, the cell phone to her ear as Jade and Court occupied the facing couch, sitting a good two feet apart, their body language telling Matt that tonight was one of their "off again" nights.

"Oh, well, *that's* not polite," Jessica said to the cell phone she now held in front of her. "I'll try another one."

"Why?" Jade asked. "They'll only get worse."

"Anyone confess yet?" Matt asked, handing Court one of the bottles and then taking a seat beside Jessica.

Jade shook her head. "No. Just one looney caller after another, more than a few of them X-rated. Jess has to be so happy with the demographics of her audience. I think they all get together in the recreation room at the local prison for the criminally insane to watch her every Sunday night."

"I heard that," Jessica said, the cell phone to her ear once more. "Is there any way we can download all these messages? You know, to keep a record of them?"

"Does it matter? I only listened to about a dozen of them, and immediately deleted them from my mailbox, but I doubt we're going to get anything of any value. Tomorrow, I get a new phone and a new number."

"Then I can keep this?" Jessica asked, closing the phone and quickly slipping it into her pocket. "Cool."

Jade adjusted the gauze wrapping on her left hand, the bandage covering the area of her palm that had suffered the worst burns the night of the house fire. "You're not seriously going to return calls to all those nutcases?"

"Yes, Jade, I am—at least the sane ones, anyway," Jessica said firmly. "I promised. Except for the calls you erased. You shouldn't have done that."

Matt looked at his bottle of beer. "And I probably should have opted for something stronger," he muttered. "Jess, let it go. Asking the public for help makes the public feel like a part of the solution, but the reality is that the calls we get almost always do nothing but add to the workload and the problem— and are no help at all in solving the case."

"And I think you're being pessimistic, and rather insulting to a concerned public. Give me that—I can still taste those onions," Jessica told him, taking the beer from him and downing a quick swallow. "*Bleech.* I don't like beer."

"Which explains why you took the bottle," Matt said, getting to his feet. "I'll get you a glass of wine. Jade?"

"No, thank you. Jessica, much as I'd love to strangle you for giving out my cell number, I have to tell you that the rest of the program was fabulous. And it couldn't have been easy for you, talking about Teddy that way. However, that said, you do realize that you cannot possibly leave this house again without Matt going with you. You may have rattled the wrong cage with that business about the killer not resting, not relaxing, because we're coming after him."

"Oh?" Jessica accepted the glass of wine and sat up

straight to look at her sister. "And that means you won't be leaving this house without Court going with you?"

"I…uh…" Jade looked at her ex-husband, and then turned to glare at Jessica. "It's different with me. I'm a licensed private detective."

"Ri-i-ight," Jessica drawled sarcastically, looking at Matt, her expression making him wonder if taking cover behind the couch might not be a good idea. Clearly his two commendations for valor didn't mean a lot when confronted with Jessica Sunshine. "You just hold up that license when the bad guy pulls his gun. I hear P.I. licenses stop bullets as well as those stupid Protection From Abuse papers stop slugs aimed at an abused wife or girlfriend. Tell her, Matt. Tell her how many women go to the cops for help and get a stupid piece of paper because, hey, it's only *domestic violence.*"

"Here we go," Jade said as she swiped Court's bottle of beer and took a long drink. "Get ready, Matt. My little sister got a Daytime Emmy last year for her feature on domestic violence, you know."

Jessica ignored her sister. "Domestic. You know what domestic means, Matt? It means tame. So it's an oxymoron for morons to believe there's such a thing as tame violence. If anyone had a brain, all the domestic-violence laws would be struck down and an assault would be treated like an assault, no matter who was attacked. And you know what a PFA means in real life? It means, hey, see this, buster? Hit me with that big ugly fist of yours again now that I've got this, and if you don't kill me, I get to have you arrested. Stupid! Then, if she isn't murdered, she finally gets sick enough of landing in the emergency room every week and kills the bastard—because she can't beat him up—and then *she* goes to prison for trying to save her own life. How can you, a cop, stand that?"

"Don't answer her, Matt," Court warned him. "It's a Sunshine ploy—redirect attention away from yourself to somebody else, especially when that Sunshine sister knows she hasn't a leg to stand on in the original argument. You know—this business of us sticking to them for the duration."

"Very funny, Court," Jade told him, pushing the beer bottle back at him. "See how indirect you think *this* is—I don't need a babysitter. Got that?"

"Neither do I," Jessica told Matt, and then smiled. "I guess I should have just said that, huh? Sorry, I've got long practice in taking the long way to get where I want to go. We all do. I think it has to do with being motherless and having to deal with Teddy for everything. All a direct approach with him ever got any of us was a quick 'Not on your life, kiddo.'"

"Really?" Matt returned her smile, although he was also ready to defend himself if she decided to turn physical. "In that case, Jess—not on your life, kiddo. You try going anywhere without me, and I'll slap you in handcuffs."

"Oooh, I'm *scared*," she shot back at him, hugging herself as she shivered in mock horror. "Jade? Tell me you're not going to stand for this, either."

"I already did," Jade said, getting to her feet and glaring down at Court. "I'm going to the bathroom. Alone. And then I'm going to bed. Definitely alone."

"Me, too!" Jessica said, hopping to her feet.

Matt watched them go, two sisters who a half hour earlier had been close to attacking each other now walking arm in arm, the best of friends and probably about to become conspirators in figuring out ways to ditch Court and himself. "We're nuts, you know," he said to Court. "The both of us."

"You more than me, I think," Court told him. "At least I know why I'm here. I feel obligated, both to Teddy and to Jade. But you could make a break for it at anytime and nobody would blame you."

"I'd blame me. Letting Jess out by herself is either like sending a sheep into the wolf's den or dropping a shark into an aquarium of minnows— I've yet to figure out which is right. But either way, I can't walk away now."

"You like her."

Matt rotated the empty beer bottle between his palms, looking at Court, a handsome, dark-haired man of the world, born to money, born to confidence, a man who seemed to know just who he was—a man who seemed totally at sea as to how to handle his ex-wife. "I *something* her. I really don't think I want to examine my feelings any more than that, at least not yet."

"Really? This is interesting, or at least more interesting than going to bed alone. Why not?"

Matt got to his feet, unconsciously rubbing at the back of his neck. "All right. Let's consider this, Court. One, I'm too old for her, in ways more important than just the difference in our ages. Two, she's Teddy's kid, and I liked Teddy, so just taking her to bed and then walking away when this is over? The thought leaves a bad taste in my mouth. Three— we're up to three now? Three, she drives me nuts. Four, she *knows* she drives me nuts, so she keeps doing it. I get the feeling I'm not in charge here, and I don't like it."

"Welcome to my world," Court said, saluting him with his beer bottle. "When it comes to the Sunshine girls, I don't think any man can fool himself into thinking he's in charge. Example, my cousin Sam. He learned his lesson five years ago, when Jolie threw his ring back at him, and did it all right when he got a second chance. I'm trying to learn mine with Jade, but I think Jolie was easier to convince than Jade will ever be, frankly. Jessica? I don't have a clue what might work with her."

Matt smiled. "Work to do what? I think we're

back to your original question—what the hell am I still doing here?"

"Oh, I think you know why you're still here, Matt," Court told him wryly. "You just don't know how it's going to end. Again, welcome to my world…"

JESSICA, DRESSED IN faded denim cutoffs and a sleeveless red-and-white polka-dotted blouse she'd hiked up and tied beneath her breasts, leaned across the hood of the Jeep in an attempt to reach a stubborn spot and scrub at it with the huge, soapy natural sea sponge she'd found in one of the garages. She was up on tiptoe in her bare feet, and just because her hair was pulled back into two ponytails and the cutoffs bordered on indecent didn't mean she'd deliberately set out to dress like Daisy Duke. Even if she had.

The interior of the Jeep was already cleaned out—shoveled out was more like it—and shone with the spray she'd found on a shelf in that same garage. The fast-food boxes and wrappers, the empty soda and coffee cups, a few bits of food she thought might make good science-fair exhibits, had filled an entire plastic garbage bag.

She lingered over the spot on the hood when her inner radar told her that someone, most probably Matt, was standing behind her on the driveway. If it wasn't Matt, either Bear Man or Court was getting a free show.

Lifting one foot off the ground, stretching her leg

out behind her for balance, she leaned a little farther and gave the now spot-free area of the Jeep's hood another few swipes with the sponge.

"What in hell do you think you're doing to my Jeep?"

Ah, success, and the first time out of the gate, too. Which was probably good, because Bear Man might not have been able to hold up under the strain.

Jessica pushed herself away from the Jeep hood, noticing that the front of her shirt was now intriguingly damp and clinging—an unexpected bonus to her plan—and turned to smile at the scowling Lieutenant Matthew Denby. "What in hell am I doing?" she chirped as she bent to dip the sponge in the pail of soapy water. "I think that should be obvious to a detective as keen as you, Lieutenant. I'm knitting a sweater."

"Very funny. Okay, I admit it, I asked the obvious and probably deserved that," Matt said, approaching the Jeep. "Now for the question I should have asked— *why* are you washing my Jeep?"

She lifted the sopping sponge and half flung it onto the ragtop, then climbed onto the running board so she could begin scrubbing at the dust and just plain crud. "There you go, Matt, a simple question, for which I have a simple answer. If you're going to force me to play Naomi to your Ruth here, then I'm at least going to ride in a clean car...Jeep."

"Play Ruth?"

She turned her head and grinned at him. "Yeah, Ruth. You know—where you go, I will go, where you lodge I will lodge, et cetera—or however she's quoted in the Bible."

"I don't think *et cetera* was used much in the Bible," Matt told her as he bent down and picked up the hose. "Move."

"What?"

"I said *move*. Who the hell taught you how to wash a car, Jess? You don't soap the entire thing and then rinse it. Not in full sun like this. The soap's drying on the hood and it'll ruin the finish. I need to rinse it off."

"Ruin the finish? Oh, I doubt that," Jessica shot back at him, not moving, but just continuing to soap the ragtop. After all, she was giving him a good view, and he should appreciate that. "This paint job was ruined long before I showed up. As a matter of fact, there's this part of me that worries that once all the dirt is gone we'll find out it was all that held this piece of junk together."

"Well," he said as if speaking to himself, "she can't say she wasn't warned."

The next thing Jessica knew she was being blasted with ice-cold water from the hose.

She let out a small screech and jumped down from the running board, keeping her back to Matt as she covered her face and yelled at him to knock it off.

"What's that, Jess? You've got your hands over your mouth. I couldn't make out what you said."

Jessica whirled to face him and caught a fresh blast of cold water straight to her open mouth. "*Not* funny! Now—*pffht!*—now *cut that out!* Matthew! I mean it! Don't make me hurt you!"

The stream of water was redirected to the Jeep and Jessica lowered her hands once more when she heard Matt's laughter. "Hurt me? And how do you think you're going to do that, Jessica?"

Wiping water from her face, Jessica approached him, not stopping until she was no more than a foot away from him. He looked so good this morning, his faintly shaggy, light brown hair glinting with gold and maybe a little silver in the morning sun, his fabulous gray-blue eyes accented by laugh lines cut into his tanned skin, his smile for once wide, unaffected.

"I don't know, *Matthew,*" she told him, moving her hands down her cheeks, her neck, and then running them over her breasts, trying to shed more water. Matt's gaze followed her hands and his smile faded slightly. "Oh, well, maybe I do know." Even before she'd finished speaking, Jessica reached up with both hands, grabbed Matt's ears and yanked his head down so that he was face-first into her chest. She wriggled her body against him for a second and then pushed him away, stepped clear of him. "Say goodbye to Hollywood, Lieutenant, because that's the last time you'll be invited to *this* party."

And then she turned on her heel and ran back toward the house, giggling at the dumbstruck expression she'd seen on his face.

"You're a child!" he called after her, stopping her in her tracks.

She turned around quickly. "And you're a man, and out for the same thing any other man is out for. You're no different. You're just more…more experienced. And a lot less polite!"

Matt walked toward her. Instinct told her it was time to go, but she seemed to be rooted to the driveway pavers. "Matt?"

"And what was this for?" he asked her, motioning toward her, clearly indicating her skimpy outfit. "You're a child, Jessica, and you're a tease. Don't try your games with me, sweetheart, because I am older and I don't play games. You may play your games with boys and not get burned, but you don't want to play with me. With me, there will be consequences. Understood?"

"Oh…just get out of my life!" Jessica shouted at him, hating how stupidly she was reacting, ashamed of the juvenile trick she'd played on him. "I don't need you and I don't want you. Understand?"

Before her brain could even register what was happening, Matt had cupped a hand behind her head and pulled her close against his body, his mouth crashing down on hers even as his other hand went to her breast.

Her lips parted involuntarily and he deepened the kiss, his tongue stroking at the sensitive roof of her mouth, tangling with her own tongue. His hand slipped up beneath the knotted hem of her shirt, his clever fingers feeling so hot against her water-cooled breast, setting her senses on fire.

This was domination, pure and simple. This was Matt telling her without words that, if he wanted to, he could have her completely under his control, mentally and physically.

Suddenly she hated him.

But then he shifted, both his body and his tactics. He insinuated his thigh between hers, applying a gentle pressure even as his mouth softened. He used his teeth to gently tug at her bottom lip, his kisses more teasing and encouraging, his thumb and forefinger working small miracles as they did unimaginably wonderful things to her now tight and straining nipple.

Jessica's hands, which had been balled into fists ready to pound against his chest, opened as she slid her arms around his back and held on tight.

He tasted of mint mouthwash, he smelled of the most erotic-smelling cologne ever manufactured, he felt like a safe haven in her topsy-turvy world. He was real, he was solid, and she needed real, she needed solid.

"Jess, I'm sorry," Matt breathed against her ear as he shifted his hands so that he was holding her, cradling her waist. "You drive me crazy, but that's no excuse."

She looked at him, caught between loss and confusion as he stepped away from her. "What? You're *sorry?*"

He nodded. "Yeah, I am. Go inside, Jessica, go get dressed, and I'll finish with the Jeep. I'll meet you in the living room in about a half hour, and we can plan what we're going to do today, all right?"

"You're *sorry,*" Jessica repeated dully. "Right. Okay. And I suppose I'm supposed to be sorry, too?"

"Jess, don't—"

"Don't what, Matt? Don't be mad? Don't feel ashamed? Don't hate me, don't hate yourself? Too late, Matt, on all counts. Too late."

Jessica turned and ran, and this time when he called her name, she didn't stop, didn't even hesitate. She didn't stop running until she'd reached her room, where she stripped out of her sodden clothes and slammed into the shower stall to stand under the rain shower for a full five minutes before she had the energy to pick up the soap.

And for all of those long minutes she'd asked herself what she should do next, how she could possibly ever look at Matt again, if there was any way they could get past what had just happened. If there was, crazy as the idea seemed, any sort of future for them.

And for all of those five minutes she heard the same words over and over inside her head: *Not on your life, kiddo.*

CHAPTER FOUR

MATT WALKED into the living room to see that Jessica was already there, waiting for him. Rockne sprawled at her feet, wearing his Notre Dame kerchief, but when he saw Matt, he got up, pointedly turned his back and walked away toward the kitchen. Great. Even dogs didn't like him anymore.

"You okay?" he asked before he realized that was probably number two on any list of dumb questions he could have asked, number one being *Are you still mad?*

"I'm fine, thanks," she said, closing the file she'd been reading and getting to her feet.

She held the manila folder to her chest like some sort of armor—or a Protection From Abuse. No, he wouldn't think that. He hadn't attacked her, damn it. Okay, so maybe he had. Sort of. And he'd be damned if he'd take the cop-out so many men took: *She was asking for it.*

"No, you're not," he said, walking up to her and touching his fingers to her smooth, too-pale cheek. "I'm sorry, Jess. I was a total ass out there. No excuses. Just my solemn promise that it will never happen again."

"Well," she said, covering his hand with her own. "That's rather depressing. I did set out to drive you crazy, you know. On purpose. If I promise not to do anything that stupid and childish again, will you promise that we can at least go back to where we were last night?"

Matt brought her hand to his mouth, kissed the soft inside of her wrist. "And where were we last night?"

"Now who's being a tease? And isn't it nice to know that neither of us is the kind to hold a grudge? Makes it easier to fight, don't you think?" she asked, grinning at him as she pushed the manila folder toward him. "Ready to go?"

"That depends," Matt said, the coiled spring in his gut slowly beginning to relax. That one woman had this much power over him was damn disconcerting. "Where are we going?"

"You tell me, since you're the one Mama Bunny talked to, remember?" she said as they walked outside, where the now clean but still not impressive Jeep had remained parked.

"It could be another dead end, you know," Matt told her, opening the door for her. "Prostitutes aren't exactly known for their love of the truth."

"Ever the optimist, aren't you, Matt?" Jessica said as she sat down on the leather seat and then shifted her legs up and into the Jeep—and nearly slid onto the floor. "Oops—slippery!"

Matt leaned inside, running his hand down the back of the seat. "What the hell...?"

"I polished the seats with some spray bottle of leather cleaner I found in one of the garages," Jessica told him, grinning as she pushed herself upright once more. "Maybe I overdid it a little?"

"That would be my first thought, yeah," Matt countered, grinning. "Strap yourself in, okay?"

He walked around the front of the Jeep, still grinning, and carefully got into the driver's seat, gripping the steering wheel as a precaution. The leather wrap around the wheel was also slippery, but he pretended to ignore that fact. "Smells good in here," was all he said.

"It does, doesn't it? So much better than *eau d'old French fries*. Your apartment is so neat—so bare— and your Jeep was so, well, definitely not neat. It makes me think you spend more time in this Jeep than you do in your apartment. Am I right?"

"Sometimes it works that way," Matt said as he inserted the key in the ignition. The engine turned over immediately, and he engaged the transmission and stepped on the gas.

His leather-soled shoe slipped off the pedal. He reacted by slamming his foot on the brake. His foot slipped off the brake.

"Jesus H. Christ, Jessica!" he shouted as he managed to stop the Jeep that had been heading for the rear of Sam's Mercedes, parked twenty feet in front of it. "You polished the damn *pedals?* Didn't you notice that they're rubber, not leather?"

Jessica had covered her mouth with both hands, her brown eyes huge and innocently shocked. "All the grooves were packed with dirt and crud. I, uh…I may have gotten a little carried away with the spray can?"

"Ya think?" Matt said, cutting the engine and yanking the keys from the ignition. And then he noticed that, although her mouth was still hidden behind her hands, her eyes were smiling. Almost dancing in her head. And, somehow, he began to see the humor she obviously had already seen. "Nobody's going to believe me down at the station when I tell them," he said, and grinned.

Now she removed her hands to say, "You're not going to *tell* anyone, are you? Matt, please don't do that."

"Oh, right. I guess you'd be embarrassed."

"No," she admitted, her grin widening. "I'm simply claiming this as my story, not yours. It'll be a real hit at parties. Everyone loves a good blond joke, you know."

"You're not really blond," Matt pointed out as he motioned for her to get out of the Jeep.

She slammed the door and glared at him as he

came around to join her. "I should have been. I was
as a child. A real towhead. It's not my fault my hair
turned to a mousy pale brown as I grew up. I'll
always be blond at heart. What do we do now, Matt?"

He headed for the door, and she followed him, not
quite the repentant puppy, but close. "Now we ask the
housekeeper where Sam keeps his car keys, and
borrow his fancy black Mercedes. More fitting for a
big media star like yourself. You won't even have to
wash it first."

"True, but you'll still be wearing that hideous jacket.
Please, please, please go shopping with me. How do
you ever expect to someday be promoted to captain or
whatever if you dress like you slept in the gutter?"

Matt ignored her and just opened the front door.

Court was passing through the foyer as they stepped
inside, scanning the headlines of the financial section
of the morning newspaper. He was tall enough and
slim enough to look good in pleated slacks of some
indeterminate dark gray with subtle pinstripes and a
smoky blue, discreetly monogrammed dress shirt open
at the collar and tapered to accentuate his slim waist
and broad shoulders.

Matt mentally cataloged his own worn jeans,
black pullover, and the brown tweed jacket he wore
to conceal his shoulder harness and the handcuffs
clipped to the back of his belt. Probably thanks to
Jessica's nagging, the thought smacked Matt that

maybe it was time he began dressing like a grown-up. Then again, Court's slacks, shirt and classy black tasseled shoes probably cost a month of Matt's salary.

"Hey, I thought you two left," Court said, folding the paper and tucking it beneath his arm.

"We were on our way, but then," Matt told him as Jessica audibly sucked in her breath, "the Jeep wouldn't start. If it's all right, we'd like to borrow the Mercedes."

"Not my Mercedes," Court said, shrugging, "but I doubt Sam will mind. As long as you don't let Jessica drive. I've heard she's got a seriously lead foot."

"One lousy speeding ticket ten years ago, and I get to hear about it forever," Jessica groused as Jade entered the foyer from the hallway that led to the morning room where they'd eaten breakfast. "What did you do, Jade—rent a billboard?"

"Not Jade. Sam told me, Jess," Court explained. "Just in passing."

"Uh-huh," Jessica shot back at him. "Why?"

"Oh, for heaven's sake, Jess," Jade said, picking up her purse and adjusting its strap on her shoulder. "Sam had that Corvette a few years ago, remember? His *compensation* I've always said, for having Jolie walk out on him—and you wanted to take it for a drive. Somebody had to warn him."

"So it *was* you, when we follow the trail back far enough," Jessica said. "Thanks, *mom*. Anything else you want to *warn* everybody about?"

"No, at least I can't think of anything right now," Jade said smoothly as she walked past her sister, winking at Matt. "Imagine how many tickets, before and since, she smiled and flirted her way out of before she met a cop who wasn't impressed. Don't let her drive. Truly," she warned as Jessica headed off down the hallway that led to the morning room and kitchen.

"Thanks for the heads up. Where are you two heading this morning?" Matt asked, to change the subject.

"Jade wants to talk to Jermayne Johnson again," Court told him.

"The brother of Terrell, our drive-by Scholar Athlete murder," Matt said, nodding. "The kid was only, what, seven, when his brother died? What do you hope to get from him?"

"With their grandmother dead now, Jermayne's the only family member left," Jade reminded him. "It's not exactly a lead, but Teddy did talk to Jermayne a week before he was murdered, just like with the other cold cases we're investigating, and I don't think Jermayne was totally honest with me when he told me Teddy said nothing of any importance."

"In other words, we're grasping at straws," Court said, pulling a set of car keys from his pocket.

Matt rubbed at the back of his neck, considering his options, and then made a decision. "Maybe there's something you need to know about Jermayne, something I found in Terrell's murder book. Jermayne had a juvvie jacket, something handled in family court before his brother was killed. Sealed of course, so it all went away when he stayed clean until he turned eighteen. Teddy moving them out of the city probably had a lot to do with that. It might even explain why Teddy got involved, took the steps he did—he was trying to save the kid. It's one of the many things I admired about the man."

"That's Teddy, all right. But he didn't have anything like that about Jermayne in his own notes. Maybe he didn't want to think about it?" Jade stood very still, her hand on the doorknob. "What did Jermayne do? It couldn't have been good, if a seven-year-old got a juvvie record out of it. I mean, it wasn't like he was caught boosting gummy bears from the corner grocery, right?"

"No, that's enough. I told you, Jade, the record was sealed, and now it's gone."

"But you know," Jessica said quietly, and he turned to see her standing right beside him, dangling Sam's Mercedes keys from her upheld fingers. He grabbed them before she could snatch them away.

"No, I don't."

"Yes, you do," she insisted. "You've got that little tic working in your right eyelid—right there, see? I've noticed it before when you were trying not to tell the truth."

"I always tell the truth," Matt said, rubbing at his eyelid.

"Still twitching, isn't it. I'm surprised both eyelids aren't twitching after that last clunker. You always tell the truth? Yeah, right, don't we all?" Jessica asked with a smile, rocking on her heels as if delighted with herself. "It's called a *tell,* Matt, and I've read all about how to look for tells, or body language. Helps me a lot when I'm interviewing people. Or, in other words, Lieutenant—liar, liar, pants on fire."

"Matt?" Jade asked. "Is she right? Do you know something? Because, if you do, then Teddy knew it, too. This could mean something. I don't know what, but anything is better than the nothing we've got right now. I mean, I'm about to give this up, move on to the Baby in the Dumpster case."

"All right," Matt admitted, knowing when he was beaten. "I shouldn't have opened my big mouth, and you can't let on to Jermayne that you know this, but I had a small talk with one of the arresting officers and she told me what she remembered about what the kid was into. And, yes, Teddy had to know, because, like I said, it happened *before* Terrell was killed. Like too many other kids, Jermayne had carried and held crank for some local gang."

"Excuse me?" Court asked. "I hate to show my stupidity, but what's *crank?* And how does a seven-year-old get a juvenile record?"

"Crank is a form of amphetamine—methamphet-amine, actually. On the street it's called speed, meth, crank, crystal, uppers, bennies, billy—"

"How in hell do you know that?" Matt asked Jessica, incredulous.

She grinned and continued, "—tweak, bitch and, my personal favorite, *whiz*. The scary part is that, in a more acceptable, legal form, similar amphetamines are Dexedrine and even Ritalin—you know, that stuff they give to hyperactive kids?"

"I may call for a prescription for you, Jess," Jade muttered from behind Matt.

"You're always so funny, Jade, a real card. Any-way, crank is a powder most times, but it can be cut, put into injectable liquid or even tablet form, and it is by far the most abused drug out there, mostly because it's both cheap and highly addictive. Get caught carrying it in salable amounts and there's no get-out-of-jail-free card, so smart bad guys find un-derage kids to hold it and pass it to buyers, with the older, go-directly-to-jail guy never touching the stuff." She looked at Matt. "How am I doing?"

"You're scaring the living hell out of me," Matt admitted. "Another special you did?"

"Yup. We called it 'Speed Run,' because people take crank for hours, getting more and more hyper until they crash, sleep up to forty-eight hours straight, and then wake up feeling like crap and desperately needing to go out on another *speed run* to find more crank so they can start the cycle all over again. I've got more, if you want it. I'm a veritable font of information. I'm flirting with the idea of trying out for *Jeopardy.*"

Court laughed and Matt looked at him. "What do you think, Court? It's too early for me to have a drink? It's not ten o'clock yet, and I already feel like I've had enough for one day."

"Yeah, yeah, Methuselah, you're all worn-out," Jessica teased, slipping her arm through his. "Now come on—as they say in all those old Western movies, we're burning daylight."

Matt waved goodbye to Court and Jade as Jessica half pulled him outside, and then she ran around to the driver's side door and held up her hand to him. "Keys?"

"This is a test, right?" he asked her, remaining where he was.

"It most certainly is. So?"

"So?" he repeated. "I'm pretty sure my departmental life insurance is paid up. I wouldn't want Mortimer to go hungry. Here—catch."

"Thank you," Jessica said as they climbed into the car and he strapped on his seat belt beside her. "You're a man of courage, and I applaud that. When I'm eighty-six and Jade's eighty-nine, she'll still treat me like the baby. It's pathetic."

"I'd like to see you at eighty-six," Matt told her as she put the car in gear and headed it toward the gates. "I'm betting you'll be the terror of the croquet courts in Boca Raton. Blond hair in a ponytail, wiggling your behind as you bend over your shot, wearing one of those short white skirts, setting off pacemakers in the appreciative male audience…"

"Sounds interesting. And, of course, you'll be invited," she told him as she waved to Bear Man, who had opened the gates for them. "You'll only be one hundred and two, right?"

"Ninety-seven, but who's counting?" Matt said as they made their way to the Blue Route. "And don't take your hands off the wheel to count that out. You're twenty-eight—I asked—and I'm thirty-nine. That was what you were fishing for, wasn't it?"

"Which way—toward I-95, right?" she asked him. "And, yes, I was being indirect again. Sorry. I should have just asked you straight out. I'm trying, I really am, but I've had those twenty-eight years of perfecting the indirect route, so it could take some time. Now, since I'm at the wheel, how about you tell me where we're going, okay?"

"Fishtown, naturally," Matt said, reaching into his pocket and pulling out the scrap of paper on which he'd scribbled the address Mama Bunny had given him. "She didn't give me an exact address, just that it's a narrow street off Girard Avenue near Palmer. Not much more than an alley, and the bottom floor is a beauty shop. Fishtown isn't a bad area of the city, and it's even better now than it was when the murders happened. In fact, technically, the murders didn't take place in Fishtown, but closer to the river. At least that's where the bodies were found."

"You work for the Chamber of Commerce in your off-hours?" Jessica asked, deftly easing the Mercedes onto the interstate.

Matt grinned. "Just shut up and drive, lady," he told her, and with the morning rush hour over, it wasn't that much longer until they hit the city streets again and were on Girard Avenue, looking for Palmer.

"I'm going to park here," Jessica said, obviously making an executive decision, because she had already pulled to the curb and put the car in Park. "Ready?"

"Actually, no," Matt told her. "First, a few ground rules. I talk, you stand there, safely behind me. Don't smile, don't pose, and for God's sake don't go fluffing your hair that way you do. It's an interview, not a seduction. Okay?"

"Oh, no," Jessica said, slumping in the driver's seat. "You're going to go all cop on the guy, whoever we talk to? Why, Matt? You know it won't get you anywhere. Keep your badge in your pocket and let me handle the questions. *Especially* if it's a man."

"Shield."

She looked at him quizzically. "Pardon me?"

"It's not a badge, it's a gold shield. I know you *journalists* like to keep your facts straight."

Jessica rolled her eyes, and Matt was hard-pressed not to grab her, kiss her senseless. "Oh, pardon me, Lieutenant, sir. Your *shield*. And can't you lose the jacket? For one, it's ugly. For two, it's getting hot out there, if you didn't notice, so it would be obvious to a two-year-old that you're carrying concealed. I won't be nasty and even mention those horrible cop shoes."

"You and Ernesto. What's wrong with my shoes?" Matt asked her once they joined up on the sidewalk. "They're cheap, they're comfortable, and they last forever."

"They're butt-ugly, the soles are too thick and they scream cop. I'm just grateful the soles are black, and not some stupid tan crepe dealies," Jessica told him as they walked to the corner and turned right to see a hand-painted sign halfway down the block: Maisie's Hair And Nails. "Ah, Mama Bunny gives half-decent directions."

Matt was looking down at his shoes, perfectly acceptable shoes, and had to hustle to catch up with Jessica, who had already moved off down the sidewalk. "The landlord supposedly lives in the apartment at the rear of the shop. We'll try there first."

Jessica inclined her head in agreement and motioned for him to lead the way, which he did, moving down the three-foot-wide, round-topped-brick corridor between the row house connected to the building housing the beauty salon. "Cool. It's like a tunnel, isn't it? Do you think there's an echo? Oh, don't make a face. I'm not going to start yodeling or anything. Man, these houses are narrow. But charming, in a Colonial America sort of way."

"Fishtown is pretty old," Matt agreed as they came back out into the sun to see a set of white stone steps leading up to a back door with the words *Keep Out This Means You* painted none too neatly on the scarred wood. "Friendly sort, huh?"

"And very direct, just like the new me," Jessica quipped, bounding up the steps to knock on the door three times with the side of her fist even as she opened one more top button on her blouse.

"I don't know why I waste my breath." The landing at the top of the steps was too narrow for both of them, so Matt stayed where he was and waited for the door to open, which it did almost immediately.

"What?" bellowed a very large man in a seriously undersize "wife-beater" undershirt and a pair of bright green boxers with small red polka-dots flapping above a set of legs that would have looked better on a chicken. "Can't youse people read? It says right there— Well, hell-ooo."

Jessica flipped at her blond hair, hanging loose below her shoulders, and smiled brightly enough to have Matt wishing he'd brought along his sunglasses.

"Hi," she chirped, striking a pose halfway between sweet innocence and "If you want it, big boy, come and get it."

"Okay, down here, Jess," Matt warned her tightly. "Now."

"My older brother," Jessica told the man, pulling a face. "Just pretend he's not here."

The man looked down the steps to where Matt stood, frowning. "Don't look much alike, do you? Youse looking for a place? I got no vacancies."

"Vacancies?" Matt shook his head and took an educated guess. "City planning office says you've got the shop, this back apartment and one more apartment upstairs. You're not exactly running a Holiday Inn here, buddy. Or have you been subdividing without bothering to apply for a permit?"

The man's eyes narrowed even as he began moving his lower jaw back and forth, as if chewing his cud. "Cop. I shoulda known."

"It was the shoes, right?" Jessica inquired sweetly. "A dead giveaway. Of course, that jacket doesn't help. Am I right or am I right?"

"Go away. You're making me miss my show," the man said.

Jessica grabbed his forearm as he made to step back inside, close the door. "No, wait. We're not here to…to bust your chops. Honest. We're here about one of the victims of the Fishtown Strangler. You remember?

One of them used to live here. Tarin White?" She let go, held out her hand to him. "Oh, I'm Jessica Sunshine and he's Matthew Denby. And you're…?"

"Pitts. Sherman Pitts," the man said slowly as he shook Jessica's hand, his gaze once more directed at her chest.

"Hi, Shermie. I bet all the ladies call you Shermie," Jessica cooed.

"No, but you can call me anything you want to, Jessica," Pitts said.

Matt had a swift mental picture of himself body-slamming Pitts to the ground and then stomping on him. Failing that, he could always haul Jessica over his knee and give her a good spanking. "And now we're all friends, aren't we?"

"Not with you, I'm not," Pitts said, talking to Matt, but still holding Jessica's hand. "Yeah, yeah. Tarin. I remember her. So what? She didn't work outta here, I'll tell you that. I don't let no hookers live here. I got a wife. Or I did till she split five years back."

"My congratulations to the lady," Matt said, holding up his shield as he motioned for Pitts to join him on the cement walkway. "Playtime's over. Down here, Shermie, now."

Jessica rolled her eyes. "Let the poor man put some pants on first, Matthew, for pity's sake."

"Oh, right," Pitts said, looking down at his boxers. "Be right back, sweetheart."

Jessica came down the steps, shaking her head at Matt. "See? He's my Shermie and I'm his sweetheart. We're pals. You could use a few lessons in finesse. You know, that 'catch more flies with honey than with vinegar' thing."

"Pitts has his own flies. Didn't you see them circling his head?" Matt muttered. "Let's go."

"Go? Why?"

"Because he closed the door, Jessica—big surprise—and he's not coming back out here again, that's why. Never let a guy out of your sight—it's rule number one. I have no warrant, no cause to ask a judge to issue one, and now, thanks to your worries about his nonexistent modesty, we've lost the guy, so let's just— Damn."

The door had opened once more and Sherman Pitts appeared, dressed in a pair of wrinkled brown slacks, his overlong gray hair combed back slickly from his forehead. "Here I am, Jessica, honey. What did you want to know?"

"Score one for the girls," Jessica said quietly, and then waited for Pitts to join them. "Thank you so much for your cooperation, Shermie. You spoke to the police when Tarin was killed?"

"Yeah, yeah," Pitts replied, nodding, his small black-bean eyes honed in like twin lasers on "the girls." He licked his lips. "They weren't interested. Tarin hadn't lived here for a long time before she died."

"Yes, and somehow your address actually seems to have gotten lost in the sheer volume of paper generated in investigating six murders," Jessica said. "So Tarin lived here, what, about a year before she died?"

"Less than that. Six, seven months? The wife would know, but she's not here, remember? Could have fooled me that Tarin was a hooker. Nice kid, kept to herself. The wife said she thought she had a boyfriend the last couple of months, but I never seen him. I told the cops that, the two that came here, and one of 'em said she sure did have a boyfriend. Lots of them, at fifty bucks a pop, and then tried to make something of it, you know? Like I was pimping for her or something, you know?"

"That wasn't nice," Jessica said sympathetically. "How dare they leap to a conclusion like that! I'll bet you weren't in a hurry to tell them anything else after that insult, were you, Shermie?"

Matt suppressed a groan, even though he had to admit to himself that Jessica had a point. Somebody had badly blundered the questioning of Sherman Pitts.

"Damn right I clammed up! Next thing they'da tried to pin it all on me, make me into the Fishtown Strangler or something crazy like that. Town was going apeshit back then, what with all those bodies and the mayor's special commission and all the hoo-ha going on. The cops were just looking for anybody to pin it on so the press would back off. I'm not dumb. I watch TV. I know. Folks like me get railroaded all the time. And the wife agreed with me. So we said what we said and that was it. Only a jackass volunteers, right?"

"Volunteers what, Shermie?" Jessica asked him. "Was there something else you and your wife thought the police might want to know?"

Pitts slid his gaze to Matt. "No. Nothing more. Besides, it was all a long time ago. Who cares anymore?"

"We do, Pitts," Matt told him quietly. "And, watching a lot of TV like you do, you know there's no statute of limitations on murder. So if you're withholding evidence in a capital crime, you might want to rethink telling us what you know."

Pitts laughed nervously, turning to Jessica to appeal for her help. "Hey, hey, let's not get all bent out of shape here. Tarin lived here, and then she left without telling us where she was going. Paid up, she was always paid up, but she just left one night without a word to us. That was a good six or more months or so before she turned up dead."

"We don't know where she lived after she left here. It was like she'd dropped off the face of the earth," Matt told him. "Leaving you as her last contact, Sherman, old buddy."

"She had a boyfriend!" Pitts looked to Jessica

again. "Like I said, I ain't never seen him, but the wife, she said there was a boyfriend. He dumped her, that's what the wife said."

"Dumped her? How did your wife figure that?" Jessica asked him.

Pitts shrugged. "Like I said, it was the wife. Me, I don't notice stuff like that. But it was winter, too, and Tarin was a little gal, always buried up to her chin in one of those big, puffy coats—you know those big, puffy coats? Anyway, the wife said she was sure of it. Tarin was pregnant." He looked at Matt. "That's why the boyfriend dumped her. He'd knocked her up and didn't want nothing to do with the kid. Now that's it. That's all I know and all I got to say."

Pitts closed the door once more and this time Matt heard a dead bolt being shot home. He looked to Jessica, who was standing very still, her face white, her eyes brimming with tears. "Come on, sweetheart. Let's get back to the car and the case folder. The autopsy report is in it."

"A baby?" Jessica said quietly, blinking up at him. "Oh, Matt, I feel like someone just punched me in the stomach. Tarin had a baby before she died. Where's that baby?"

Matt hustled them back through the narrow tunnel and onto the street, then turned her in the direction of the car. "We don't know if Sherman's wife was right, Jess. Teddy doesn't have a copy of the entire autopsy report, but I know the summary page was in his file. Let's not jump to conclusions until I read it."

"Yes, you read it," Jessica agreed. "I don't think I want to. It was enough for me to know that she was one of the strangler's victims."

He watched as she walked to the driver's side of the Mercedes and decided not to fight her on that one for the moment, but just climbed into the passenger seat and picked up the manila folder that had been placed on the floor. He paged through quickly, locating the photocopy of the medical examiner's preliminary findings.

Perimortem bruising, contusions indicative of a struggle. Ligature marks on ankles, wrists, neck. Hyoid bone fracture. Rape kit negative but vaginal tears indicate forceful penetration, possibly postmortem. Question as to whether ejaculation achieved. Appendectomy scar. Healed fracture of left femur. Nonremarkable striation of pelvic floor consistent with childbirth. Recent episiotomy scar. Toxicology report pending.

"Sherman's wife was right. Tarin White was pregnant when she left the apartment and gave birth not too long before she died. Sorry, sweetheart," he told Jessica, closing the folder.

Jessica had inserted the key in the ignition, but she hadn't turned it. She simply sat with both hands in a white-knuckled clasp of the steering wheel. "Oh, God. And Teddy knew that, didn't he? Just like he knew Kayla Morrison had a young daughter—I went to see her a few days ago, you know, Keely. She's a teenager now, and a real accident looking for a place to happen, poor kid. That's why he was concentrating on these two victims. None of the others had children. A couple of them had no family at all."

"Knowing what I know about Teddy, and after meeting you and your sisters, yeah, that makes sense."

Jessica put her hand on Matt's arm. "We've got to find this guy, Matt. Now more than ever. I don't care if it all happened so long ago. I don't even care if this case is totally unconnected to whoever murdered Teddy. Somebody killed Tarin White and took her from her baby." Her eyes widened. "And the baby! Where's that baby, Matt?"

"Good question. Tarin might have gone home, wherever that was, to have the baby, and left it with relatives when she came back to Philly. Or the kid could be in the system somewhere. Then there's private adoption…"

"Tarin was black. Are there adoption agencies that deal only in African-American babies, do you think? I mean, it's a place to start."

Matt motioned for her to start the car. "It's still not

easy to get access to adoption records, Jess. Nobody came forward to claim Tarin's body and she would have been buried by the city, except that an anonymous citizen donated the cost of a plot and headstone. I remember reading that in her file."

"*Somebody* who knew her, I'm betting. What else explains the donated plot and stone?" Jessica said, turning onto Girard Avenue once more. "Didn't anybody ever check that out?"

"Why would they? Tarin was one victim out of six. Somebody was touched by the deaths and wanted to help, end of story. We concentrated on finding the killer, not on the victims who, when you get down to it, were just a part of the pattern of the killer. The only thing I'm wondering now is how Tarin White paid for the expensive dental work I read about somewhere else in the report. I mean, she wasn't exactly living at the Ritz. Red light."

"I see it," Jessica said, slowing the big car in the left-turn lane. "Okay, so we're not just running over the same ground the cops did back then or that Teddy did twice a year for the past dozen years. We'll take a new path, go looking for the child."

"Why?" Matt asked, looking out the window, vaguely aware that a jacked-up diarrhea-yellow Dodge had pulled abreast of them at the red light. "We're looking for a serial killer, Jess, not working just one murder."

"True. But Teddy was concentrating on Kayla Morrison and Tarin White. They're the only two out of the six he has notes on these past three years or so in his twice-yearly rework of the cases. There had to be a reason. Maybe that both had kids and Teddy was taking it personally, but then again, maybe it was for some other reason. What are you doing?"

"Nothing. Quiet," Matt said as he lowered the window, letting in the sound of a stereo with a seriously stressed bass. "Well, I'll be damned. If it isn't my old friend, Mister Byrd. How's it hanging, Tweety? I've been keeping an eye out for you, so we can have us a little talk. Pull it over and park it and we'll— *Shit!*"

The Dodge peeled out just as the light turned green.

Jessica put the pedal to the floor and followed, cutting back into the middle lane and cutting off the car originally two behind Byrd's.

"Cripes, Jess, what are you doing?" Matt yelled, clinging to the roof handle as she pushed the car through an impossibly small opening and came up hard on Byrd's tail. "Let it go. I've got the description and plate number."

"No. You want him, we'll go get him. Who's Tweety?" Jessica asked, her eyelids narrowed as she rode the Dodge's bumper, both cars hitting sixty miles an hour in just a small stretch of open road.

"Nobody. Back it down, Jess, break off the chase."

"Not until you tell me who he is and why you want him," Jessica yelled, and then added, "Hold on, he's turning."

Matt's body slammed into the passenger door and he actually closed his eyes, waiting for the shock of impact that had to follow the screech of the Mercedes's tires laying rubber all the way through the turn. He opened them to see that they were on another straight stretch, and the Dodge had begun to pull away, so Jessica accelerated. "Jesus, Jess. Okay, okay. Byrd's one of the weakest links in the gang that's been giving Ernesto and some others grief. I only wanted to talk to him."

"Ernesto? *Our* Ernesto?" Jessica asked him, swerving slightly to avoid a double-parked cab. "But Ernesto said he was okay."

"He's not *our* Ernesto. And he's a good kid, sure, but he lies like a rug," Matt said, watching as the Dodge took another wide corner. "Just break it off now, Jess. This is too dangerous to civilians. I'll get Tweety some other time."

"But I…oh, all right, if you really think so," Jessica said, the speedometer beginning to ease back below sixty, thank God. "No, wait—he's pulling over. Look, Matt! We've got him! He's getting out, he's—"

"He's bailing, the little shit. Pull over," Matt ordered her, already unbuckling his seat belt. The car hadn't quite come to a stop when he threw open the door and began a foot pursuit, following the fleeing Tweety Byrd into a small neighborhood park. Down a flight of stone steps, up a long hill, pushing through trees and cutting around benches, avoiding mothers and baby strollers, slowly gaining on the kid, who stupidly kept slowing up to check behind him to see if Matt was still following.

The kid's baggy pants were also beginning to slow him down, and Matt could see Tweety's striped boxers slowly making an appearance. But the kid kept running.

"Shit, shit, shit," Matt swore, feeling his holster chafing his side. "Tweety—down on the ground, now! You don't want to piss me off, Tweety! I'm too damn old for this! Ah, hell…"

Matt launched himself at Tweety's back, crashing the teenager to the ground, landing hard on top of him, knocking the breath out of both of them.

"One, two, three—and it's a pin! And the new intergalactic pro-wrestling champion is none other than our—"

Still trying to command his lungs to suck in some air, Matt looked up to see Jessica standing next to him, her arms shot high into the air. "Shut…up," he gasped out as he reached behind him for his handcuffs.

"Yes, sir, officer, sir," Jessica said, still sounding too damn jolly to Matt. "Cuff him, Dano!"

"That's *book* him, Dano. But you're too young to know that." Matt reached for Tweety's left wrist and pulled it behind his back, slapped on the cuff before reaching for the teenager's right wrist. The kid was so skinny, he had to snap them all the way. "You're not too bright, are you, Tweety? I just wanted to talk to you. But now you're under arrest."

"I'm arrested? What for, sir? I didn't do nothing, sir. It's my cousin's car, sir, I swear it. I just borrowed it. Maybe…maybe I didn't tell him, but he'll be fine with it. Honest! What you cuffing me for? I told ya I didn't do nothing wrong."

Matt looked up at Jessica, who was still grinning. "You ripped off your own cousin, Tweety?" he asked, although he knew it was probably a rhetorical question. "Took yourself out for a little joyride. Shame on you. And now we pile on disobeying an officer, failure to halt, reckless endangerment—that's speeding on a city street, Tweety. What else? Don't worry, I'll think of something. What do I want to bet you're on probation now? You could go away for this, Tweety, and you're nineteen now, so you'll be heading to Graterford if you pull a tough judge. You're in some serious shit, Tweety, that's what you are. Come on, get on your feet. Thatta boy."

"It's my cousin's car! I swear it on my momma! And you chased me when I wasn't doing nothing."

"Matt? Maybe it is his cousin's car."

"Jess, stay out of this," Matt said, reaching into his pocket for his cell phone to call dispatch to run the Dodge's plates, and for a black-and-white to take Tweety downtown. Then he hesitated, as if he'd had second thoughts. After all, he wanted information, and he knew Tweety was the weakest link in the gang that claimed the eight square blocks around the apartment complex. "Your cousin's car, Tweety? Then why did you take off?"

"*You* know," Tweety said, tears running down his cheeks. "You're all torqued because your homeboy Ernesto told you about the books. You just want to beat my ass because of that stupid fag."

"Ernesto's got a brain, so you call him a fag. And I suppose being dumb means you're a *real* man? Great logic you've got going there, Tweety."

"Okay, okay. Nobody hurt him. It was just the books. I swear it!"

Matt wasn't sure what the kid was talking about, so he went fishing. "You shouldn't have done it, Tweety."

"Wasn't me who done it! I just watched. It wasn't me sat on Ernesto while his books got shoved down the sewer. Stupid books, stupid fa—stupid pinhead Ernesto. My momma's gonna kill me, man, she's gonna freaking *kill* me!"

Matt couldn't decide who he was madder at—Tweety and his cohorts, or Ernesto, who should have told him he'd been attacked. "They were Ernesto's books, Tweety. He's trying to make something of himself. Why does that bother you so much? What did the kid ever do to you?"

Tweety hung his head, his lank, greasy hair falling over his face. "I dunno, man. I dunno…"

"I think I do," Jessica said, so that Matt rolled his eyes and motioned for her to back away yet again. "No, Matt, listen. Ernesto is getting out. Isn't he, Tweety? He's working hard, trying to make a better life for himself, and you wish you could have a better life, too, don't you? And you can! You're not stupid, are you, Tweety? Don't hate Ernesto for working hard. *You* work hard, Tweety. Are you still in school? No? Too bad. But you still have time. Instead of destroying someone else's books, why not open a few of your own? It's not cool to be ignorant, Tweety. It's cool to be smart."

"Oh, brother." Matt fished the key to the handcuffs out of his pocket and released Tweety, who looked at him in astonishment.

"You're letting me go, man?"

"Hell, yeah. After having to listen to that pitiful lecture, lockup would seem like a vacation. Go on, Tweety, go. Take that car back to where you found— Take it back to your cousin. And just for the record, Ernesto didn't tell me about the books, so you don't tell anybody about the little talk the two of us had here today, all right? We have a deal?"

"Yes, sir," Tweety said, rubbing at his thin bony wrists.

"Good. Because if I hear anything different, I'll come down on you like a ton of bricks, *capice?*"

"Uh-huh," Tweety said, nodding furiously, and then he took off, running back down the hill and toward the street, holding on to the waistband of his baggy jeans with both hands.

"Happy?" Matt asked Jessica as she watched the teenager go, a smile on her face. "Open a book? God, I'm working with a cockeyed optimist. I'm only glad I sent Tweety away before you asked us all to join hands for a few verses of 'Kumbaya.'"

"Better an optimist than a pessimist," Jessica told him as they walked down the weed-choked hill, side by side. "What are you going to do about Ernesto?"

"Find out what books he lost and replace them for him. Read him the riot act for not coming to me for help, even if I understand why he didn't. What else can I do?"

"Teddy would have moved him out. That's what he did with Keely Morrison and her grandmother. That's what he did with Jermayne Johnson. It's probably what we should do with Ernesto. It would be a tragedy if he ended up like Terrell."

"Teddy couldn't save the world, Jess, and neither can you. There're too many Ernestos out there to help them all, and way too many Tweetys."

"I suppose so. But you're trying, aren't you?"

Matt rubbed at the back of his neck. "Yeah. I suppose I am. A little. Damn."

Jessica slipped her hand in his, bumping shoulders with him as they walked along. "You're a nice man, Matthew Denby. I think I like you."

Matt closed his eyes for a moment, warmed by her words, even as they semi-frightened him. "Good. I like you, too, Jessica Sunshine. Even if you are certifiable. Now give me those keys, because I don't like you enough to let you get behind the wheel again, not with me in the death seat."

Jessica laughed and handed over the keys. "It was fun, though, wasn't it? Do you think Tweety stole that car?"

"Who cares? It was a piece-of-crap car."

"Oh, that's cold, Matt. All right—so do you think he'll take it back where he found it?"

"He's probably scared enough to do that and, correction, it's not cold. It's a cop on vacation, one that isn't looking for a bunch of paperwork on a piece-of-crap car. Now what are you doing?"

Jessica gave the top of his sleeve another pull, and Matt heard stitches breaking away. "You ripped your jacket seam when you tackled Tweety. I'm just making sure the rip is past repairing. In the interests of saving you from appearing on one of those television fashion-police shows where they grab people who look like they dressed in the dark and give them a makeover, you understand."

"I've seen those. You have to be nominated to get on one."

"I know. I've already written the letter. Don't make me mail it. You really need some new clothes, Matt."

"Yeah, I think so, too."

"And so many people don't believe in miracles." Jessica's smile was like a punch to his gut, a not entirely unpleasant one. "Today? No, we should go back to the house, think of what we should do next about Tarin's baby. Tomorrow. And you won't change your mind and back out. Promise?"

"I promise. One new jacket, maybe another pair of jeans. A couple of shirts. I think I shrunk a bunch of them somehow."

"Either that, bucko, or you *grew*. And shoes. Please, God, let the man buy a new pair of shoes," Jessica said, slipping into the passenger seat.

"Anything else?" he asked as he turned the key in the ignition.

"Well, we could talk about a new car."

"You don't know when to stop pushing, do you?"

"Nope. Never mastered that particular talent," Jessica said, imperiously motioning for him to pull away from the curb. "Onward, Supercop, we have work to do!"

CHAPTER FIVE

"So I HEAR YOU WENT drag racing down Girard Avenue with Sam's Mercedes." Jade collapsed onto the chaise in Jessica's guest bedroom. "I'd say I don't believe it, but I do."

Jessica rubbed at her shower-wet hair with a thirsty Egyptian-cotton towel as she sat cross-legged on the bed. "Matt may be cute, but he has a big mouth. And it was a police chase. It wasn't a drag race. There's a difference."

"There are a lot of differences. The major one being that you're not the police." Jade took a sip of tea and carefully replaced the cup on the saucer. She'd already told Jessica that the china was Meissen, probably from the eighteenth century, as Sam Becket was a high-end antiques dealer, which meant that there wasn't a nice, sturdy earthenware cup with a yellow smiley-face or funny saying on it in the entire house. "And when you're not the police, what you did, Jessica Marie, could more aptly be called imbecilic."

"I prefer to think of myself as a free spirit,"

Jessica said, tossing the damp towel onto the carpet and beginning to run a wide-toothed comb through her hair. Rockne sniffed at the towel and then lay down on it, sighing.

"And how does Matt think of you?"

Jessica cocked one eyebrow at her sister. "What do you care?"

"I don't, I suppose," Jade admitted. "No, that's not true. I do care. Jess, he's not a boy you can play with. You do know that, don't you?"

"I've heard that rumor somewhere," Jessica admitted, knowing that Matt had already warned her about the same thing, knowing that she didn't care. "But all men are boys at heart, don't you think?"

"No, I don't. Look, I'm no expert on relationships, but—"

"How's that working out for you, anyway, Jade? You know, you and your ex living under the same roof."

Jade ran a hand through her long straight hair, pushing a thick lock behind her ear. "All right, smart-ass, point made. I'll butt out if you do, too, agreed?"

"I never disagreed," Jessica told her, feeling pretty pleased with herself. With Jade, it was a long time between verbal wins, so she'd savor this one. Besides, she didn't know how she felt about Matt, but she did know that what she did feel wasn't the sort of conversation she wanted to have with either of her big sisters. "How did you and Court make out today with Jermayne Johnson?"

"It was pretty much a waste of time, I'm afraid. Jermayne still swears that he and Teddy talked about the Phillies' chances for the division title this year, and not much of anything else. I don't believe him and neither does Court, but Jermayne isn't budging."

"Did you go at him about that trade-school idea? I think Teddy really wanted him to go to school."

"He wants nothing to do with it, said Teddy didn't owe him anything, that it was the other way around. And he said—muttered almost under his breath— that he didn't need any help. That's when Court finally started to get a little suspicious."

Jessica fished Jade's old cell phone out of her bathrobe pocket and began looking through the incoming calls. There were dozens, and she idly scanned the numbers, the area codes. "Suspicious how? Wait. I mean—suspicious *why?*"

"I don't know. Court said it would be hard to explain to someone as hardwired for facts and just the facts as I am—which would have started another fight, except I'd made a resolution this morning not to fight with him for at least twenty-four hours and I didn't want to blow it in three. Anyway, it was just a feeling he got, on top of the feeling I admit to having that Jermayne is still hiding something from us. Court said…well, he said Jermayne's eyes kept going off to the side, and that meant he was lying. You know, he says he doesn't need help, but his eyes say yes, he does. I think Court, for all he says he doesn't, watches too many television shows—after listening to you and the way you carried on about Matt's eyelid."

"No, no. Court's right, Jade. That's another *tell,* just like Matt's twitchy eyelid. When people aren't telling the truth, ninety-nine percent of the time their eyes shift left and down. They can't help it, it's body over mind. I love to watch politicians being interviewed and watch their eye movements. If we voted by eye movements, believe me, half the guys in office wouldn't be! Now, find me someone who can lie while looking me straight in the face, and I'll show you a sociopath, and when itch comes to scratch, I'd rather vote for a liar than someone who doesn't give a damn about anybody or anything except himself. Anyway, since you also think something's fishy with Jermayne, which would you rather have, Jade? A liar or a sociopath?"

"I'd rather have answers," Jade said, ever the practical one, as she picked up the cup once more. "I'd rather we could solve Melodie Brainard's murder and Teddy's murder and put all this behind us, get on with our lives. I can't stand this…this uncertainty."

"That's my big sister," Jessica said, nodding. "Likes her ducks all lined up in tidy little rows and hates secrets. Which makes you a good P.I., I guess, but I don't know why you don't have one beaut of an ulcer, the way you let things tear at you."

"Nothing's tearing at me," Jade said, putting down the cup again with more force than she'd probably intended. The cup hit the saucer with an audible *clink.* "Damn, I nearly broke it. I've had enough of that."

Jessica scooted off the bed, pulling down the short hem of the terrycloth robe. "Easy, Jade," she said, kneeling in front of her sister. "Look, can we talk about something?"

"Sure. Anything," Jade said, and her gaze shifted left and down. At least her sister wasn't a sociopath.

Jessica smiled as she took Jade's hands in hers, squeezed them gently, aware of the bandage still covering the worst of the burns. It was an odd feeling, but a nice one, finding herself in the position of the calm and cool one, the grown-up. "I know about the Belleek, Jade," she said simply. "I wasn't going to say anything, but watching you with Sam's china and all…"

Jade closed her eyes, lowered her head. "It was… it was stupid. I think I lost my mind for those few minutes. Something. Court and I talked about it after Jolie told him what she and Sam found in my bedroom, and I'm okay with it now. But it was a stupid thing to do."

"Tell me what happened," Jessica said quietly.

"I already told Court."

"I know. But now you can tell me. It's different, telling another woman, especially a sister. Someone who shares your pain at losing Teddy."

Jade shook her head, her curtain of dark hair falling forward to partially hide her features. "Nothing will help. He gave me that china. I loved every piece, every memory attached to each piece. And I destroyed it. What I did was unforgivable."

"You were mad at him, weren't you? For dying. For letting you be the one to find him—"

"No!" Jade's head came up sharply, and then she lowered it again. "Yes. I was so mad. Not just at him…"

"When you called me—it was close to one in the morning, wasn't it?—I couldn't take it in. Teddy, committing suicide? And accused of having murdered some woman? It didn't compute, you know? None of it. You know that I was in Chicago, following a story for a new special I hope to do, and you were calling from Philadelphia to tell me my world had just turned upside-down. You know what I did, Jade? I just started packing. You know, like I was going on another story? I arranged transport to O'Hare, I called for my bill, I brushed my teeth… and I packed. Going through the motions."

Jade had lifted her head again, and Jessica saw the tears in her deep brown eyes. "One foot in front of the other," she whispered. "It's what he always told us."

"Yeah. It's what he always told us. Except I

couldn't do it. I was all set to go. The car was waiting for me downstairs. But when I tried to put one foot in front of the other? My knees just collapsed under me, and the next thing I knew I was on the floor, sobbing so hard I couldn't breathe. Everything I thought I was, everything I believed I'd built myself up to be—it all came apart like a house of cards, and I was just a little girl again, wanting my daddy…"

Jessica let her words trail off, trying hard not to cry. Because this wasn't about her. This was about Jade. Jessica had done her crying—wild, uncontrolled weeping—and she would always miss her father. But she had expressed her grief, and at least moved closer to acceptance. She'd get all the way there once they solved Teddy's murder, always missing her father, but able to function, get on with her life, just as he'd have wanted her to do. Just as he'd have wanted them all to do. Jolie had held on for a while, aware that she was always *on stage* for the paparazzi, but Sam had broken through her shield the day of the funeral and made her face her pain and sorrow.

Jade? Jade was strong. Jade didn't bend. And as she and Jolie had discussed, they both knew that if Jade didn't bend soon, she was going to break.

"Here, we'll share," Jade said after several long tense moments, handing Jessica a tissue from the box on the side table. "That's what you want me to do, isn't it, Jess? *Share?*"

Jessica wiped at her eyes, blew her nose. "Yeah, sis. That was the plan. Or am I still just the baby sister?"

"You'll always be the baby sister. But that doesn't mean I don't know you're grown up now. Most of the time."

"Gee, thanks. I wish we could have gotten to you sooner, Jolie and I. I can't imagine what it was like to be in that house, alone."

Jade raised her head, looked past Jessica. "There was quite a crowd for a while. Until they took Teddy away. It was awful, Jess, but you'd have to know that. I came home late and saw the light under the door to his office. I called for him, thinking he must have fallen asleep, hoping he'd fallen asleep. He was always upstairs at that time, following the pattern he'd set so long ago. Rockne had been lying just outside the office door, and he came to me, whining, wagging his tail like mad. Why was Rockne locked out of the office? That's what I wondered, and I got even more nervous, more reluctant to open that door. I said a quick prayer that Teddy hadn't had a stroke or a heart attack or something, and opened the door, to see him slumped back in his desk chair, his eyes wide open, the wall behind him sprayed...sprayed with..."

"You called us."

Jade nodded. "After calling 9-1-1, yes. And those *idiots*," she said, her voice going tight. "Open and shut, they said. Teddy had strangled Melodie Brainard a few hours earlier—they had him dead to rights on surveillance cameras at the Brainard estate. Then he'd come home, gotten himself drunk, and used his service revolver to kill himself. They wouldn't listen to me, wouldn't believe me when I said it had to be a mistake, that Teddy had been murdered. They wouldn't believe that Teddy would never do that to me, make me be the one who found him. And then… and then they all left."

"They should have called for someone to stay with you. Mrs. Grady, from next door. Somebody."

"I told them not to call anybody. I, uh, I went upstairs, trying to find a way out of what I knew there was no way out of—a way to fix everything somehow. Does that make sense? Anyway, I kept thinking about how I'd found him, the way I'd found him. Were the police right? Did he really kill himself, knowing I'd be the one to discover the body? You can't love somebody and plan for that somebody to find you with the back of your head blown off, damn it!"

Jade looked past Jessica once again. "And they'd said he'd killed Melodie Brainard. Killed the wife of the front-runner for mayor of Philadelphia, for crying out loud. What was he doing at the Brainard estate? What secret was he keeping from me, when he promised there would be no more secrets? We were partners, equals. He'd *promised.* I came home, Jess. He needed me, and I came home. I've always taken care of Teddy, ever since Mom left. It's what…it's what I've always done. I left Court so that I could take care of Teddy, I left every dream I'd ever… Oh, God."

"You were mad at him," Jessica said in a whisper. "You were mad at the whole world, weren't you? The cops, Teddy, everybody. But mostly Teddy, for having lied to you, kept another secret from you. You had to let that anger out somehow, Jade."

Her sister smiled. "I picked a hell of a way to do it, didn't I? All the pieces of Belleek Teddy brought me from his trips to Ireland, all the pieces he gave me for my birthdays, for Christmas. I was very methodical, you know. I opened the door to my closet, pushed the clothes to both sides, and then lined up every last piece of Belleek and threw them, one after the other, at the wall at the back of the closet. One after the other…and the next…and the next. When I was done, I simply kicked a few scattered shards into the closet and closed the door."

"Ah, Jade…"

Jade smiled wanly. "I even have neat tantrums, don't I? Planned out. Nothing spontaneous. I've never done anything spontaneous, have I?"

"You eloped to Las Vegas with Court," Jessica said.

Jade's smile widened. "And look how that worked out, huh? I wish he'd leave, go home to Virginia. He's only here because he's a fine Southern gentleman and he thinks it's the right thing to do. We're both such responsible adults I'm surprised we don't make the rest of you sick to your stomachs."

"Boy, are you one screwed-up female," Jessica said, grinning. "Court loves you, Jade. I don't know why, but he does."

Jade abruptly got to her feet. "Change of subject," she said, commanded. "I saw you looking at the list of messages. Are you ready to give that up yet? You know nobody but crackpots is going to contact us."

Jessica knew when to call it a day with Jade. In fact, she'd gotten further than she'd imagined she would. The rest was up to Court, if he cared to go there, if he was feeling brave. She pulled the cell phone from her bathrobe pocket and scrolled down the incoming mail list again.

"I hate to admit it, but I guess I do have to give this one up as a bad job. Matt was right. There're just too many calls to be able to respond to all of them, and the two dozen or so I listened to earlier, after we got back from Fishtown, were all pretty lame, unless Jolie wants somebody who calls himself Studly-the-Muffly to suck her toes. Creepy. I deleted a whole bunch of them, and now the mailbox is full again. Although I won't say on air that I'm not returning calls. Easier to let everyone think theirs was the only one I didn't answer, right? I mean, I can't possibly— Uh-oh."

"Uh-oh what?" Jade asked, picking up her cup and

saucer in preparation for leaving the room, to get changed for supper, probably.

"I think I recognize this number. That's what's *uh-oh.* Hang on, Jade, I'll see if she left a message."

"She who? That's my phone you know. Give it to me."

"*Was* your phone. You gave it to me, remember?" Jessica held up a hand to stop her sister as she punched in numbers with the other hand, pausing to put the phone to her ear to listen to instructions, then pushing more buttons. "I'll put it on speaker. I love these new phones. You can do anything with them. Get ready."

She pushed one last series of buttons.

"Jade? Jade, you called?"

The Meissen cup and saucer hit the floor unnoticed, shattering into a dozen pieces, and Rockne shot to his feet, yelped and ran out of the room in a big red blur. *"Mother?"*

The message continued: "I can't believe this. Sunny and I can't believe this. We're in Reno for a… well, never mind. I didn't check our messages until last night. I called immediately, but your stupid phone said your mailbox was full. At any rate, we're devastated of course, just broken up about the news. Sunny made reservations for some ungodly early hour, and we'll be arriving at Philadelphia International a little after three o'clock your time today. We have to bring all our baggage, so we'll have to go through the mess of claiming it, but we should be at the house by five. You don't have to fix anything fancy, although I'd appreciate it if you remembered that Sunny is a diabetic now." There was a slight pause, and then, "We're truly sorry, Jade. Teddy was a…he was a good, simple man."

Jessica closed the phone and tossed it onto the bed. "They're *devastated*. Yeah, right. I think I'm going to be sick."

"I broke Sam's cup," Jade said, dropping to her knees and picking up some of the larger pieces. "What is it with me and china and bad news? We have to go meet them at the house, Jess. Cripes, I don't even know if that second set of crime tape has even been removed yet. Get dressed."

Jessica looked at the mantel clock. "It's almost four now. If we drag our feet, we can keep them standing at the curb for a while. Well, *you* can. I'm not going."

"Oh, yes, you are. Jolie's not here. I'm not facing them on my own."

"Jolie wouldn't go, either. The last time Mom called her, it was to ask for money. Jolie's still waiting for Mom to sell some crap story to the tabloids since she didn't pony up. And don't forget Uncle Sunny. That's what she calls him? You want to know what I call Teddy's brother? I call him a stinky, smelly, wife-stealing son of a—"

"Jess, don't go there. Please. Not right now."

"Don't worry, I won't go there. But that's because I'm not going anywhere. I'm most especially not going to within five miles of Mommie Dearest and her little *Sunny* boy."

MATT SNEAKED a quick peek at Jessica as he maneuvered the Mercedes through rush-hour traffic on the Blue Route. "That's quite the look you've got on your face, Ms. Sunshine. Halfway between a two-year-old sucking on a lemon and the misery of constipation."

"Not funny, Matthew," Jessica said, her arms folded tightly across her chest. Defensively across her chest. "I'm only doing this because I know I shouldn't ask Jade to do anything I wouldn't do."

"You want to tell me about your mother?" Matt asked.

"Not particularly, no," she said, and then sighed. "What do you want to know?"

"I can't be sure, since I don't know what has you so spooked," he said rationally. What wasn't rational was how he felt seeing Jessica so obviously upset and hurting. She really was getting to him, even when she wasn't deliberately trying to get to him. Maybe even more so.

"Okay, okay—but I'm not spooked. She doesn't scare me," Jessica said, sitting up straighter. "Anyway, back to what happened. It's the sad old story of the overworked husband who's never home and the unhappy lonely wife. I can still hear her yelling at us for being a pain in the neck, for being such ungrateful brats, and then threatening us that one day we'd come home and she wouldn't be there, and then, boy, would we be sorry about the way we and Teddy treated her. I'd come into the house every day after school, shaking inside and calling for her, wondering if this was going to be the day she took off."

"Jesus. That's verbal child abuse, you know?"

"It sucks, I know that. She rarely smacked us, but she sure did have a way with words. And then one day she did it, she left. I was six, maybe seven, the first time. Sometimes she went to her relatives in New York. Sometimes nobody knew where she'd gone. Sometimes for a couple of weeks, sometimes for a whole month. But Teddy always took her back. Until the last time, when she got Teddy's brother to leave with her, all the way to Hawaii—she always wanted us to move to Hawaii, and Teddy would always just promise that they would when he retired. She just had to wait, raise the kids and let him get in his thirty years."

Matt remembered Teddy's colorful Hawaiian shirts. He always wore one. Maybe they had been his version of a hair shirt? Cripes, people sure could complicate their lives. "But this time she didn't come back, right?"

"Nope. For weeks Teddy sat in the dark in the living room, waiting for headlights to come down the street, waiting for her to come home. It damn near killed him."

"And did real wonders for you and your sisters, I'm sure," Matt said, not looking forward to the family reunion awaiting them. "How old were you when she left for good?"

"I don't remember."

Matt longed to cut across three lanes of traffic to pull the car onto the shoulder and take Jessica in his arms, just hold her, comfort her. "I don't believe that."

"But I'm telling the truth. I truly don't remember. I don't want to remember. The only thing I did know for sure was that now I came home from school, shaking, hoping she *wouldn't* be there. Jade was my mother, when you get right down to it. Pretty much from the beginning. Jade braided my hair, Jade fixed me peanut-butter-and-jelly sandwiches for my lunch box and helped me with my homework, Jade explained what was happening to my body when I started to…when boys started bumping up against me all the time, and then laughing like loons. By the time Mom left for the last time, I really didn't count on her to be there, anyway. If you want to know who was hurt in this deal, besides Teddy, it was Jade. Big time. Jade let Jolie and me have a childhood, but she never got one for herself."

"I suppose you're right," Matt said, following Court's car off the Blue Route. "Tell me about Jolie."

"Jolie sort of floated through it all. She was always a daydreamer, making up fantasies and then acting them out. She hid in her imagination, an actress playing a role. She was Cinderella, and Mom the wicked stepmother. But she just plain hates Mom now. We all hate her, I suppose, in our own ways. Girls are supposed to have a mother, a mother who cares about them, you know? If she'd died, that would have been terrible. What she did was worse than dying. She left, and without a word to us, not even a hug goodbye. And she never even called to see how we were, her own daughters. Not a birthday card, not a Christmas present, not even a go-to-hell on her way out the door. And now here she is, show-ing up too late to be of any good to anyone, and dragging along my rotten uncle, who shoved a knife in his own brother's back. You shouldn't have come along, Matt. This isn't going to be pretty."

"That's okay. I'm used to breaking up riots," Matt said, trying to ease some of the tension in the car.

"Oh, there won't be any riot to break up. Just watch. Jade will be all cool and civil, and offer to take them to the cemetery or something. And she expects me to follow her lead, which I'll do—for Jade. I just can't figure out why Mom bothered to come back at all. There has to be a reason, and it sure isn't so she can weep over Teddy's grave. You know, how people always wait until it's too late to ask for forgiveness?"

"You don't think people can change, Jess? You don't believe she might be truly sorry for what she did to you?"

Jessica shot him a look. "You tell me. Do you think people can change?"

"I'd like to think so," Matt said slowly. "Although, in my line of work, I don't see much of it."

"No, I guess you don't, and that's sad. But you want to know what's really sad? When Jade couldn't contact Mom, the three of us actually batted around the idea that she had come back to see Teddy and had somehow killed him. How's that for twisted?"

"You were grasping at straws. It's understand-able. Jess?"

"Hmm?" she said as she lowered the sun visor and checked her makeup in the small lighted mirror. "I want to make sure I look terrific. She'll hate that I look terrific. I can remember her sitting at this vanity table she had, checking for wrinkles and then com-plaining that Teddy was making her old before her time, making her do housework, forcing her to have a third—never mind."

"A third baby. That's what you were going to say, wasn't it? She let you hear her say something like that? Cripes, Jessica, let's rethink this, all right? I make a right turn up here, and we can go into the city, get some dinner, catch a movie. Court's with Jade."

Jessica slammed the sun visor back into place. "I told you, it doesn't bother me. I'm a success. I didn't turn to drink or drugs or putting out for the entire football team under the bleachers. Jolie's all right, she's a big movie star, just like she always dreamed she'd be. And Jade's…and Jade is… No, Matt, I can't let Jade face her alone. Not even with Court. He's too much of a gentleman."

"But I'm not," Matt said, pulling to the curb behind Court's car. "Just give me the signal, and I'll show you how much I'm not."

"I don't want to rely on you, Matt," Jessica told him, putting her hand on his forearm. "I like to think of myself as being mega-independent."

"So I'm just to stand there and pretend to be invisible?"

She smiled. "Oh, you'll know when to jump in if it turns out that I need you—probably to hold me back. But thanks for the offer." She leaned across the console to kiss him.

Matt cupped the back of her neck in his hand and pulled her closer, kissing her for courage, kissing her to remind her she was one damn desirable woman, kissing her because, more and more, all he wanted to do was kiss her. Hold her. Let her deeper into his solitary life that had seemed so rational and workable until she'd come into it.

"Wow," Jessica said when the kiss was over, her face now only a heartbeat from his. "I think I could get into this big bad protector thing. I really do like you, Matt. You should probably be running away as fast as you can."

"I'll take your advice under advisement," he told her, tracing the curve of her cheek with his index finger. "Okay, I've considered it. I'm not going anywhere."

Jessica's smile slammed a figurative fist into his gut. "I don't need another father, Matt."

"That's good, Jess, because my feelings toward you are not in the least paternal. And I'm not that damn old. I'm not even as old as I was a week ago, before I met you."

"That sounds interesting." Jessica pressed her palm to his chest and then slowly slid that hand lower, slipping it lightly down past his belt, skimming him before easing her fingertips along his thigh and sitting back in her seat once more.

Matt's immediate physical reaction to her daring touch, her purposeful tease, surprised even him. "You're trying to kill me, aren't you?"

"God, no. I have other plans for you, Lieutenant, and they very much depend on you staying alive. Can I say that I don't want to be alone tonight once we're rid of Mommie Dearest and hope you understand, and I don't have to draw you a road map? Matt? Answer me."

"Sorry, Jess," he said, one hand on the door handle. "I was just mentally reviewing our route back to Sam's house to figure out if there are any drugstores on the way."

"Drug— Oh," Jessica said, her smile bordering on the wicked. "See if you can find a large, economy-size box, okay?"

"Are you being optimistic about me or about yourself?" Matt asked her, and quickly got out of the car in time to see an obvious rental car pull up directly in front of the Sunshine house. The driver's-side door opened and Matt involuntarily sucked in a breath as Teddy Sunshine, complete with loud Hawaiian shirt, stepped out.

No. Not Teddy. His brother. But the resemblance was uncanny, from the graying, sandy-colored hair to the potbelly above a nonexistent ass and skinny legs. Thank God Teddy had never worn shorts with his Hawaiian shirts.

Matt raced around to Jessica's side of the car to be able to grab her if she took one look at her uncle and passed out or something. He stood blocking her view as she got out and slammed the door, putting his hands on her shoulders to keep her in place. "Are you sure you're ready for this? Your uncle...just hold on to me, okay?"

Jessica smiled at him as she reached up to remove his hands. "And they say I'm the dramatic one. Come on, step out of my way, Matt. I can handle this, I'm a big— *Oh, God, oh, sweet Jesus…*"

Matt grabbed her as she sagged slightly at the knees. "Steady, sweetheart."

"I'm all right, I'm all right. I…I just wasn't expecting that. Jade hasn't gotten out of the car yet, Matt. Let's go be with her before— Ah, and there she is. Queen Claudia. Wonder where she left her tiara."

Matt didn't know exactly what he'd been expecting, but Claudia Sunshine didn't fit any of his preconceived notions. Yes, he saw a definite resemblance to Jade. The dark hair. The slim build. The patrician features. She couldn't be much more than twenty years older than her firstborn daughter. But there was a tightness to her features that probably had something to do with a surgeon's knife, although the scalpel hadn't seemed able to remove the sullen downturn of the woman's mouth.

"You favor your father in coloring," Matt said as they walked down the sidewalk to join up with Jade and Court, the four of them staring at the two newcomers much like Wyatt Earp and Doc Holiday might have sized up the Clanton brothers at the O.K. Corral. "Who moves first?"

"I suppose I do," Court said, and he drew Jade with him toward her mother, leaving Matt to look at

Jessica, who made another wonderfully comic face and followed.

"Mrs. Sunshine," Court said. "How was your flight?"

"Terrible," Claudia Sunshine said in a smoke-husky voice. "They made Sunny all but strip to his underwear because he kept setting off the alarms. Does he look like a terrorist? I ask you, does he?"

"No, ma'am, he doesn't," Court said, extending his hand to Teddy's brother. "Mr. Sunshine."

"Sunny. Everyone calls me Sunny," the man said, shaking Court's hand a little too heartily. "Teddy's gone, huh? I can't believe I'll never get to talk to him again."

"Yeah," Jessica said none to quietly. "He only had, what, over a decade or more to make a call? There's just never enough time, is there?"

"Jess, don't," Jade said quietly. "Come on, say hello. We can't just stand here like lumps."

"I can," Jessica said almost happily, and Matt smiled. She wasn't going to make this easy on her mother and uncle. "Then again, I just got an idea. Stay sharp, Matt, please. I'll apologize later, I promise. Profusely, if you play along."

"Mother, hello," Jade said, stepping forward three precise paces. Leaving a good six feet between them, Matt noticed. If that last bit of bridge was going to be crossed, it would have to be by Claudia Sunshine.

"Hello, Jade," her mother said briefly, looking past her oldest daughter and straight at Jessica. "Jessica Marie. Where's Jolie? I'd hoped to speak with her."

"Jolie and her checkbook are in California," Jessica snapped out, stepping up to put her arm around Jade's waist. A united front, Matt supposed. Either that, or role reversal, with Jessica playing the stand-in mommy this time. He also supposed he ought to introduce himself, but Jessica beat him to it. "Lieutenant Matthew Denby, here they are, as promised. You said you wanted to ask about their whereabouts the night of the murders, I believe."

Matt's eyes widened for a moment—he was surprised they hadn't popped out of his head—but he recovered quickly, he hoped, and reached into his pocket to flash his shield even as he stepped in front of Court, who was hiding a smile behind his hand. "Yes, thank you, Ms. Sunshine. Strictly routine, you understand, folks, a process of elimination. If the two of you wouldn't mind coming down to the station while we verify your alibis, I—"

"*Alibis!* Sunny!" Claudia exploded. "What the hell is going on here? I told you it wasn't worth it. I *told* you I didn't want to come back here just to see a stupid stone and some hole in the ground. We could have done this all from Honolulu." She narrowed her eyes at Jade. "*You.* You've always hated me. This is your idea, isn't it?"

"No, actually," Jade said, "but I wish it had been, because at least now we know the truth. You're not here because of Teddy or because of us. Why did you come back, Mother?"

"I'm assuming I can back off now?" Matt whispered to Jessica, whose rich brown eyes were all but dancing. "What did we accomplish?"

Jessica put a finger to her mouth to warn him to be quiet, then said, "We've proved that they're not here to mourn Teddy, but because Teddy's dead. And they want to get inside the house, or else they would have asked us to meet them at some hotel. Thanks for playing along. Loved the badge flash, by the way. Very impressive."

"Yeah. I practice. What's your mother saying?"

"…to me. Just like the silver belongs to Sunny, since it came down to the oldest son. Sunny's the oldest son now."

"Oh, I don't believe this. I freaking do not believe this," Jessica said, and she took a full step forward before Matt could grab her arm and hold her back. "They're here to sack the place. Like…like grave robbers. Hey! Hey, Claudia! Sunny! Up yours, okay? All the way up!"

"And here I left my riot gear in the Jeep," Matt muttered as Jessica shook her arm free of his grasp and made a beeline to within a foot of her mother, going chin to chin with her on the sidewalk. "Court?

Hang on to Jade, okay, and I'll see if I can keep Jessica from a domestic-violence charge."

"There's no need," Jade said, her voice calm, if a little tight. "Mother? Your rings and the diamond bracelet are all in a box in Teddy's room. I'll go get them."

"The hell you will!" Jessica shouted. "She left him, she left the rings. I'd rather grind them up in the garbage disposal! Matt, tell her. They're no longer her property, right?"

He couldn't help it. He had to wonder—how did a nice homicide cop like him get mixed up in a domestic dispute? Oh, yeah, now he remembered. Jessica. Life sure hadn't been dull since the first time she told him to go mind his own damn business…and then pulled him straight into hers.

"Actually, if they were gifts from your father, then technically they are the property of—" he began, only to have Jessica cut him off.

"She left them behind when she took off. She gave up any right to anything she left behind on the day she bailed. Starting with *us!*"

"Down, girl," Matt warned her. "As I was saying, technically, the rings, the bracelet, anything that was a gift to your mother is her property. The question is, since she chose to leave them in your father's pos-session all these years, without asking for them back... Did you ask Teddy to send the jewelry to you, Mrs. Sunshine?"

"Talk to him? Why would I talk to... Yes! Yes, of course, Officer, I told him I wanted what was mine. Didn't I, Sunny?"

"Teddy could be hard," the man with Sunny's worn pleasant Irish face said, looking only slightly ashamed of himself. "Not to speak ill of the dead, but he gave Claudia a bad time for a lot of years. He refused to see that he was...well, that he was trying to cage an exotic bird. Saddling her with that house over there, saddling her with... Not that Claudia wasn't a wonderful mother."

"Jessica, I'm giving her the jewelry," Jade declared flatly. "We don't want it. What would we do with it? The sooner we're done with this, the sooner we can leave here."

Matt put his hand against Jessica's back and could feel her trembling, with fury most likely. "Make it a trade-off, Jade," he said quietly. "Sunny's the softer target, I think. The jewelry for the Sunshine family silver. Go ahead, try it. I'll back you."

In the end, it was Court who completed the negotiations, all taking place on the sidewalk outside the Sunshine family home as birds sang in the trees and children rode their bikes in the quiet residential street. World War III was averted.

Jade retrieved the jewelry in a plastic grocery bag

and handed it to Matt, who checked it and then literally tossed it off to Court, who passed the bag to Claudia Sunshine. A strange chain of custody, but Jade was looking fragile, ready to break, and she probably hadn't wanted to get within touching distance of her mother and uncle again.

Sunny and Claudia conferred, and then Sunny agreed yet again that he hadn't really wanted the family silver all that much, but as long as they were coming back to Philadelphia for the jewelry, they might as well give it a shot. Full of sentiment, Teddy's baby brother was.

"There, see? A reasonable solution. A compromise. Leaving only the matters of your father's Social Security, police pension and his life insurance," Claudia all but crowed just when Matt thought they might be home free. "After all, I am his widow, and therefore entitled to all survivor benefits."

CHAPTER SIX

"DON'T," JESSICA WARNED as Matt moved to cover her hand with his own as they drove back down the Blue Route. "Please…just don't."

"Families can be brutal, Jess," Matt told her gently. "I saw it all back when I was working in a black-and-white. I've seen knock-down drag-outs over Grandpa's favorite but pretty much worthless pipe."

"At least somebody had a sentimental attachment to their grandfather's pipe. My mother is about as sentimental as a shark. No, a vampire. A bloodsucking vampire. Claudia the Vampiress. I've never been so angry or so embarrassed in my life. His *widow?* You know, out of all of it, I think that's the worst. I'm his daughter, and I had no idea there had never been a divorce."

"Do you think he was still hoping she'd come home?"

"Oh, God, Matt, don't even think that! He wanted his wife back, and I brought home a dog for him, instead? And you know what? Rockne turned out to be twice as loyal—ten thousand times more loyal—than the woman who'd vowed to love and cherish Teddy all of their lives. Poor old dog."

"Rockne or Teddy?" Matt asked, hoping to lighten the mood a little.

"Both of them, I guess," Jessica said, swiping at her eyes with the back of her hand and then sighing. "Okay, I'm done. The house is legally Jade's, all three of us are the beneficiaries in Teddy's will. But what about the police pension and the rest of it, Matt? Does Claudia get it?"

"Do you care?"

Jessica slumped slightly in her seat. "No. If Teddy didn't make any other arrangements, he probably wanted her to have it, the old softie. He didn't divorce her. God. Nothing dies harder than love, does it?"

"Or hope," Matt said, tapping his horn at Court and Jade and then easing onto the exit ramp and heading onto the Schuylkill Expressway. "Otherwise, why would we still be chasing a happy ending to Teddy's story?"

"Is that what we're doing now? Or are you looking for a drugstore?"

Matt slid the Mercedes into the slow-moving rush-hour traffic. "I'm not holding you to that, you know. You've got enough on your mind right now."

"And you don't think you can take my mind off those problems? I think you're underestimating yourself, Matt. Or at least I hope so."

Matt shot her a look. "That's quite a mouth you have on you, young lady," he said, grinning. "A man less confident of his…abilities, might wrap it up and call it a day."

"But not you," Jessica said, returning his grin. "Not my big bad cop. You were really good back there, by the way. Did you see Claudia's face when you asked them to go down to the station with you? That was inspired. You're really quick on the uptake. I would have looked pretty bad if you hadn't figured out what I was doing and played along."

"Partners support each other."

"Partners? I seem to remember you telling me you like to work alone. But now we're partners?"

"As long as you remember who's in charge, yes, I suppose we are." He eased onto the apron of the road and slipped onto an exit ramp, ignoring blasting horns. "Damn. I keep forgetting I don't have my bubblegum machine to stick on the dash. Remind me to get it out of the Jeep, okay?"

"You cops really call that red light a bubblegum machine? Neat. So where are we going in such a hurry?"

"My place. I want to catch up with Ernesto before we go for supper," he told her, shooting her a quick look. He didn't want to say he mostly was hoping to take Jessica's mind off her encounter with her mother and uncle, as well as giving Court and Jade some time alone back at Sam's house. "Consider this a training lesson, partner. I talk, you listen. And, please, no heartwarming pep talks."

"Yes, sir, Lieutenant, sir. But don't be too hard on Ernesto, Matt. He's trying to stand on his own two feet and not come running to you for help. Believe me, I understand the feeling. Oh, and by the way, thanks for trying to do something to take my mind off Vampiress and Uncle Sunny—just in case you think I don't know what you're doing. He looks like a whipped dog, doesn't he? Sunny, that is. Hard to believe he's the younger brother. He looks older than Teddy by at least a decade, like maybe even Paradise isn't so great if Claudia comes along with the poi and grass skirts. Serves him right."

"Are you done now?" Matt asked as he pulled into the parking lot, already looking for someone to watch the Mercedes so he didn't come back to it to see it stripped and sitting on its axles. "Ah, just the man I was looking for," he said, shoving the gear into Park. "Jess, you remember Tweety Byrd, don't you?"

"You're not going to chase him again, are you?"

"Nope. I'm going to pay him to stand beside the car and tell everyone it's mine. If he doesn't take one look at me and make like a shepherd."

"Make like a shepherd? Is that police talk?"

"Sorry, no. It's just something my dad used to say—make like a shepherd and get the flock out of here."

"Oh, that is so lame." Jessica smiled. "Are you a betting man? Because I'm betting that Tweety's too interested in the car to even look at you, let alone run away."

Matt got out of the car and called to Tweety, who visibly jumped, but was smart enough not to try to run. It was nice to know even Tweety could learn his lesson. The ten-spot ripped in half, with one half going into his pocket, the other half to Tweety, probably also helped.

"You're such a cliché sometimes, Matthew," Jessica told him as they walked to his building. "A ripped bill? Didn't Bogart do that once in one of his tough-guy movies?"

"Bogart? As in Humphrey? I don't know. You watch old movies?"

"During Jolie's infatuation with Lauren Bacall, yes. We all watched old movies. It was her I-want-to-be-the-new-Barbra-Streisand phase that nearly did us all in. If I never hear 'The Way We Were' again, I will die a happy woman. Which apartment is Ernesto's?"

"Right here, 1-A." Matt knocked on the door and counted to ten, giving Ernesto time to put down his book, leave his bedroom and peek through the keyhole. At the count of nine he heard the first of the trio of dead bolts being snicked back, before the door opened a few inches.

"Buenas tardes, mi capitán," Ernesto said, only one eye and part of his cheek visible in the opening.

"Yeah, right," Matt said, getting a bad feeling. "Open up, Ernesto."

"Gee, I'd really like to accommodate you, Lieutenant, but I've got the mother of all trig finals tomorrow, and—"

Matt pushed open the door, eliciting a startled "Hey!" from Ernesto and a "Should I be taking notes on entering without a warrant, partner?" from Jessica.

The apartment was small, only four rooms—the living room housing a ripped chair, a sagging red imitation-leather couch and a wide-screen HD television set—but almost painfully neat. Ernesto's work, not his mother's. Matt didn't want to know how the mother had earned the money for the television set.

"Who did it?" Matt asked as Ernesto first tried to cover his left eye, and then gave it up as a bad job, dropping his hand to his side to reveal the "mother" of all black eyes. "And don't mess with me, Ernesto. I already know about the books."

"Oh, Ernesto!" Jessica went straight to the boy, attempting to touch his face and then quickly drawing back her hand when Ernesto flinched. "Does that hurt? Stupid question, of course it hurts. No, no, don't cover up. I won't touch it. Shouldn't you have ice on that? Or a piece of raw steak? Matt, shouldn't he have ice on that?"

"Still the same pretty lady, huh, Lieutenant?" Ernesto quipped, grinning and then wincing and touching the black-and-blue skin beneath his eye. "And they said it would never last."

"Shut up, Ernesto," Matt said without emotion, his brain ticking away, seeking some sort of solution. "Where's your mother?"

Ernesto shrugged. "You think she tells me? I haven't seen her in longer than I haven't seen you. Why?"

"When do you get out of here? When's your last day of school?"

"I'm done, man. It's the middle of June. I lied about the trig exam, okay?" Ernesto looked at Jessica. "What bug's up his—uh, what's his problem?"

"Just play along, Ernesto," Jessica said, looking at Matt with those damn huge brown eyes. Those trusting, slightly dancing brown eyes. There were times she reminded him of Rockne. "I think the lieutenant is having a Terrell Johnson flashback, that's all."

Matt ignored her. "When do you leave for Penn State?"

Ernesto shot another look at Jessica and then shoved his hands into his pockets. "Pretty soon. I've got a room in one of the dorms and I'm taking some summer English lit course my adviser suggested I get out of the way before the real fun starts. I'm doing fine, Lieutenant. Really. It was a couple of books. I shouldn't have tried to stop them, that's all. *Mi avería*. My own dumb fault. I just need to stay out of their way, that's all."

"You heard him, Matt. Ernesto just needs to stay out of this gang's way. Sam won't mind," Jessica whispered. "I'm sure he won't. When we talked about Terrell, he was really upset. Said it was a criminal waste of a good kid."

Matt pinched at the bridge of his nose. He was overreacting. It was a black eye, that's all. Ernesto wasn't Terrell Johnson, and nobody was going to find his body on a city playground, his life and bright future blown away by a bullet to the face.

"Pack your stuff, Ernesto," Matt said, and the hell if he was overreacting. "You're coming with us."

"I'm coming with… Where to?" Ernesto backed away from them, looking both confused and scared, like anyone abruptly removed from their environment, whether it be a healthy one or not. "Look, man, I don't need to—"

"Get me pen and paper, so I can write your mother a note," Matt interrupted. "Come on, Ernesto, move. You've got ten minutes."

"I couldn't pack my makeup in ten minutes," Jessica said. "But come on, Ernesto, I'll help you. You're going on one heck of a vacation, trust me. Do you know how to swim? No? Don't worry, I'll teach you. I know Sam keeps swimsuits in the pool house. And the pool's heated, so we can have your first lesson after dinner. Are you hungry? I know I'm starved…"

Matt watched the two of them go, Jessica's arm around Ernesto's slim shoulders. Well, he'd diverted her mind from the confrontation with her mother and uncle, hadn't he? He'd also probably diverted himself out of a drugstore run.

"HOW'S JADE DOING?" Jessica asked Court as they walked across the terrace on their way to the pool. The surface of the water was almost painfully bright in the sunlight, even as the shadows of the tall slim evergreens edged closer to the pool as the sun dropped toward the horizon. She had to squint to make out the two figures in the water.

Court shook his head. "Not good. She can't get anywhere with Jermayne, which doesn't surprise me. That kid doesn't give an inch. So rather than take a break, take care of herself, she's digging into the Baby in the Dumpster file. I can't think of anything more depressing, can you?"

"Only seeing Mommie Dearest and Uncle Sunny this afternoon, which is why I asked how Jade's doing. But I'm over it," Jessica said, sighing. "Jade was much too easy—handing over that jewelry. Although the plastic bag was a nice touch. Thanks for going along, and being the sane, diplomatic one. You didn't have to do that."

Court's cleanly sculpted jaw—so aristocratic, like the rest of him—seemed to set in a hard line. "Am I wasting my time, Jess?"

Jessica didn't know what to say. She liked Court, she really did. She loved her sister. "I don't know, Court. What are you trying to accomplish?"

He shot her a quick self-deprecating smile. "Good question. You read about situations like this. People who love each other, truly love each other, but just can't live with each other. I don't want Jade and I to be two of those people."

"You could always boss her around all day and night, and then she wouldn't love you anymore," Jessica quipped, trying to lighten the suddenly somber mood. "Sorry. I get nervous when things get serious. I don't know, Court. Having never been in love, I don't know what you're feeling, either of you."

"Then let me help you," Court said, smiling. "Angry, frustrated, impotent—emotionally, that is—confused, baffled, angry. I already said that, didn't I? Angry is a big one, though. Sometimes I don't know whether I want to kiss her or shake her. Miss Independent."

"Look, Jade's stubborn, there's no denying that, but she's also scared. Teddy dying? She just lost her anchor, and her reason for being here in Philadelphia in the first place, rather than, say, with you in Virginia.

Sure, there's still the business, but let's face it, the business isn't doing all that well."

"It's not?" Now Court had lost his hangdog face and his eyes were alive, interested. "Is she in financial trouble? And now, with your mother laying claim to Teddy's money…"

"He had us as beneficiaries on a couple of small life-insurance policies, Court, and Jade does own the house free and clear. I'm just saying, nobody's getting rich on the Sunshine Detective Agency. Not that Jade would tell you any of that even if she was living under the Walt Whitman Bridge in an old refrigerator box."

Court nodded, his hands thrust deep into the pockets of his designer slacks. "Okay, okay. Change of subject. Tell me about Ernesto."

"There's nothing much to tell. Sam's delighted that he's here—Matt called him earlier—and he leaves in less than two weeks to start classes at Penn State. In the meantime, staying here means he isn't around a bunch of bullies who seem to hate him because he's smart."

"The world's crazy, isn't it," Court said rather than asked. "Maybe it was simpler back in the old days. People like my ancestor built a fortress and then defended it against all comers, and damn laws and conventions if they got in his way."

"You're talking about the pirate? Ainsley Becket,

wasn't it?" Jessica asked, one eye on Matt as he stood at the side of the pool with Ernesto, showing the almost painfully thin boy how to keep his arms outstretched before diving off the side. Matt was such a nice guy, one of the good ones. He didn't look half-bad in that borrowed bathing suit, either.

"Yes, Ainsley. He decided what was his, and then he protected it by any means necessary. You have to admire that. And watching Jade these past weeks, I believe I can understand where Ainsley was coming from when he did many of the things he did. When Morgan visits, I'll ask her to tell you some of the stories she told me."

Jessica turned to look at Court. "Morgan? Your cousin? She's coming here? When?"

"At this point, she isn't sure. She found a few more Becket relatives in Michigan or somewhere, and wants to do a little more investigating before she comes stateside and we have some sort of reunion. It could be a while, as she's hoping to include Sam, and he'll be leaving for Ireland with Jolie pretty soon."

"Did she learn anything else about the Empress? Just the hope that this Ainsley Becket guy could have hidden a priceless pirated emerald—hey, try saying that fast five times: priceless pirated, priceless pirated—somewhere for someone to find two hundred years later excites the heck out of me! I think I'd hate it if she found it before we could all go on a treasure hunt. I've never been to England, you know. I'd love to take a camera crew with me."

"And I'd have to choke you if you tried," Court said amicably. He pulled back the cuff of his dress shirt and checked the time on his Rolex. "Jade still wants an eight-o'clock meeting, to talk about the cold cases. It's seven now. I'll go see about refreshments."

"Sounds like a good idea. I'll go tell Matt," Jessica said, and moved off toward the pool area, singsonging "Priceless pirated, priceless pirated..." under her breath.

She walked over to the tiled edge and then jumped back to avoid the splash as Ernesto did an awkward belly flop into the water. "Doesn't quite have the logistics of diving down pat yet, huh?" she asked Matt as she wiped a few drops of water from her face.

"Please, don't let him hear you say that. I've already had to listen to some mathematical equation or something meant to fix trajectory, angle of impact and something else I don't remember. The kid makes me feel like a brainless high-school dropout."

"So that's why you just about pushed him into the pool?"

"That would be the reason, yes," Matt said, slicing his long fingers through his damp hair. His hair curled when wet. Nifty. Sexy, even. "Where were you?"

"Oh, I had an errand or two to run," Jessica said

as Ernesto clung to the side of the pool, shaking his head like a terrier and grinning like a loon.

"A few errands," Matt prodded. "Really?"

"Uh-huh, really. Some more pink highlighters—a person can't have too many pink highlighters—a family-size bag of Snickers—"

"A person can't have enough family-size bags of Snickers," Matt interrupted, grinning.

"Smart-ass," Jessica said, pretending she was going to slap his arm. "So, the highlighters. The candy. A coral lipstick to match my new blouse. It's amazing, the variety of products they sell in drugstores these days."

Matt looked her up and down, his expression remaining neutral. "Drugstores. You went to the drugstore."

Jessica couldn't hold back her grin. "Yeah. How about that. The drugstore."

Ernesto pulled himself up and out of the pool. "You two really have deep conversations," he said, grabbing a towel from a nearby chair. "Next to 'C is for Cookie,' I can't think of anything more interesting I've ever heard. I'm going to go up to my room and shower now, if we're done having fun pushing the little Spanish kid into the pool to see if he floats."

"Sorry, Ernesto," Matt said, giving the teenager a hearty slap on the back that sent the thin boy staggering slightly before recovering. "But you really do talk too much."

"Yeah," Ernesto teased. "Like my big cop friend— all talk and no action. Isn't that right, Miss Sunshine?"

"It's Jessica, and no comment," she said, looking up at Matt. Who could blush. Who knew! "We're getting together at eight, in the living room—that huge room just off the foyer—to talk about the cases we're working on. Matt? Can Ernesto join us?"

Matt sighed, looked at Jessica, looked at Ernesto, looked at Jessica again. "I meant it. The kid talks. Incessantly. I don't think they gave him that black eye because of the books. It was because of his big mouth."

"I also know how to listen," Ernesto said, looking appealingly at Jessica. "I'd like to hear about these cases you guys are working on. I think it's really neat. You know, trying to prove your dad didn't kill anybody, and that someone killed him. And I'm good at puzzles. I can help."

"Now see what you started," Matt grumbled as he bent to pick up another towel. "Let's go. I want to shower, too, before our own little Einstein uses up all the hot water."

"In this place?" Jessica laughed. "Sam must have a water heater the size of your whole apartment, Matt. We couldn't run out of hot water if we stayed in the shower for hours."

"Don't give me ideas I don't get on my own," Matt whispered in her ear as they let Ernesto walk ahead of them toward the steps to the terrace, Rockne following the boy, his tail wagging furiously, for Teddy's lonely dog seemed to have decided to adopt Ernesto. "Although, I probably should be open to suggestions."

"Wearing that swimsuit, you sure ought to be," Jessica told him, snapping the back of the waistband of the navy-blue trunks. "Please tell me you're not like Teddy was and wear your tidy-whiteys under your swim trunks."

Matt slapped her hand away just as, in Jessica's mind, things were about to get interesting. "You're a menace, do you know that? How long do you think this meeting will go on tonight?"

"I don't know," Jessica said, giving up the fight. "Court says Jade is giving up on the Terrell Johnson Scholar Athlete thing and starting with the Baby in the Dumpster case. So we may have to talk about that one for a while, much as I hate the entire subject. Jolie's case is solved, we're getting nowhere with the Fishtown Strangler and have less than nothing to report. About an hour?"

"So, by nine o'clock? Too early to make an excuse and go to bed. You want to go for a drive? A moon-light swim?"

"A swim? Are you nuts? It doesn't stay all that warm at night yet."

"But the pool's heated. I heard you tell Ernesto it was."

"Nope, sorry, still a big no on that one. Jolie's the real gung ho swimmer in the family, not me. But the drive sounds nice. Where do you want to drive to?"

Matt looked away from her for a moment. "Now that you mention it, I'd like to take another look at Joshua Brainard's house and grounds. To see how well it's lit at night."

"You mean where Melodie Brainard died. The last place Teddy was seen alive, even if it was only on camera, entering and leaving through the front door. I thought you said it was the camera aimed at the backyard and pool that was out of commission, not the lights. Besides, that's not our case, remember? It's none of our cases, not until we solve the rest and hopefully find ourselves a suspect."

"Melodie Brainard's murder was my case, until the brass took it away from me and wrapped it and your father's death all up in one big murder-suicide bow. A pal got me a look at the murder book, Jess, and it's pitiful. Hardly any forensics, precious little crime-scene investigating. Nobody even walked the perimeter of the fence that goes all around the grounds, looking for a break, a point of entry, a bubblegum wrapper, nothing. We're talking a ten-acre property, with only the visible part of the fence fancy fieldstone. The rest is chain-link. That Teddy would be dumb enough to walk in front of cameras if he was on his way to kill Mrs. Brainard just doesn't compute. One bolt cutter, and he could have entered from anywhere, if he had murder on his mind. Not that the murder book has anything about motive in it anywhere. Just that Teddy must have snapped somehow."

"The back of your neck is turning red," Jessica pointed out quietly, even as her own hands closed into fists. "They just wanted Teddy to be guilty and the whole thing to go away. Crime of passion, all that crap. As if Teddy didn't go there intent on murder, but something went wrong and it happened, and then he killed himself because he couldn't live with the shame. In other words, a bunch of bull that makes good copy. Poor Mr. Brainard—now, on with the show, let's elect this guy. Is Joshua Brainard that powerful?"

"He's the fair-haired boy, running for mayor, promising the cops he'll be their man, sure. But it's his father who holds the real power, and not just with the police. Daddy Brainard and his megabucks have been around City Hall for a long time, and he knows where all the bodies are buried. He pulled in some favors for his sonny boy, and that was it, the lid was on and nailed down. There hasn't been a single follow-up story about Melodie Brainard's murder, not one mention of her in any reporting done on her husband's campaign. It's like she never existed."

"We managed to get some press on her. Well, Jolie did. But you're right. There should have been some follow-up, somewhere, and there wasn't. It's like

Melodie Brainard is just another anonymous victim, like the victims in our Fishtown Strangler case."

"Uh-oh, I hear that tone again," Matt said as they walked through the empty living room and headed for the staircase in the foyer.

"What tone? I don't have a *tone*."

"Yeah, you do. It's a sort of…well, it's a sort of 'I'll save you!' tone. Jessica Sunshine to the rescue. Truth, justice and the American—"

"Oh, shut up. I'm not a crusader. I'm a journalist. I look for stories, period."

"You look for *causes,* little girl," Matt told her, actually ruffling her hair as they climbed the stairs together. "I kind of like that about you."

Jessica pushed at her hair even as she grinned at him. "Well, in that case, maybe you're right." She went up on tiptoe and kissed his cheek. "You taste like chlorine. Go shower, and I'll meet you downstairs for Jade's big meeting. Should I wear heavy shoes?"

"Now you've lost me. Heavy shoes?"

"If we're going to go checking the perimeter of the Brainards' fence. Isn't it all woods and marshy gook and a couple of streams behind the house? Oh, and we'll need flashlights. Wouldn't it be great if we found a hole in the fence? Then we could say that Melodie's murderer entered the grounds that way. And with the security camera near the pool out of commission, that explains how he strangled her and tossed her in the pool, then left again without being detected. I cannot *believe* you guys didn't check the fence."

"I was pulled off the case within an hour, remember? I'd barely given the order to secure the perimeter when the brass showed up and took over."

Jessica winced. "Sorry, Matt. I didn't mean you, you know that. You said you wanted to help us because you knew Teddy. I'd also like to think you're sticking around because…well, because of us. But this is also personal, isn't it? You're pissed at the way the Brainard end of the case was handled."

"Guilty as charged, yes." Matt leaned down and kissed her cheek. "I'm a homicide cop. Homicide cops stand for the victim. I don't think anybody's standing for Melodie Brainard. Or for Teddy."

"Except us," Jessica said, standing up very straight, feeling a new resolve invading her every molecule. "Except us, Matt."

He ran the side of his index finger down her cheek. "You got it, Maid Marion. Now, if you don't mind, Robin Hood has to go take a shower. I'll see you downstairs."

"It's not just the swim trunks. I really like you, Matthew Denby," Jessica whispered as she watched Matt enter his room and close the door behind him.

CHAPTER SEVEN

MATT LOOKED AROUND Samuel Becket's living room, wondering how long Jade's meeting would take, wondering how long it would be before he and Jessica could make the drive over to the Brainard estate—wondering how he'd be able to concentrate on anything except the gleam in Jessica's eyes when she'd announced she'd done some shopping at a local drugstore.

And he called himself a professional? Not anymore. It had been amateur night ever since he'd first laid eyes on Jessica Sunshine.

Court handed him a cold longneck beer he accepted gratefully, then watched as his new friend sat down beside Jade, who was sorting through some papers on her lap. Jessica sat on the facing couch, scribbling notes on a legal pad and looking for all the world as if she wanted nothing more than to be where she was, playing at supersleuth. Or caped avenger. Either one was enough to set Matt's guts to churning.

Ernesto was sitting cross-legged on the floor beside the large round coffee table, an adoring Rockne sprawled half across his legs, the expression on the Irish setter's face one of unabashed adoration. The old dog had been mourning Teddy, almost at the expense of his health, and it was good to see that he was coming around. It was also sort of neat to see Ernesto interact with the animal, nice to see Ernesto, well, Ernesto just being a kid.

Right. Like Ernesto and his active brain could ever be just a kid. Matt reached down and grabbed at the open manila folder in front of Ernesto. "Give me that," he said, frowning as he saw that Ernesto had been reading the autopsy report on Terrell Johnson. "What the hell's the matter with you?"

"What?" Ernesto complained, looking up at Matt. "I've dissected a frog in school, you know. I watch The Discovery Channel. There's nothing there that's going to make me go running to puke somewhere. The dude got his face blown off. I'm guessing there wasn't an open casket, not from that description of the wounds."

"You're a ghoul, *mi amigo,*" Matt told him.

"*Sí, mi compadre.* And you're not *mi madre.* Trajectory is interesting, isn't it?"

Matt opened the folder and paged through to the medical examiner's report. He skimmed it and then turned the page, to the photocopy of the drawing of a male head, full face and profile. A line had been drawn through each, showing point of impact and subsequent travels of the bullet. "Okay, genius, I'll bite. What about the trajectory?"

"The shot came from below. Entered here, on the jaw, and traveled upward, to dance around inside the guy's brain. Death was instantaneous, I'm guessing, even before his knees began to buckle," Ernesto said, getting to his feet to use his index finger to trace the drawn line of trajectory. "How tall was Terrell Johnson?"

Jade put down her own notes and looked at Ernesto. The boy, after all, was talking about her case. "He was a basketball player. He was tall. Why?"

"He played center, Matt," Court added. "I think we can assume he wasn't less than six-five, six-six. Isn't his height in the report?"

"Yeah, found it," Matt said, shuffling through the pages until he found the relevant information. "Six-seven. Two hundred and thirty-four pounds. Big boy for high school. And smart, or he wouldn't have been named a scholar athlete. No wonder everyone wanted him."

"I Googled him," Court said, also getting to his feet. "The plan was to red-shirt him, see if he was all done growing, maybe pack some more pounds on him, and then decide if he'd be a power forward or center. Sort of small for a center, these days. Is this going anywhere?"

Ernesto rubbed his hands together. "Actually, sir, I

believe we can conclude that Terrell's murderer was considerably shorter than the victim. Then again, if we're talking who shot the guy, that doesn't narrow the suspect pool much, does it? I'm considerably shorter than the victim, for one, and so is most of the country, the average height of the Caucasian male being—"

"No lectures, okay? Nobody cares," Matt broke in, rolling his eyes.

"No? But it's interesting," Ernesto persisted. "I mean, you can take all American men, say between the ages of eighteen and twenty-six, and get one figure as the mean. Or you can break the figures down into Caucasian, Hispanic, Black, and get another figure. We Hispanic types bring the height down a bit, and the Blacks pump it up a bit more, so it does sort of even out. You can break down the Caucasian figures, too, but you see what I mean, right? Genetics are still genetics, no matter how long it's been since any of our ancestors lived in Italy or Ireland or Sweden or wherever. Nutrition plays a part, of course, outside of genetics. And there's still the age factor. The average age of the onset of puberty has been declining, so—"

Matt had put his hand across Ernesto's mouth. "Lesson one, folks. Don't ever ask Ernesto a question."

"The murderer also could have been sitting down," Jessica said. "On a chair, or maybe just on the court, so that the murderer's size doesn't really enter into the equation. Right?"

"And another country chimes in," Matt said, sighing.

"Well? Am I right? Guys always do that—play a while, then sort of collapse on the court to catch their breath. So one of them's sitting there, and Terrell's still shooting around, and the guy is mad—maybe because Terrell's so clearly the better player—and he reaches into his pocket or gym bag or something, pulls out his piece and *bam,* blows Terrell away. People kill for dumber reasons."

"There were no powder burns, so the shooter wasn't too up close and personal, Jess. The police believe it was a drive-by," Jade said. "Terrell's body was found right next to the chain-link fence, close to the street."

Ernesto raised his hand, as if he was in a classroom. "May I?"

Matt and Jessica exchanged looks, Jessica smiling, Matt rolling his eyes. "Oh, go for it, Ernesto. God knows you want to."

"I've already examined the drawings of the position of the body on the court in relationship to the location of the fence and the street. The shot could have come from either side of the fence, but I have to think the killer was on the same side of the fence as Terrell. Factoring in a moving car, the crap-ass condition of Philly's side streets—potholes, you understand—and the average proficiency of a teenage shooter trying to funnel a bullet between the links of a chain fence? I'd say the odds of getting off a clean shot, also factoring in the broken streetlight on the street side of the court, the hour and amount of darkness, and the probability of success drops to about one in ten thousand six hundred and forty-three, give or take. Now, if the weapon had been a semi-automatic, an Uzi, then okay, anybody can get lucky with a spray gun. But a single shot? No homey's *that* good. Mostly, they're too busy posing, you know, turning the hand sideways and trying to look tough? You cops need to have some street-smart guys on the payroll, obviously. It's all clear to me."

"Great," Matt said sarcastically. "You're hired— just as soon as you can manage to grow some hair on your face."

"Don't tease him, Matt. I think I can see a couple of whiskers there somewhere. What about a ricochet, Ernesto, have you *factored* that in at all?" Jessica asked, turning on the couch, her legs tucked up beneath her. "Maybe the bullet hit the fence, then ricocheted off the court to hit Terrell? Ricochets can be more deadly than a direct hit, and that could explain the trajectory?"

"I'm not even going to ask how you know that," Matt said, rubbing at the back of his neck. "Because then you'd tell me. And, Miss Know-It-All, the bullet was a .22, and did a .22's usual dance inside Terrell's skull. There was nothing left but fragments, nothing to tell us if it was a ricochet or what the hell it was."

"He's right, Miss Jessica," Ernesto said, having chosen to address her that way, which seemed to make him more comfortable. "It's all supposition. Now, same as back when the guy was shot. But I'm betting the shooter was inside that fence with him. So either we decide that the shooter was a lot shorter than Terrell, or we play with scenarios that put the shooter on the ground and Terrell standing over him. Like, hey, there could have been a fight, and Terrell knocked the guy down, and he pulled out his piece and shot from his back."

"Court?" Jade asked, for Court hadn't said anything for quite some time. "You look so solemn. What do you think?"

"Nothing I want to be thinking," he said, getting to his feet. "Look, Jade, we've played out whatever string we've had on Terrell's murder. No matter who shot him, no matter the reason or the trajectory—all of that—the chances are greatest that it was a gang-related killing, even if Terrell wasn't in a gang. A dozen years later, those gang members have grown up and scattered. Out of town, in jail, shot dead themselves and buried. We'll never close that case, and it's pretty clear that his brother, Jermayne, is no use to us. It's time to drop our investigation, which has gone nowhere, anyway, and move on."

"You just don't want me going to that neighborhood again," Jade said accusingly.

"Damn straight I don't. That's no secret."

"The Baby in the Dumpster," Jessica said quickly, frowning at Jade. "Do we have to, sis? For one, everybody and his brother have investigated that case, for years. And number two, it makes me incredibly sad. Especially when I look at that computer rendering of what the baby would look like if he'd lived."

"You want Court and I to join you in working the Fishtown Strangler case, instead, Jess?" Jade asked, and Matt had to cover his mouth with his hand and pretend to cough to keep from laughing at the horrified expression on Jessica's face.

"Us?" Jessica asked, getting to her feet, pretty much with the speed of someone who just realized a fire had been lit beneath her. "You want to join *us*? Well, wow…gee…that would…I mean, that would be *swell*. All of us working together and all…"

"Okay, okay, forget it, before you swallow your tongue," Jade said. "Where are you going?"

"For a drive," Matt replied, as Jessica slipped her arm through his. "It might help to clear our heads if we take our minds off these cases for a few hours."

"A good idea," Court said, looking at Jade. "You and I could drive down to Penn's Landing, Jade. Take a walk near the water?"

Jade shook her head. "No. I want to read over this file for a while, so I can hit the ground running tomorrow morning. It's the thickest of the files, thanks to all the false leads and intense investigation, and I'm having trouble deciphering some of Teddy's progress notes. For instance—Matt, there are several instances where Teddy wrote the same word beside a block of information. I'm wondering if it's a police shorthand of some sort."

Matt shook his head. "What did he write?"

Jade riffled through the pages, pulled one out and held it up. "Well, like here, where the information concerns the chain of custody of the blanket the baby had been wrapped in—it's missing, by the way. Teddy underlined that information and beside it wrote—" she spelled out the word "—*f-u-b-a-r*. What's fubar?"

Jessica turned her head into Matt's shoulder, giggling.

Court pinched the bridge of his nose between his thumb and index finger, suppressing a small, amused smile.

Matt mentally looked around for a convenient hole to fall into. Jess was down to earth, sometimes even wonderfully earthy. He didn't know Jolie well enough to categorize her. But Jade, he had immediately decided, was the refined lady of the trio of Sunshine sisters. The sort you never swear around, the kind of person no one in his right mind would dare tell an even slightly off-color joke in front of, the sort of aristocratic lady males of all ages always felt it necessary to protect, open doors for, throw their coats over puddles for—and never explain the meaning of fubar to, even if she begged.

Ernesto looked up at Matt and then shrugged. "I know that one, Miss Jade. It's fu—"

"Fouled up beyond all recognition," Matt said quickly and probably a little too loudly, as Jessica now hung on to him with both hands, snorting with laughter. "I believe the term originated with the military."

"Oh." Jade looked at Court, and then back at Matt, unblinking. "Thank you, that explains it."

"That wasn't the right word, Matt," Jessica gulped out at last, her eyes dancing with mischief. "I know the correct word."

"And you'll keep it to yourself," Matt warned.

"No, I won't. It's *repair*. Not *recognition*." And then she grinned, her eyebrows raised comically on her forehead. "What? You expected me to say something else?"

"I never know what to expect from you," Matt admitted honestly. "I didn't know the blanket was lost, Jade. There's no excuse for that."

"From what I've read of the file," Court said, "it was a case of too many cooks, as my father used to say. The local police, the state police, the FBI, five or six other state and federal agencies all joining in—because the case was so nationally exposed, got so much media attention. I doubt what happened back then would occur today. I can remember speaking with Teddy about it one time, and he said that changes in procedure were made because of that case. Not that those changes help us much."

"Is anything left?" Matt asked Court. "There's got to be tissue samples, something for DNA comparisons. And what we can do with DNA has changed since the murder, too. What couldn't be done a dozen years ago might be possible now."

"If we had someone to compare that DNA *to*," Jessica said, "and we don't. A mother, a father, a sibling. What are you thinking to do, Jade?"

Her sister shrugged. "I'm not sure, to tell you the truth. It's why we left this case alone while we worked on the others, remember? There's really not much we can do. And it really doesn't look like Teddy had any new success to report. His last update on his progress notes was a week before he died, and all he wrote was something he'd have to be alive to explain to us."

She reached behind the pile of pages, to the last page, and pulled it out. She handed it to Matt. "See if you understand this. I promise, 'fubar' isn't anywhere in what he wrote."

Matt took the paper and held it over his head as Jessica reached for it. "Down, girl. Age before beauty."

"I'll take that as a compliment, grandpa," she said, and contented herself in leaning in close against his arm as he read Teddy's notes. "Here, use these."

Matt glared at the wire-rimmed pair of reading glasses Jessica had produced from her purse. "Where the hell did you get…? I don't need reading glasses."

"No. You need longer arms," Jessica quipped, winking at Ernesto before going up on tiptoe to slide the glasses onto Matt's ears. "I watched you trying to read Tarin White's autopsy report in the car. Being a good, caring person, I picked up a pair of these little half-glasses at the drugstore when I was there. It's nothing to be ashamed of, Matt. Hit forty, and the eyes start to go. It's perfectly natural. There's a technical term for the condition, but you probably don't want to know it, right? Anyway, they're plus two—I think they should be strong enough. If not, I can just hold the paper across the room, so you can read it better."

"She got ya, Lieutenant. Loving this!" Ernesto said, going up on his knees and holding up his right arm. "High-five, Miss Jessica!"

Jessica complied, and Matt muttered "fubar" under his breath before he went back to reading Teddy's notes, not ready to admit it was now easier to make out the closely printed words.

"Okay," he said a few moments later, "I think I've got it. We have to remember that Teddy was writing these notes for himself, so he wasn't interested in writing them in a way that anyone else other than him had to understand. Last June, he wrote 'no clear timeline.' That's true enough. If you all remember—

and who can forget—the body had been frozen. The medical examiner determined that. So we have no clear idea of TOD."

"Time of death," Jessica supplied helpfully.

"Why is there always an echo when you're around?" Matt asked her, adjusting the glasses on his nose. "In December, he wrote 'dead-end hospitals NE.' He was checking out hospitals in the northeast section of Philly, I'm guessing. But we went through birth records back when the body was found. And scanning his notes for previous years, I'd say the northeast was the last quadrant. He'd run out of hospitals to check. Doing this stuff on his own had to take a lot of time, a few greased palms and a good deal of finesse, since he didn't have a badge to flash anymore. So this last notation, the one he made just before he died? I'm thinking he'd widened the search to outside the city limits. Like I said, we checked birth records, but there's nothing like a face-to-face to prompt a memory of something that might be important. Teddy was a great proponent of shoe-leather investigation."

"Let me see," Jessica demanded, tugging on his arm. "Where is…? Oh, okay, I see it. 'Abington. Write-off. Single black female. Child male. Questionable alias.' Well, that's something, I guess." She looked up at Matt. "You think he found where the mother gave birth? I mean, that's what I'm getting out of it. There is a hospital in Abington. So Teddy thought he'd found out where the baby was born?"

Matt was still looking at the progress notes. "Jess, get the progress notes for the Fishtown Strangler."

"What? Why? Why do you—"

"Just do it," he said shortly, adjusting the glasses on his nose as he moved the paper closer and then farther away, trying to make out the date of Teddy's last progress note. *June 3*. Yeah, the third.

He took the page from Jessica and checked the last update on the Fishtown Strangler. *June 5*. A week before Teddy died. The visit to Abington had led Teddy straight to one of his other unsolved cases. Part of him wanted to smile, another part of him wanted to throw something heavy against a wall.

"Matt? What's wrong?"

"I don't know. Nothing. Everything. The dates are so close together, you know? Of the two entries Teddy made? No. It's crazy. It's too much of a coincidence. But both crimes did occur the same year."

"You're beginning to get on my nerves, Denby," Jessica said, and then brought home her frustration by giving him a sharp poke in the ribs. "Come on, out with it. What's too much of a coincidence?"

He rubbed at the back of his neck and then stopped, because Jessica was bound to notice the gesture. "Our fifth victim, Tarin White, gave birth, right? Teddy knew that. We can't find the baby, that's a one-in-a-million shot, but we know she gave birth a couple of months before she died. And we've got one dead baby—for whom we've got no TOD at all and never will. I think…I think Teddy had decided there was a connection between the two. Something he found out at Abington Hospital, someone he talked to, something someone remembered? I don't know. But I think he thought he found something."

"We need a calendar," Jessica said. "Quick, somebody, get a calendar. Jade, you've got your computer. Find us a perpetual calendar on it, and let's get a timeline going here for the year of the crimes, okay? Ernesto? Stick close, kiddo. I have a feeling you'll be good at this."

"Sure," Ernesto said, rubbing Rockne behind the ears. "You know, everything comes down to numbers sooner or later. Gestation periods? That I'm not so sure about, okay? Fruit flies, I know their gestation period. Elephants. But not human, sorry. Now, what you got?"

"Fruit flies? Sit, Ernesto. Don't talk." It took some time and some counting on his fingers as he held his hands behind his back, out of sight, but Matt and the others finally came up with a timeline that could, but then again could not, fit. That could, or could not, connect Fishtown Strangler victim Tarin White to the Baby in the Dumpster case.

Matt pointed this out to everyone else.

Jessica jumped all over him, figuratively, because

she liked the scenario, sad as it was, but Jade agreed with Matt, as did Court. They were somewhere between *possibly* and *pipe dream*. But it might explain why no one ever came forward to report a missing child—or identify the baby's body. If the mother was already dead, if the Fishtown Strangler turned out to have expanded his terror to both mother and child...

Ernesto was still playing with the intricate hand calculator Court had brought him from Sam's home office. At the moment the kid was swearing it had every bell and whistle anyone could ever hope to own, and if it could make a decent beef burrito, he'd marry it. Matt made a mental note to be sure Ernesto had just such a calculator before leaving for Penn State.

"You ready to go?" Matt asked Jessica quietly, for Court and Jade were deep in conversation now, and he doubted they'd miss the pair of them if they left. Jade did look up for a moment, waved goodbye and immediately went back to explaining to Court that a trip to Abington and the hospital there definitely was a good idea, to see if they could locate whomever Teddy had spoken to on his visit.

Jessica glanced quickly toward the French doors leading out to the terrace. "It is getting dark. Sure, let's go. I put two flashlights on the foyer table."

"Ernesto," Matt said, looking down at the boy. "Thanks."

Ernesto grinned up at him. "Hey, *amigo,* no

problem. Uh…do I have kitchen privileges, do you think? I keep thinking about that chicken Mrs. Archer gave us for dinner. Don't we, Rockne?"

"I'm sure Mrs. Archer wouldn't mind. Except, if you don't mind, I've got plans for Rockne," Jessica told him. "Come here, boy. Come here, Rockne. Wanna go bye-bye, hmm?"

Rockne's tail began to wag frantically and he followed Matt and Jessica to the foyer, and the leash she had sitting on the table next to the flashlights.

"Why are we taking the dog, Jess? More importantly, do I want to hear your answer?"

"Probably not," she said, hooking the leash to Rockne's collar. "Now, as your daddy used to say, let's make like shepherds, okay, before Jade thinks of something else she wants to ask you."

"ALONE AT LAST," Jessica quipped, sinking into the front seat of Sam's Mercedes, as Rockne, strapped into the seat belt in the back, pressed his nose against the side window. "And we're getting somewhere, aren't we?"

"Are we?"

Jessica sat up straighter, frowning at his tone. "What? Now you're going to be a wet blanket? We've got some good ideas working here, Matt."

"Good ideas," he repeated as they drove past Bear Man and out onto the two-lane macadam street.

"Hunches. Possibilities, probabilities. Your mind travels in more directions than Pennsylvania's own Senator Arlen Spector's infamous Warren Commission theory on the twists and turns of the magic bullet that killed Kennedy. And here I thought you guys in the *media* believed in the need for two sources before you went with a story. Or am I wrong?"

"Oh, brother." Jessica hated it when people rained on her parades. "Why can't you just go with the flow? I mean, it's not as if we've been having success after success to crow about here, you know. It's exciting to think that Teddy may have stumbled on something that rattled the wrong cage, and that we might be getting somewhere. That we might soon be able to prove that our father didn't kill anybody, including himself."

"That's not the way it works, Jess," Matt said, and she longed to repeat that jab in the ribs she'd given him earlier. "We don't deal in hypotheticals."

She folded her hands beneath her breasts. "That explains a lot."

"Meaning?"

Jessica shrugged. "I don't know. Meaning all those unsolved homicides in the city, maybe?"

Matt shot her a dirty look—it was definitely a dirty look. "You do that on purpose, don't you?"

Knowing that her hopes and plans for Matt and her and the rest of the evening might be in jeopardy meant a lot to Jessica. Still, she couldn't resist. She batted her eyelashes at him and asked innocently, "Do what, Matt?"

"Make me nuts."

She relaxed. "Oh, I can't take the credit for *that.* It's probably the shoes. I know they'd make me nuts. Not to mention the jacket."

"You know something, Jess? For two cents, I'd pull this car over and make love to you, here and now. If you really want to know what's nuts, *that's* nuts. I'm nuts."

Jessica pretended to dig in her purse for change. "Would you be open to taking a nickel?"

Matt grinned even as he shook his head. "Why am I suddenly feeling all nostalgic for Eddie Frantz and his smelly cigars?"

"Okay, *partner,* score this round even. Now tell me what else is making you nuts—bothering you."

"I'm probably asking for trouble here and should give up while I'm ahead—I personally think I won that round—but it's been driving me nuts the way we're going about this whole deal."

"For instance?" she asked through stiff lips.

"Okay. For instance. The Fishtown Strangler accounts for six victims, and don't even open your mouth to say seven, because I'm not buying a connection to the Baby in the Dumpster. Not yet. At any rate, we're investigating two of the Fishtown victims.

Two. And we didn't even begin in order. You went after Kayla Morrison on your own before you and I went after Tarin White. White was strangled before Morrison. Like that."

"Like that, huh? Oh, well, if that's all that's bugging you," Jessica said, relaxing, "it's really simple. The other four victims had no family, for one. Sad lonely women out on the street and now dead. They could have landed here from Mars, for all anyone ever knew about them. Second, Teddy had worked all six women—all six cases, I should say—and for the past several years, he was concentrating only on Tarin and Kayla. And if you really must know, I started with Kayla Morrison because *M* comes before *T* in the alphabet."

Matt drove on for a full five seconds before peeking into the rearview mirror, smiling. "Rockne, did you hear that? The lady thinks she's being logical. It's really a privilege to hear how her mind works, isn't it?" he said without heat. "Jess, nobody takes murder victims in alphabetical order. It's not like you're taking a number at the deli counter for your order of sliced bologna."

"I do. Work that way, that is," Jessica said, not insulted in the slightest. "And I'd do it again, because I've felt twice as dedicated to finding the Fishtown Strangler after meeting Kayla's daughter and mother. The daughter's fifteen or so now, and wild, looking for trouble and on the brink of destroying her whole life. And her grandmother can't control her. There's such anger there, and such grief that won't go away. Those two really need our help, some closure, you know?"

"Every victim's family needs closure, Jess, honey. That's one of the reasons I do what I do."

"So we're not so different, are we? And what does it matter how we do what we do as long as we get results?"

Matt pulled the Mercedes to the curb and turned to look at Rockne. "Never argue with a woman, buddy. You can't win."

Jessica leaned over and kissed Matt's cheek. He smelled like that sexy cologne again, and she had to fight herself back to the moment and not think about her hopeful plans for later in the evening. "Sure, you can. If we let you. So, where are we?"

"About a block from the Brainards' front gate. I figure we'll leave the car here and walk the perimeter of the fence, circle back here. And that's all we're going to do, Jess, understand? I just want this off my mind—that I left a job half done."

"Oh, sure, I get it. We're just looking, checking things out." She put her hand on the door handle and then hesitated. "You want to kill the dome light first, Lieutenant, or do you think we're safe enough to open the door?"

"Kill the dome light? Why the hell did I bring her

along?" Matt muttered to himself as he walked around the car to the curb. "I've got to stop thinking with my hormones."

Jessica prudently pretended not to have overheard him. *He was so cute...*

CHAPTER EIGHT

ROCKNE TUGGED on the leash, sniffing at the ground as they made their way along the high stone wall and then turned into the woods that surrounded the Brainard estate.

"Is he part bloodhound or just looking for a place to lift his leg?" Matt asked, taking the leash from Jessica, who was having enough difficulty trying to turn on her flashlight, now that they were away from the street and detection by passersby.

"You don't want to know the answer to that," Jessica told him, smiling up at him, her expression turning comical as she stumbled over a tree root and nearly went headfirst to the ground. "Oops! How many acres are we going to be walking around? A person could get hurt out here in the dark."

"Ten, and just keep that flashlight aimed at the ground in front of you and you'll be fine. And you might want to consider lowering your voice."

"Oh, yeah, right. Sorry. But the reason I wanted to bring Rockne is that, if there's a hole in this fence, you can count on him to find it. He's always looking for escape hatches."

"I feel his pain," Matt grumbled, transferring his flashlight to the hand that held Rockne's leash so that he could offer his arm to Jessica. Who took it, naturally, her body now pressed close against his as they made their way down the fence line. "I may be walking along here like I don't have a care in the world, but inside? Inside, I'm running for my life."

"From *moi?*" Jessica asked him, grinning up at him again as she gave a small shake of her head, sending her hair to swooshing gracefully before settling into place once more. Making him doubly aware of the soft full side of her breast against his arm. "Why, Lieutenant, sir, I'm flattered."

"You're a menace. What's worse, you know it. What tops that—you're enjoying yourself," he told her, trying not to admit that he also was beginning to enjoy himself. He almost always seemed to be enjoying himself when Jessica Sunshine was around. He'd even begun to ignore that little voice inside his head that kept repeating *run away, run away.*

"More compliments! Matthew, how you do flatter a girl. Rockne, don't do that, you almost tripped me," she ordered as the Irish setter cut across in front of them and began pulling toward the fence.

"I think he's found something," Matt said, surprised to feel his heart beginning to beat a little faster.

He hadn't really expected to find anything, and certainly not so fast. "What is it, boy?" he asked, aiming his flashlight at the fence. "What do you see?"

Jessica let go of Matt's arm and went to her knees beside Rockne. "And we have liftoff. Look, Matt, somebody cut the fence. Right here. I don't think we would have seen it, if not for Rockne. I'm so impressed—you're a genius, Rockne."

"Get up. Don't touch anything. Rockne, back off, now," he ordered quickly, tugging on the dog's leash, even if he didn't believe that whoever had cut the fence hadn't worn gloves so there'd be precious little trace evidence. And there'd probably be no useful footprints for anyone to find, either, especially nearly two weeks and as many rainfalls after the crime.

"Oh, right, sorry," Jessica said, getting to her feet and quickly backing away from the fence, although she kept the beam from her flashlight directed at the neatly cut three-foot-high slash in the chain link. "No animal did that, right? It's too perfect. Somebody used a wire cutter."

Matt only nodded, running the beam of his flashlight in a circle, looking for bent or broken weeds, trampled grass. "We're not going to get the crime-scene unit out here, not with everyone swearing the case is closed. Jess, shoot your flashlight around, look for anything that might show us the direction taken by whoever cut the fence."

"I'm doing it," Jessica said, excitement in her voice. "I'm shaking, Matt, I really am. I hoped, I really did—but we've actually found something." She looked up at the dark sky. "Hang in there, Teddy, we're going to fix this, we really are. We found a real honest-to-God clue. Haven't we, Matt?"

Matt stepped next to her and put a hand on her back, rubbing the tense muscles between her shoulder blades. She wasn't kidding—she really was shaking. "Yeah, we sure did, kiddo. I wish I could say it means something to anybody but us. I can't see any trail out here anywhere, and this is public land, anyway, part of the park, so anybody could have approached from anywhere. It doesn't prove anything. It doesn't even prove that the person who cut the fence did it in order to get onto the grounds and kill Melodie Brainard, or if they did it two years ago just for the hell of it. In fact, the only way we can even make ourselves feel better about anything would be to see if there's anything on the other side of the fence, any recently disturbed vegetation, cigarette butts, that sort of— Hey, come back here! Jessica, stop!"

He'd had to open his big mouth, hadn't he? Matt grabbed the stiff chain-link fencing so that no sharp edges could cut through Rockne's coat, and then bent and followed the two of them onto Joshua Brainard's private property, once more mentally kissing his gold shield goodbye.

"What in hell do you think you're doing?" he asked as he stopped beside Jessica, who was standing on tiptoe, trying, it seemed, to look into the clearing beyond the trees that currently concealed their presence.

"I'm looking at the side of the Brainard house— what do you think I'm doing?" Jessica whispered fiercely. "Getting my bearings, you know? Come on, the backyard is this way."

"We could be destroying evidence tramping around here, Jessica," Matt said, hanging on to Rockne's leash and hoping the damn dog didn't start barking and reveal their presence.

"You already said there probably won't be any more evidence, and that nobody would come looking, anyway. I just want to see how much open ground would have to be covered between the edge of all these trees and the pool, okay? Stay down— it's pretty well lit back here, isn't it?"

"Yeah," Matt said, a sinking feeling invading his belly as he remembered some of the little he'd learned about the Brainard estate's security system before being pulled off the case. "Although I'll lay you eight-to-five that the motion detectors make crouching down to avoid being seen pretty much a moot point."

"Well, hell, Denby, why didn't you say that earlier?" Jessica asked accusingly, just as if she'd applied for his permission before sneaking through the opening in the fence.

"Maybe it's not on," Matt said, ignoring her remark. "It wasn't working that night, along with the out-of-commission security camera. Brainard's been pretty busy. Burying his wife, giving four stump speeches a night to his adoring audiences. He might not have thought about calling in a repair crew."

"Then maybe we just got lucky, right?" Jessica pushed on until she could part a huge rhododendron bush in front of her and they could both look across an expanse of perfect lawn and up the gently sloping hill to the huge terrace and Olympic-size swimming pool where Melodie Brainard had worked out twice every day, until the night of her death. "Wow, some setup. And a lot of open territory for an intruder to travel without Melodie seeing him and locking herself in the house or something. Makes me think she might have known whoever killed her."

"She knew Teddy," Matt pointed out, knowing he wasn't being helpful. But, hell, didn't Jessica realize he'd already thought about several different scenarios, including the old she-knew-her-killer one?

"She knew lots of people. I tell you, I'm really impressed here. I've seen snazzy country clubs that aren't set up this well."

"Melodie Brainard was a champion swimmer when she was younger. I suppose the pool was built

especially for her. It's heated, and there's some re-
tractable domed-roof dealie that's hidden under a
slab of cement or something. Money might not buy
love, but it's pretty good at getting you most everything else. We found her body in the pool, dressed in
a bathing suit, but she was strangled before she hit
the water."

"Uh-huh," Jessica said, nodding even as she shooed
a mosquito away from her face. "I read the newspaper stories. Pretty woman, too, even if she and her
husband weren't exactly living the perfect marriage.
Jolie told me Brainard admitted to her and Sam that
he and his wife had—and I quote—'grown apart, lived
their separate lives.' You know, if we could dig up a
secret love nest for our candidate for mayor, it would
go a long way toward making him a suspect. Especially if he didn't have a prenup, because the guy is
worth millions. Isn't the marital partner always the
first suspect in these cases?"

"Right, sure, great idea. Maybe you could do one
of your shows on the subject," Matt said, feeling a
prickle at the back of his neck. "Let's go somewhere
and talk about that, okay? There's something about
trespassing on private property that slows my
thinking process."

"Chicken," Jessica teased, her bright eyes showing
him that she actually fed on this sort of clandestine
adventure even before she said, "I'm kind of getting

off on it, myself. We're not going to get cau—" Her head snapped up as lights strung in the trees all went on at once, turning the night nearly into day. "Okay, scratch that. Run for it!"

Matt grabbed her arm. "No, we're not going to *run for it*. We're caught, Jess. Let's try to make the best of it. Come on, let's show ourselves."

"And I'm to let you do the talking. I know the drill," Jessica said as Matt pushed aside a large branch and motioned for her to precede him into the clearing. The Irish setter followed, his head down, his tail between his legs. Great. The dog had more damn sense than the dame, the redhead more smarts than the blonde—or something like that.

Matt stood with a hand against Jessica's back as Joshua Brainard made his way down the grassy slope, a shorter, broader man beside him, the bodyguard's hand pointedly hidden beneath his sports coat.

"Raise your hands, keep them where the muscle can see them," Matt whispered as he raised his arms. "Mr. Brainard, my apologies. We're clearly trespassing. My name is Matthew Denby, and I'm a lieutenant, Homicide Division. If you'll allow me to use my left hand to reach into my breast pocket, I'll pass over my identification. Do I have your permission, sir?"

"Two fingers only, slow and easy," the bodyguard growled. "And shut up that dog," he added. Rockne had gone into Best Friend and Protector mode, and was both barking wildly and reared up on his hind legs, straining at his leash, now taut thanks to the fact that Matt had his hands high in the air.

"Gosh," Jessica whispered out of the corner of her mouth, "this is all so TV cop show." Before Matt could stop her, she'd stepped forward, dropping her hands, to say, "Jessica Sunshine, Mr. Brainard. You might recognize me from my show, *The Sunshine Report?* Do you know someone sliced a hole in your security fence?"

Brainard motioned to his bodyguard to heel or sit or do whatever bodyguards do when not needed. "Ms. Sunshine, of course," he said, clearly slipping into his public persona. "I had the pleasure of meeting your sister last week when my friend Sam Becket brought her to my office."

"Really?" Jessica said, tilting her head to one side, just as if she hadn't already gotten chapter and verse on that not-quite-delightful meeting. "She didn't say. You're probably wondering why Lieutenant Denby and I are, well, standing on your lawn, aren't you? There's a ridiculously easy explanation."

"I'd like to hear it, Ms. Sunshine," Brainard said, inclining his head slightly, his smile still in place, but beginning to look a little frozen.

Matt stepped in front of Jessica before she could dig them both in any deeper with more of her facility for twisting facts to suit her own position—it was already time to roll up the pant legs, as the old saying went, because it was too late to save the shoes.

"I was the primary on your wife's case, Mr. Brainard, until the chief decided to shove the case up the ladder and out of my hands. I'm human enough, sir, to feel that might have been a mistake and that there might have been, well, a rush to judgment. It bothered me, for instance, that there was no real check of the fence that borders your property to ascertain if an intruder had found a way to get onto the grounds. I should have kept my opinion, and my plans, to myself." He held out his hands as if begging for understanding. "But you've seen Ms. Sunshine, Mr. Brainard. I guess I'm just a sucker for blondes."

The bodyguard laughed and leaned closer to Joshua Brainard to whisper—and the bodyguard wasn't good at whispering— "Not to mention the rack, right, boss?"

"I'll murder you later," Jessica whispered—she was better at whispering—before she gave her blond hair a practiced flip and subtly sucked in her breath, not so subtly pushed back her shoulders. Matt had a sudden urge to strip off his jacket and toss it over her.

"Matt's just trying to protect me, Mr. Brainard," she said, waving a hand at her throat as if the evening was a lot warmer than it was. "The whole trespassing thing was my idea. At least once I saw the cut in the fence. I mean, the opening was there, I was there. It seemed logical that I, you know, take a peek?"

"Go inside, Leslie, I can handle this," Brainard ordered his bodyguard, who immediately began to protest that he was needed where he was.

Jessica snorted. Yes, snorted. *"Leslie?"*

"Shut up," Matt warned her, whispering between clenched teeth. "Our boy Leslie's got a great big bang-bang under that jacket."

"He's not going to shoot us. How would Brainard explain that to the press? Relax. And let go of Rockne's leash. I want to see if he's going to bite Brainard's leg off or something."

Matt looked at her for a moment before he figured it out, what she'd planned. "You always expected to see Brainard tonight, didn't you? Find a way through the fence, go knock on his door, whatever it took. All so we can see if Rockne recognized him, to see if Brainard maybe had been at Teddy's house that night. Damn it, Jess, you can't do that. You can't have your own agenda, not if we're going to work together."

She looked at him, her brown eyes flat, her expression tense. "Let go of the leash, Matt. Rockne's still pulling, still barking. Let's see what happens."

Swearing under his breath, Matt let go.

Rockne the wonder mutt immediately took off across the lawn to where a brown rabbit was taking a moonlight snooze, and the chase was on.

"My money's on the bunny. Next theory?" Matt asked a clearly crestfallen Jessica.

"Oh, shut up. Leslie put up a good fight, but he's leaving now. Let's see if Brainard sent him to his room—or to call the cops to come get us."

"I'm figuring that depends. How many buttons are you willing to open, Jess, in the name of getting your own way?"

"You're really angry, aren't you."

"Still playing detective? Yeah, I'm really angry."

"Then I don't have to worry about making you angry when I ask our friend Brainard a few more questions, do I?"

"Ms. Sunshine?"

"Yes, Mr. Brainard—and it's Jessica, please. I mean, I am standing in your backyard, aren't I?"

"Ah, yes. Thank you, Jessica. I realize what your sister was doing, and I'm sure you're attempting to do the same thing. Clear your father's name. I can't fault you for that. If my father had been accused of murdering someone and of committing suicide to avoid prosecution for that crime, I would probably do a little investigating of my own, unable to accept such a theory. But we're not dealing in theory here, Jessica, are we? We're dealing in facts."

"Are we, Joshua?" Jessica asked silkily. "As the good lieutenant here has already said, the investigation into both your wife's murder and my father's wasn't very intense or comprehensive. The hole in your fence, for instance?"

"I've known about that slice in the fence for some time, Jessica," Brainard said as Matt stood by quietly, watching the man's face, the expressions that came and went on that face. "Some young vandals cut through it several months ago and amused themselves by throwing all our patio furniture into the pool. One of them actually defecated into the shallow end, as a matter of fact—a common occurrence I was told, as sickening as that seems. A police report was filed at the time. I'm guilty of being too busy with my campaign to have as yet ordered the repair of the breach. That's all there is to that."

Matt watched as Jessica's shoulders slumped for a moment and then straightened again. "And the motion detectors, the security camera? You didn't have time to think about ordering those repaired, either? That's difficult to believe, especially after your property was vandalized."

Brainard smiled yet again. "My property, Jessica, is *vandalized* as you call it, more often than I can keep up with the repairs. Squirrels, Jessica. They routinely chew through cables, wires, and outwit any contraption that is set up to discourage them. If you'd care to see the repair invoices, I believe the last repair of one of the main cables is dated not two weeks before my wife's murder. I sometimes think the squirrels in this neighborhood all have advanced degrees from MIT. If the motion detectors weren't programmed only to signal movement at a height of five feet, the alarms would run constantly."

"Let's go, Jess," Matt said, putting his hand on the back of her waist again. "Mr. Brainard, thank you. You didn't have to be so accommodating."

"It's all right, Lieutenant, I understand. As I said, I've already met Jessica's sister. I wouldn't expect less determination from her sibling. There's a third, I understand. Should I keep the porch light burning, expecting her to stop by sometime soon?"

"Well…." Jessica's smile was brilliant and, to Matt's rapidly understanding eye, one that should make any sane man duck for cover.

But Joshua Brainard might still be trying to get himself another vote. "Yes, Jessica? You have a question?"

"I do, yes. You see, we've—my sisters and I— we've been racking our brains to think of a single reason why your wife and our father would ever have come in contact with each other, let alone that he'd strangle her. I, we, thought perhaps, having time to give the whole thing some more thought, you may have discovered a reason that might, well, that might satisfy us? I mean, then you wouldn't have to keep the porch light on, would you?" she ended, doing that tip-of-her-head thing again.

Brainard shook his own head. "No, I'm sorry, I can't help you there. According to my father, whom

Melodie confided in more than me, I'm sorry to say, your father had come to her with vague questions, even warnings. He stalked her, Jessica, and if I'd known it, I would have put a stop to it. As it was, Teddy Sunshine had badgered my assistant into scheduling a meeting with me, but then your father canceled it. The day my wife died, he canceled that appointment, instead choosing to go after my wife yet again. But I told your sister all this. Her response, as she obviously didn't care for mine, was to attempt to drag me and my late wife through the mud, having brought her own photographer to waylay me, possibly lend her publicity, which, I suppose, is very common for Hollywood types, so I forgave her, and Sam. I would hope you don't have similar intentions."

And now we know why you're being so nice, Joshua, Matt thought, watching Jessica closely, waiting for the zinger. She also was being too nice during this semi-polite exchange. A zinger was coming. He'd seen her Chickpea the Clown interview and a few others, so he knew how she worked. The zinger question was coming, it was just a matter of when.

"Through the mud, Joshua?" Jessica purred, repeating the man's words.

Matt bent down to grab Rockne's leash now that the dog had come back to them…and maybe to hide behind the dog, at least hide his smile behind the dog. *And here it comes…*

"You know what I see when I look at your wife's case, Teddy's case, Joshua? I see a cover-up. A big, fat, official cover-up. And as a journalist, I have to ask myself—who has something to hide here? Is a run for mayor of Philadelphia more important to you, Joshua, than finding out who killed your wife?"

"Your father killed my wife," Joshua said tightly. "I have complete faith in the Philadelphia Police Force. If they're satisfied, I'm satisfied. And no threat of more bad publicity, of some muckraking two-bit cable-news reporter or hotshot sex-goddess movie star is going to change my mind."

So much for Mr. Nice Guy, Matt thought, wincing. But Jessica just kept that same blond-barracuda smile on her face.

"Bad publicity? Ah, Joshua, you haven't seen bad publicity."

"Is that a threat, Ms. Sunshine?"

At Brainard's tone, Rockne bared his teeth, growled low in his throat. "Easy, boy," Matt said, taking a step of his own toward Brainard, who now dug his manicured fingertips into his palms.

"I don't know if it's a threat, Joshua," Jessica purred. "I imagine it would be, if you have something to hide. Do you have something to hide?"

"Say good-night, Gracie," Matt said, grabbing her by the elbow and turning her back toward the trees.

"He's hiding something," Jessica said breathlessly

as Matt pushed her ahead of him through the slit in the chain-link fence. "Did you see his eyes? Left and down, left and down. He knows something, or maybe just suspects something. Either way, there's something rotten in Denmark."

"And there's a nutcase in suburban Philadelphia," Matt bit out. "Keep moving."

He opened the car door, slamming it shut the moment Jessica lifted her legs into the car, and then quickly strapped Rockne into the seat belt in the backseat. Five seconds later, the Mercedes was rolling away from the Brainard estate, the headlights off. Matt only turned them on once they were past the large wrought-iron gates.

"What are you doing?"

"Sam doesn't need his car recognized, that's what I'm doing. Or do you think our pal Leslie wasn't standing at those gates, camera in hand, watching for us?"

"They already know our names, genius," Jessica reminded him. "And Sam was with Jolie when she met with Brainard."

"So I'm overreacting, getting as crazy as the rest of you. Sue me, remembering that by next week I'm most probably going to be out of a job, flat broke and looking at a civil suit from our fair-haired mayoral candidate," Matt said as he turned onto a more well-traveled street. "But first, let me agree with you.

Brainard knows something, or at least suspects something. The kicker to that is, I don't think he cares enough to do any digging. He's too wrapped up in getting himself elected in November."

"Which is it, Matt? He's guilty? Or he's worried?"

Matt pulled into the drive-through of a fast-food restaurant. "I don't know. But I don't think he's going to get my vote. I'm a law-and-order kind of guy, but maybe also too much of an idealist. I'd like to think a man running for mayor has some personal integrity."

"Lots of luck holding on to that pretty thought." Jessica pushed her fingers through her hair, tucking it behind her ears. "A year in my line of work and you'll have no illusions left. So, what are we eating? A Double-stuff Heart Attack in a Bun, or a wilted salad with dried-up cheese all over it?"

"Pick your poison. My treat."

"I'd rather we went back to Sam's and I find something in the kitchen to whip up for us. Concern for your arteries, you understand."

"And she cooks, too," Matt said, grinning. "What did you have in mind?"

"Eggs? I'm very good at eggs."

Matt made a face. "Big deal. I can scramble an egg. All right, let's go," he said, pulling the Mercedes out of line. "You can cook, and I can start working on my résumé."

"Oh, would you stop? It wasn't all that bad. And

Brainard isn't going to report you. He likes publicity, sure, but not bad publicity, and people would be bound to start asking why a decorated lieutenant was pulled off Melodie Brainard's murder investigation."

"Decorated?"

"I looked you up, so now you can sue me. And, nope, Brainard's not going to say a word, at least not right now. In a couple of days? Maybe. But by then anything he says will be looked at as sour grapes and self-serving, so he won't say anything then, either. Just some vague, official statement, and that's it."

Matt was getting that funny prickling feeling at the back of his neck again. "In a couple of days? You mind explaining that?"

"Sure would, handsome. Ah, you know what? We should have stayed in line, gotten Rockne a couple of hamburgers. Sorry, Rockne," she said, looking into the backseat.

"You aren't worried about Rockne's cholesterol?"

"When he can still move that fast after a rabbit? No, I don't think so. Are we going to make love tonight?"

Matt nearly drove over a curb. "Damn it, Jess, don't do that. Not to me, anyway. Save your in-from-left-field zingers for the guests on your show."

"First you complain that I'm too indirect, and now you're complaining about zingers. All right, how's this for easing into the subject first? Are we going to go shopping for some new clothes for you tomorrow morning—after we make love tonight?"

Matt turned on the radio, and dialed up the volume. From the look of Jessica's smile, he knew she'd taken his nonresponse as a *yes*. Which, heaven help him, it was.

CHAPTER NINE

MATT WAS obviously faking sleep on the couch when Jessica entered the living room, two plates and two cups of coffee balanced on a silver tray. He had his arms crossed on his chest, his chin tipped forward and his feet propped on Sam's priceless antique coffee table.

He looked huggably adorable. And sexy as a rumpled cop could look, which, as it turned out, was pretty darn sexy.

Jessica carefully went to her knees beside the table and slid the tray onto the surface before slipping a hand beneath the hem of Matt's slacks and lightly tickling his calf. "Rise and shine, sleepyhead. Your delicious bedtime snack is here." She grinned. "And it brought some eggs for you to eat, too."

Matt opened one eye and sort of peered down to where most of her forearm now was hidden under his pant leg. "Gosh, Mrs. Robinson, are you trying to seduce me?"

She laughed. "I know that line—it's from *The*

Graduate. I bought it on DVD last year. But I think, if you want to be exact, it's 'Mrs. Robinson, you're trying to seduce me? Aren't you?'"

Matt pushed himself up on the couch. "And are you, Mrs. Robinson?"

"Well, the way to a man's heart is supposedly through his stomach," Jessica said, unfolding a heavy cloth napkin and spreading it on his lap, "but that isn't really where I'm aiming. Hungry?"

"I think so, yes," he said, looking at the tray. "Smells good. What is it?"

"Eggs Benedict, you plebian," Jessica said, picking up one of the plates. "It's true, then, if it doesn't come in a take-out box or have powdered sugar and sprinkles on it, cops don't know nothin' from breakfast."

"Guilty as charged." Matt took the plate from her and held it in front of him. "Looks pretty. What's in it?"

Jessica rolled her eyes. "You mean it, don't you? You've never eaten eggs Benedict. All right. Eggs Benedict, Lieutenant, consists of eggs, Hollandaise sauce, and Canadian bacon, served on a lovely toasted English muffin. Mine are better than most, the secret being the addition of a crucial smidgeon of Worcestershire sauce many leave out. Take a taste."

Matt did as she said, and smiled around a mouthful as he chewed and swallowed. "You made this? You? All by yourself?"

"I also can walk and chew gum at the same time. Yes, all by myself. I'm a great cook, a real catch. Now some coffee."

"Why? You put Worcestershire sauce in that, too?"

"I'll ignore that crack. No, I use one hundred percent Arabica beans. Most coffees are either robusta beans or a combination of Arabica and robusta, but one hundred percent Arabica is the best. I carry my own beans with me when I travel. And the cutest little hand grinder Jade gave me for Christmas a few years ago."

Matt picked up the coffee cup and took a sip. "Okay. That's pretty damn good. I'm impressed, which means something, because cops know their coffee. What else can you do?"

Jessica grinned. "Ask me later, once you're done eating and we go upstairs."

"I'll do that," he said, his incredibly sexy eyes sort of smoldering as he looked at her, which Jessica considered an encouraging sign of good things to come. "Because you know what, Jess? I give up, partner. I know a losing battle when I see one, and I'm not going to fight this one anymore. I'm not completely nuts."

"Well, that was romantic," Jessica said, caught between her rapidly rising libido and her sensitive nature when it came to the intensely personal.

He put down his now empty plate. "I'm sorry,

Jess, that was crude, and I apologize. I want you. I've wanted you since that first night, when you looked at me and told me to go away, you didn't need my help. I want to hold you, I want to kiss every inch of you, taste every inch of you, possess every—"

"Hold that thought," Jessica interrupted breathlessly, grabbing the tray and getting to her feet. "Second door on the left at the top of the stairs. Ten minutes. Okay?"

Without waiting for his answer, she took off like a shot for the kitchen, her hands shaking as she rinsed the dishes and loaded them into the dishwasher. Then she ran to the powder room off the kitchen, nearly skidding across the tile and into the front of the pedestal sink.

She rinsed her mouth with mouthwash she found in the medicine chest, slapped cold water on her cheeks, pulled out the neckline of her blouse and sniffed at her skin to be sure that her Chanel No. 5 was still her most predominant scent after traipsing through the woods an hour earlier. It was.

Wow. She was already tingling with anticipation, already pleasantly aroused. That had never happened to her before. Who knew there could be such a thing as culinary foreplay?

She looked at her reflection in the mirror, drew in a deep breath and exhaled it slowly, and told herself, "You wanted it, kiddo, and now you're going to get it. Don't look now, but it's showtime. Go get it!"

Halfway down the hallway toward the foyer, she

saw Jade coming toward her, a cup in her hand. Just what she didn't need, a roadblock on her way to showtime. "Uh…hi," Jessica said brightly. She winced as she heard her voice. Too brightly.

"Hi, yourself. Going to bed?"

"Thinking about it, sure," Jessica told her, speaking too quickly, trying to control her breathing. "You?"

"Avoiding Court, if you must know," Jade said, frowning.

Wrong. Jessica didn't need to know. She didn't even want to know. Not right now. *Showtime, showtime.*

"I'm feeling particularly in charity with him tonight, and he knows it. I don't want to make a mistake we'll both regret."

"Good thinking. Well, good night." Jessica cared about her sister's problems, she really did. *But not right now. Right now, she was freaking tingling, and it had been a long time between tingles!*

"Jess, are you feeling all right? You look a little…flushed."

"Me?" Jessica responded, silently cursing her fair skin. "Nope. Feel fine. Maybe a little warm? I…I was cleaning up the kitchen."

"I thought I smelled eggs, earlier. Should I go to bed with him, Jess?"

Damn. "I don't know, Jade. What do you think?"

"I think we're compatible in bed and drive each other crazy out of bed."

"Then don't do it."

"It has been so long. More than a year now, Jess, without sex. That's not natural, is it?"

"It is for me," Jessica said, suppressing a sigh. "Well, you two were married. It's probably natural that you—"

"I shouldn't say this, not to my baby sister," Jade said, turning the cup in her hands, "but Court is a marvelous lover."

Man, Jade sure did pick her times for True Confessions. "Then do it."

"He'll expect more than I can promise him."

"Then don't do it."

"I sleep with my teeth clenched these days, I swear it, knowing he's just down the hall."

"Then do it. Definitely. Do it. Okay, good night again!"

Jade looked up from contemplating the bottom of the cup. "What's going on here? You've been dying to get me to talk about Court and me, and now I'm telling you my deepest feelings and you're edging toward the stairs. Jessica? Don't tell me that you and Matt are…well, of course you are! Everybody is. Jolie and Sam. You and Matt. So what in hell am I doing heading for the kitchen and another cup of warm milk?"

"Beats me," Jessica said, shrugging. "Well, gotta go." She turned, took two more steps toward the foyer, the stairs and the waiting Matt, and then stopped, sighed, and turned around again. "You really want to talk about this, don't you, sis?"

"No, not really," Jade said, shaking her head. "Go on, go upstairs. I think I'll warm some more milk and take it and the Baby in the Dumpster file upstairs to bed with me."

"Ah, Jade, really?"

"Yes, really. It's the smart thing to do. But while we're talking about smart things to do…are you sure you and Matt should be, you know? You're my sister. I don't think he's the marrying kind, and I don't want to see you get hurt."

"Married? Who's talking about getting married?" Jessica was genuinely shocked. "We're just going to have sex. People do have sex for reasons other than love, you know."

"I guess so. I'm just old-fashioned, aren't I? It's shocking, though, to hear my own sister's so…so modern."

"Yeah, that's me. Modern. Everything's up-to-date in Jessica City and all that," Jessica said, wishing her sister would just shut up, because the last thing she, Jessica, wanted at the moment was to think too much about what she was about to do, and how it would end between her and Matt. It's never good to be looking at the ending when a person is just at the beginning, right?

"Well…good night," Jade said, turning toward the kitchen.

Jessica watched her sister go, wondering if she should follow her, and then the clock in the foyer struck the hour. Her ten minutes were up, and had been up five minutes ago.

She headed for the stairs, not breaking into a jog until she reached the turn in them, halfway to the second floor.

THE DOOR OPENED just as Matt had begun a serious "What the hell do you think you're doing?" discussion with his better self. He watched, amused, as Jessica closed the door behind her and then sort of collapsed against it, her breasts rising and falling rapidly as she seemed to try to catch her breath.

"Let me guess. You're being followed?"

"Close, but no cigar." Jessica shook her head, slowed her breathing, but still stood with her hands behind her back, that back against the door. "Not followed. Just found out. I saw Jade downstairs. I didn't tell her anything. She guessed."

"Oh, terrific. Should I be expecting Court to come pounding on the door anytime soon, demanding to know my intentions?"

She smiled a rather nervous crooked smile. "Sam's house only makes a person feel like he's living in another century. Court would never do that. And if

Jade changes her mind, he'll be a little busy himself for the next couple of hours."

Matt raised one eyebrow as he eased himself away from the bedpost he'd been leaning against and walked over to stand in front of Jessica. Damn, was the woman in love with that door? "Is that so? Good for Court and Jade."

"Uh-huh," Jessica said, leaving her spot at the door and walking a few feet past him before turning to look at him again. "Can I be honest with you, Lieutenant?"

Matt shrugged, wondering if she'd changed her mind and wanted him to leave. "Go for it."

"Right. Go for it. Okay. Here's the thing—I haven't had sex in over a year, Matt, which is pretty much par for the course for me, if you must know. I'm not as modern as Jade thinks I am."

"Jade?"

"Never mind. Let's just say I don't do this very often, all right?"

"All right. We'll say you don't have sex very often. And…?" he prompted when she lowered her head.

He heard her sigh. She looked up at him again. "And I'm horny as hell, okay? I didn't know I was," she added quickly. "I really didn't. But the other night? When we kissed? I can't stop thinking about it…and you…and wanting you to do it again. Only this time… do we have to, you know, go so slow? Because I'm really not sure if I can go all that slow, and—"

The next thing he knew, Matt had her in his arms, and her back was against the door again, and they were kissing, and they were pulling at each other's clothing, and he was vaguely aware that the door was softly sort of banging in its frame, and he somehow was backing into the room, and their knees seemed to telepathically communicate that it was time for them to bend, and they were kneeling on the floor in the middle of some probably priceless antique carpet and he was still kissing Jessica and she was still kissing him back.

He was unbuttoning her blouse.

She was ripping his T-shirt free of his slacks.

He was unsnapping her bra, watching, amazed, as her breasts spilled free. "Sweet Jesus…"

He kissed her again.

She worked at his belt and zipper.

He was pressing her back, against the carpet, even as she bit at his shoulder.

She was lifting her hips, helping him remove her panties. Screw her skirt, it could stay where it was…

One leg of the panties caught at her ankle. He heard the thin material rip as he pulled it free. The act excited the hell out of him and seemed to ignite something even more desperate in Jessica, who was now almost frantically pulling at the waistband of his slacks.

He cupped her face between his hands and kissed her, kissed her again, their tongues dueling, their teeth nipping, their breaths mingling as she moaned low in her throat, as he caught the soft sounds and swallowed them, sending the effect of her voiced pleasure straight to his aching groin.

Her breasts were full, her nipples pert and pouting, responding to his lightly pinching fingers, the drag of his tongue as he laved at first one nipple, then the other, his tongue flicking rapidly, in pace with his racing heartbeat.

Somehow he managed to pull the foil packet from his pocket before his slacks were out of reach. He fumbled like a teenager, finally opening the packet with his teeth as Jessica ran her hands over his hips. He all but collapsed onto her, breathing like a racehorse approaching the finish line.

She reached down one hand, searching for him, finding him, opening her legs to him as each provocative thrust of her hips urged him to come to her, plunge deep inside her, move with her, soar with her.

She tore at his back with her rounded nails. He slammed into her, again and again. Deeper, faster.

If one of Sam's fancy crystal chandeliers was attached to the ceiling just below them, it would have been swinging back and forth, its crystals jangling as if southeast Pennsylvania had just been hit by a major earthquake.

"Matt…" Jessica moaned his name against his ear as he felt her body tense, release, again and again. "Matt…Matt…yes, yes, yes…*now!*"

Like he had a choice? She was killing him. He was a willing victim. He was putty in her hands. Thank God *all* of him hadn't turned to putty.

He was older, he should be more controlled. He wasn't. He needed her, he had to have her, he had to finish this before his heart exploded.

Jessica slid her frantically skittering hands down to his buttocks and pulled him to her one last time, and Matt felt himself break into pieces, instinct taking the place of rational thought. He covered Jessica's slightly open mouth with his own, needing her kiss even more than he needed the shattering climax that ripped through him moments later.

It took full minutes before they stopped holding each other, kissing each other, regulated their breathing and cleared their minds enough for Jessica to begin chuckling and for him to join her.

They were in the middle of the floor, half naked, the both of them, totally satisfied, sated and beginning to feel just a little bit silly.

"Well, now…that was…interesting," Jessica said as he slowly rolled off her, to sit beside her as he tugged down his T-shirt and pulled up his shorts and slacks. "What happened?"

"You want an instant replay?" he asked as she, too, sat up, fumbling with her front-closing bra. "It might kill me, but we could think about it in an hour or so."

"It's something to think about." She rubbed at her backside. "I think I've got a rug burn. Can we at least change playing fields? You know, move to the bed?"

"I don't think that's outside the rules, sure," Matt said, helping her to her feet, to see that she was now holding the ripped panties. "Sorry about that."

"I'm not," she said, going up on tiptoe to kiss his cheek. "You were wonderful."

"And more than a little bit rusty, I'm afraid. Look, Jess—"

She put a finger to his lips. "Shh, don't say anything, okay? We did what we did, I don't think either of us regrets it—you don't, do you? Good, I'll take that grin as a no. Where it goes from here, if it goes anywhere at all—that's up to the future. I'm…I'm just really glad you're a part of my *present*."

Matt kissed her fingertips, one by one, looking deeply into her eyes. "One day at a time, hmm?"

"Like somebody once told me, one foot in front of the other," she said, smiling.

JESSICA AWOKE reluctantly, holding up a hand a few inches from her eyes to block out the sunlight that had crept across the bed because she hadn't closed the drapes the previous evening. She'd had better things to do, she thought, smiling even as she turned onto her side to kiss Matt good morning.

The smile faded when she saw the indentation in the other pillow, but no Matt.

It was probably smarter that he had gone back to his own room after she'd fallen asleep after the most amazing, sensual, mind-shattering, drawn-out love-making of her life, but the pang of loneliness that hit her was still pretty surprising. She hadn't slept with anyone else in the bed since she and Jolie had shared a room for a while when Teddy and their mother had slept in separate rooms.

She'd needed Jolie's presence then, to keep her from being scared that their lives were falling apart.

She needed Matt's presence now, but she wasn't about to think about why, or if her life would fall apart if he were to leave her the way her mother had, and never look back.

"Work," she said out loud, putting an edge of steel into her voice she didn't really feel. "When in doubt, when in pain, when alone—work, Sunshine. It hasn't failed you yet."

She reached for the cell phone on the side table and punched in the number of her friend at the *Philadelphia Inquirer.* The reporter owed her a favor, and it was time to collect.

MATT KNEW he wouldn't be honest with himself if he didn't wonder how well his and Jessica's first few moments together might come off this morning, but when she walked into the breakfast room, her blond hair bouncing on her shoulders and the usual open trusting smile on her face, he stopped worrying.

Although it would make him less nervous if Jade would stop sneaking looks at him when she thought he wasn't looking.

"Hi, everybody," Jessica said, grabbing a plate from the sideboard and piling it with strips of bacon and three slices of cantaloupe. "So what's on the agenda for today? Anything that can't wait? Because Matt and I are going shopping."

"We are?"

"Yes, Matthew, we are. You promised." She sprinkled a good tablespoon of sugar over the cantaloupe slices. "Or I threatened. One of those two."

Matt smiled at Court, who was looking at him commiseratingly. "So what are you two doing today? Jess and I are going shopping."

Jade said, "I want to take a look at your Fishtown Strangler notes on Tarin White. It's a real long shot, I know, but if Tarin White was the mother of that poor dear child…"

"There's bound to be tissue samples from both White and the baby somewhere," Matt told her, deliberately trying to keep Jade and Jessica from pinning all their hopes on that sort of coincidence. "But don't count on the department paying for testing and comparison. That takes convincing a DA we've got a good reason to have him order the testing, and even then, if we get the paper authorizing it, the results wouldn't be back for months. Then there's the possibility that the samples have degraded so badly over the years that there's nothing left to test. Exhuming the bodies? Lots of luck with that."

"Just chock-full of optimism, isn't he?" Jessica said as she munched on a slice of bacon. "So you won't mind, Lieutenant, if I've taken our most recent theory another step or two? Good. I'm thinking more about Tarin White right now, you understand. Tarin White and her expensive dental work and donated plot and headstone. You're following me, aren't you, Matt?"

He sat forward, his forearms on the table. "Yeah, I think I am. Find the sugar daddy and maybe we've found the *daddy*. DNA from a living donor, matched against that from tissue samples from the baby, and we might get something. We'd certainly get a DA's attention, just because we'd be introducing a new player—the father."

"I'd like to get an explanation of why he never came forward to say that his love child, or whatever the baby was, had gone missing, and that maybe the Baby in the Dumpster was his kid."

"Good point, Court," Jessica said. "What kind of man thinks first to protect himself and not his own child?"

"That's pretty simple. A married one," Matt told

them, getting to his feet. "Okay, Jess, let's go get this over with."

Jessica licked her fingers as she, too, stood up. "Would you listen to the man? You'd think I was marching him to the guillotine, not the mall. I'm figuring King of Prussia Mall, Jade. What do you think?"

"I think the last time I went to King of Prussia I came back with my credit card still smoking from overuse. Be careful, Matt. I've begun to think that malls are like casinos, pumping in extra oxygen so you feel all happy and ready to open your wallet."

"I'll keep that in mind, Jade, thanks," Matt said as Jessica pulled a face at him. "One new sports coat, a couple of shirts, a pair of jeans. That's *it*."

"And shoes. Please, God, shoes. I mean, you're being seen with me, and I have some sort of reputation to uphold, you know," she told him as she waved goodbye to Jade and Court. Once they were out of the morning room and around the first turn in the hallway, she stopped, grabbed him by the shirtfront and kissed him hard on the mouth. "Good morning, hot stuff," she then said against his lips.

Matt cupped her bottom in his hands, pulled her closer. "Good morning, yourself. And thank you for a very good night."

"Back at you," she said, easing out of his embrace. "Okay, now I'm ready to go."

"So am I," Matt muttered as he followed her, "but I imagine you're talking about going to the mall. I guess we're still using the Mercedes? I don't know if my ragtop would be allowed on the King of Prussia parking lot. I know my W-2 won't be greeted with open arms."

"Oh, stop," Jessica scolded him as they headed out the front door to the big black car parked in the circular driveway. "For one thing, the clothes aren't *that* expensive, and for another, if you invest—yes, *invest*—in quality clothing, it lasts longer."

"Economics 101 from Shopaholics University?" Matt teased. "Or would that statement come from a textbook called Fifty Ways to Rationalize Blowing the Budget?"

"Neither," Jessica purred as he helped her into the car. "It's from a song I wrote called 'I Love Spending Other People's Money.' Want to hear it?" She put her hands to her breast as she began to sing, "'I lo-ove spend-ing *other* people's mon—'"

He closed the door on the sound of her voice, shaking his head and chuckling as he rounded the car to the drivers' side and climbed in. "No encores," he warned her as she sat, now with her hands folded in her lap, looking as innocent as sin-on-a-stick.

He waited until they'd pulled out between the gates before he told her about the phone call he'd gotten just before he'd gone down to breakfast.

"Talked to my captain this morning. Or, should I say, I listened while he talked."

Jessica's head whipped around to look at him with wide eyes. "But you're on vacation. They're not calling you back to work, are they?"

"No, they're not. As a matter of fact, the captain would like me to *extend* my vacation, if I promise to do that extending on some island far away from Joshua Brainard's estate. If I don't, the possibility of a *permanent* vacation could be considered."

Jessica winced. "That rat! I didn't think he'd do that. Brainard, that is. Tattle on you."

"He wasn't tattling on me, Jessica. You could say he was reporting a B and E, if you don't count that we didn't really break anything or enter more than his backyard."

"And we didn't steal anything," she added hopefully, as if that mattered. "Is Brainard going to press charges?"

"No, it wasn't that kind of call. It was more like Brainard complaining to his even more powerful than him daddy, and Daddy calling his pal, the current mayor, and the mayor calling the chief, and the chief calling the captain, and the captain calling me. By the time the captain got to me, the yelling had gotten pretty damn loud. I go near Joshua Brainard again and it could, probably would, cost me my shield."

"Oh, Matt, I'm so sorry. It's all my fault."

"I didn't have to follow you onto Brainard's property," Matt said as he headed for the King of Prussia exit. "And I sure as hell didn't have to take you along when I went to inspect that damn fence in the first place. I knew what I was doing, and I knew the possible consequences. Melodie Brainard was my case, damn it."

"And that's the only reason you went back there?"

Matt sliced her a quick fierce look. "You should know the answer to that. No, it wasn't the only reason. I'm as wrapped up in this whole thing as you are, Jess. Melodie Brainard, Teddy, the unsolved cases, the whole nine yards. Not to mention that I seem to be lusting after one gorgeous nutcase of a blonde."

"I'm not a real blonde," she told him quietly. "The nutcase, again, I'll let stand. So what are we going to do?"

Matt pulled into the large parking lot, slipping the Mercedes in between two SUVs just outside the entrance to Neiman Marcus. "We're going to buy the still-a-lieutenant some new clothes. They might help if he has to go job-hunting. Because I'm not walking away from this, Jess. I'm in too deep now."

"With the case, the cases."

He put the car in Park and reached for her, cupping her chin as he brought his mouth to hers. "Something like that…"

Two hours and more frustration than he believed any man should have to endure later, they were leaving one last men's shop when Jessica pulled on his sleeve and pointed across the selling floor. "The Case of the Vanishing Bride at ten o'clock."

He turned in the direction she'd pointed, immediately recognizing the slim, almost fragile-looking David Pearson, the groom supposedly left at the altar so many years ago, as the story had been all over the local news when Jolie and Sam had cracked the case. It was even easier to recognize Cathleen Hanson, the Vanishing Bride herself, because she looked a lot like Jessica. Eerily like Jessica, although more than a decade older. Beside them was a boy of about twelve, who was lucky enough to resemble his mother more than he did his father.

"Let's go say hi," Jessica prompted, already pulling Matt across the selling floor. "Hey, hi! David, Cathleen. I'm Jessica Sunshine—Jolie's sister?"

"Yes, I remember you," David Pearson said as he held on to a pair of jeans he had been holding in front of him as if the denim might bite him, his smile slight and a bit nervous. "Your sister brought you to my office."

"Right." Jessica introduced everyone around, just as if they were meeting at some cocktail party, and then asked Cathleen, "So how are things going?"

"Fine, thank you," the other woman said, drawing her son against her side. "We're…we're going camping. My…our son enjoys camping."

Matt had a few quick thoughts about the advisability of David Pearson out in the woods, but didn't voice them.

Jessica, of course, had no such qualms. "Really? I guess I shouldn't say this, David, but you know, you really don't look like the woodsy type."

Matt figured Jessica's first clue had been Pearson's knife-creased dress slacks, the little green alligator appliqué on his shirt…and the powder-blue cardigan tied around his throat by its sleeves.

Pearson flushed. "I'm not, Jessica." He looked at his son, the son he hadn't known he had until a few days ago. "But I'm trying. All three of us are trying. Aren't we?"

Cathleen nodded her head, her own smile tremulous. "We're getting to know each other again."

"Well, I think it's wonderful," Jessica said, spreading her arms as if to embrace the three together, yet not completely together people. "And I'm just glad my dad and sister were able to help."

"We appreciate it, we really do," Pearson said, blinking rapidly behind his wire-rimmed glasses. "I've had my lawyers file for divorce. Angela isn't fighting it."

"I should damn well guess she's not," Jessica said, turning serious for a moment, and then she smiled once more. "Well, let's not talk about all that. I just wanted to say hi, and how happy I am to see you. Have a real blast on your camping trip!"

"If I were keeping a list of awkward moments, that one would be right up there near the top," Matt said as they walked out of the store. "Your dad went looking for a body, found a live woman—and her child—and Pearson learns that his wife was involved in that disappearance up to her neck."

"I know. It was freaky. I'm hoping, in a couple of months, to have them on my show for an in-depth interview. But not yet. I'm just laying groundwork right now. Never hurts, you know. Stop frowning— I'm not a ghoul. I said a couple of months, okay? Change of subject, because that one's a downer. So, you like the jeans we bought, right?"

By this time, they were heading back across the parking lot, both of them loaded down with plastic shopping bags. "The jeans, yes. You, I'm not so sure about. Although the salesman seemed to think it was all pretty funny."

"Oh, give it a rest, will you, Lieutenant? You do know I wasn't actually going to check for myself, right?"

"No?" he asked her, punching the remote so that the trunk of the Mercedes popped open. "Then what does saying 'How do they fit in the crotch' while reaching for me mean, Ms. Sunshine?"

She giggled. "Okay, so I was reaching, I admit it. A temporary loss of inhibition undoubtedly brought on by having reached for your crotch before— Don't *look* at me like that!" She winced comically. "But I wasn't kidding when I told you they fit you really well in the backside. They're going to want you for the next Hot Cops calendar. Honest."

Matt sort of growled, low in his throat.

"Oh, come on, it was a joke! But may I say that it was very nice of you to buy that calculator for Ernesto. Our little genius is going to be over the moon."

"As opposed to me sending *you* over the moon, you mean?" he asked her before leaning in to kiss her cheek. "Relax. I had fun. I don't remember having fun blowing my savings account before this, but I had fun. And the sneakers are comfortable, much as I hate to admit it."

"And they don't light up when you walk in them, or glow in the dark, or have a basketball player's name stenciled on them. I told you there were sneakers for people older than Ernesto and younger than your grandpa."

"Yeah," he said as they headed back to the highway, "but I was sort of leaning toward those fluorescent purple ones for a while there."

"Yeah, right. Matt?"

"Hmm?" he asked, intent on merging into the passing lane.

"I'd like to go home—to Teddy's house—if you don't have anything else planned. I was thinking about something that happened a lot of years ago, something I saw one night when I snuck into my parents' bedroom, hoping they were both in there because Mom had…well, never mind. Teddy was alone, but he wasn't in bed. He was kneeling on the floor in front of his open closet, looking at something in a strongbox. I backed off and went back to bed."

"And never went snooping to see if you could open the strongbox?"

She shook her head. "I'm pretty daring now, I admit it. But sometimes a kid figures there are things she'd just be happier not knowing about, you know? And then I decided that Teddy must have been locking up his service revolver in that strongbox, so I did just go *look* in the closet. But no strongbox. I thought—I think now, anyway—he must have kept it hidden beneath the floorboards in the closet. To keep the gun safely away from us kids."

"Did you talk to Jade about this? If anyone would know, I'd think she'd know," Matt said, already mentally plotting out the shortest route to Teddy's family home.

"No, I didn't, because I forgot about all of it until something else made me think about it this morning, although you're right. She would know if anyone would, since Teddy gave her the master bedroom after

Mom left for good and moved himself into Jade's old room. Jade said there was a strongbox on Teddy's desk that night, open, and the service revolver he used to…the gun was there, too. But she never said anything about where he normally kept that strongbox. Maybe…maybe she never knew about some hiding place in her closet, if there really is one."

"Just like you never knew about the wedding rings, the diamond bracelet?"

Jessica looked at him sharply. "Oh, right. You're thinking Teddy kept those in that hiding place, too? That makes sense. So then Jade would know about it."

"Speculation, Jess. Let's go see what we find."

"Thanks," she said, sinking down in the seat. "I want to go look, but I don't want to go looking by myself…"

CHAPTER TEN

JESSICA FISHED a key chain from her purse and handed it to Matt, who opened the door. She could have done it, but her hands were sort of shaking, which was ridiculous. She'd grown up in this house. She'd slept in her old bed when she'd come home, and up until the day of Teddy's funeral, before moving to Sam's place, before someone had tried to burn the house down with Jade inside it.

She wrinkled her nose when they stepped into the small foyer. "Still smells like smoke. Jade said she wants to hold off the insurance adjuster until we're not so busy, but I don't know what anyone can do to get rid of this smell. Not to mention that, if she's thinking of selling the place, which would be my plan, it's pretty difficult to get a buyer when someone has...died in the house."

Matt slipped his arm around her shoulders and she let herself ease against him. She had never before felt so *safe* in someone else's presence, never so secure; she could just melt into Matt and stay this way forever. "I know. Murder or suicide, it affects how people think about a house. Do you really think Jade wants to sell?"

"Jade doesn't…she doesn't share what she thinks all that often. I know what *I* think, and that's that she should make up with Court, who obviously loves her as much as she loves him, and move permanently to his house in Virginia. Give up this private-investigator stuff and call it a day. She only did it in the first place because she wanted to help Teddy. Of course, if I said any of that to her, I'd have my head handed to me after she read me a lecture on how much she loves her job, so I'll keep my opinions to myself."

"No you won't," Matt said, kissing the top of her head and then taking her hand, leading her to the stairs.

"True. But you didn't have to say it," Jessica groused as they made their way upstairs and into Jade's bedroom. "You go first," she told him, pointing to the closet. "Just ignore the broken pottery on the floor because that's a whole other subject I don't want to talk about right now."

"I already know about Jade's little meltdown the night Teddy died." Matt opened the closet door and looked inside for a light. Finding it, he pulled the chain and the inside of the closet lit up enough to showcase the broken Belleek. "Damn. That's a cold, controlled temper I wouldn't want to cross," he said, using his foot to push the broken pieces to one side.

Jessica slowly approached the closet. "Still waters run deep?" she suggested, peering into the closet. "What do you see? Anything?"

Matt went down on his haunches, carefully running his fingertips across the hardwood floor. "No, nothing yet— Wait a minute. Okay, here. There's definitely a cutout here. I was right, Jess. Jade couldn't have lived in this room and missed it. And," he said, prying open the rectangle of floorboards, "it's empty."

"So that's that," Jessica said, sighing. "I was so hoping there'd be something in there, you know? An extra notebook, something like that. Maybe something with Melodie Brainard's name on it, because she wasn't one of his cold cases. You know?"

"I know, sweetheart," Matt said as he got to his feet, brushing his hands on his pant legs because some small bits of broken china had clung to him. "How long ago did Jade take over this room?"

"Uh…I don't know…a couple of months after Mom took off for the last time. Why?"

"Because Teddy was still on the force back then, that's why. Would he still lock his service revolver away in this room once it belonged to his daughter?"

Jessica felt a small surge of hope skitter along her spine. "Good thought, Lieutenant!"

"Thank you. I keep telling you, that's why they pay me the big bucks," he said as she led the way across the landing and into Teddy's bedroom. "Same drill? We look in the closet?"

She gestured toward the closed closet door. "Go for it." Then she lowered her gaze, because she knew what she'd see when Matt opened the door. Teddy's stupid, adorable, silly Hawaiian shirts filling at least half the small closet. It had been bad enough to see her uncle in one of those colorful shirts.

"See anything?" she asked, still inspecting her toes in their strappy sandals and pretending to herself that she was judging if it was time for another pedicure.

"Not much, unfortunately. Same sort of setup as in Jade's room, also empty. You went through his clothing?"

Jess looked up at him. "Through his clothing?" she repeated, twisting her hands together. "No, I don't think so. We, um, we buried him in his dress blues. There was no reason to go through his clothing."

Matt was already shifting hangers, checking in pants pockets, shirt pockets.

She turned her head, unable to watch. Why did this search seem like such a *violation?* They were just clothes, just stupid Hawaiian shirts and way-too-baggy khaki slacks. One day soon they'd have to gather them all up, take them to Goodwill or some other charity. The shirts weren't Teddy. Teddy wasn't here.

"Okay, got something," Matt said, shaking Jessica

out of her sad thoughts so that she nearly raced across the room to grab whatever he'd found.

"What is it?" she asked as he held what looked to be a business card out of her reach.

Matt lowered his arm. "It's the business card of one Norman Myster, D.M.D. Cosmetic Dentistry. Pretty impressive address, too." He turned the card over, squinting at what was written there. He moved the card further from his eyes and squinted again.

He was so damn adorable. "Where are your new reading glasses, Methuselah?"

"I forgot them," Matt said, handing the card to her. "You try to make it out. Is it Teddy's handwriting?"

Jessica felt a tug at her heart as she looked at the nearly illegible scribbles. "It's his. His printing is fine, but his handwriting is…was…pretty unique. I had to practice for a long time before I could forge gym excuses in his handwriting. I hated gym, and I hated the communal showers even more. I was the only girl in school who got her period twice a month. Thank God our teacher was a man. No woman would have bought that fairy tale."

"Fascinating as this all is," Matt said quietly, "can you read what Teddy wrote?"

She nodded, smiling. "I can't be one hundred percent sure, but I think it says 'lying sack of shit.'" She looked up at Matt. "Sounds like Teddy, doesn't it?"

"As poetic as he ever was," Matt agreed, taking

back the business card. "And he was really on a roll, in case that hasn't hit you yet. The Disappearing Bride, the dentist? I can't believe he committed suicide Jess, I just can't. Not when he was obviously at last making progress, lots of progress. He had to be feeling the old juices running, feeling like a real cop again. Sadly, that might have made him careless. You up for a trip to the dentist's office?"

"To see if Norman Myster, D.M.D. and lying sack of shit, did all that expensive work in Tarin White's mouth? You bet my old braces retainer, I am. Let's go."

Matt pulled out his cell phone. "First, let's see if the good doctor is in."

He wasn't, and wouldn't be until after three.

"Well, damn, the guy went out for a three-martini lunch, just when I was all hot to nail his lying hide to the barn door," Jessica said, trying hard not to get her hopes too high. But if they could scare Norman Myster into telling them who paid for Tarin White's dental work, they might be on their way to solving the Baby in the Dumpster case. It was heady stuff!

"That's all right, Jess. We should probably go have some lunch, anyway. What do you want—fast food or fast food?"

"As long as whatever we get has a good supply of red meat, I'm willing to overlook your cholesterol level for today," she told him as she led the way out onto the landing once more. "Okay?" She waited for his answer. "Okay?"

"In a minute," he said, and she turned around to see him peeking into the other bedrooms. "I've seen Jade's room and Teddy's. Leaving yours and Jolie's. Let me guess, this one's yours."

Jessica smiled as she hung on to the doorjamb and looked in at the white French provincial furniture, the soft pink eyelet canopied single bed, the small herd of stuffed animals piled on the bed and displayed on the wide window seat, the cheerleading trophies and ribbons taking up almost one full wall of the room. "What was your first clue, Lieutenant?"

"The poster of Dan Rather when he was a correspondent in Vietnam, actually," Matt said, walking into the room. "Was it that you wanted to grow up to do that sort of job, or was it his smile and Texas drawl?"

"A little bit of both, I guess. He looked pretty good in fatigues forty years ago, with that jungle in the background. I'm more into Christiana Amanpour these days, actually—that is one gutsy woman. But we can't forget those who blazed the way. Edward R. Murrow, Huntley and Brinkley, all those guys. I'm just small potatoes and I know it, but I am trying to keep the banner flying. Hey—you want to hear my Walter Cronkite impersonation? I've watched a million reels of old tape of him handling the Kennedy assassination, all sorts of big stories." She lowered her chin and her voice, to intone gravely, "Good evening, this is *Wal*-ter Cronkite reporting from—"

Matt held up his hands. "Stop, please. My parents have fond memories of Walter Cronkite in his heyday. Don't blow them." He walked over to the dresser and picked up a photograph of Jessica in her high-school cheerleader outfit. "God, you were cute. I'm surprised the players could keep their minds on the game."

Jessica felt herself beginning to blush. "Thanks. Would you believe I spent my teenage years thinking I was ugly as a stump? Boobs too big, legs too long, smile too wide—too many teeth to fit into my mouth. I think, when I have babies, I want all boys. Girls can be so difficult."

Matt didn't say anything as he replaced the photograph on the dresser, but then turned to her, his expression grave. "Is that you speaking, or your mother? Or maybe what you think your mother thought about raising three girls?"

"I don't know," Jessica said, plunking herself down on the side of the narrow mattress. "Wow, Matt, that's *deep*. Ever think about hanging out your psychologist shingle?"

"Sorry, sweetheart, that wasn't fair," Matt said, joining her on the bed. "I shouldn't get into pop psychology."

Jessica leaned her head against his shoulder.

"That's okay. And you've given me something to think about. Although I'm already pretty sure it's easier to raise boys than girls. Wipe your feet, don't bounce the ball in the house, put down the lid—what else do boys have to know?"

"How to behave in a girl's bedroom?" Matt suggested, slipping his arm around her.

Jessica smiled as she peeked up at him. "Oh, that's easy. Please allow me to demonstrate…" She reached up a hand to cup it behind his neck and pulled him down for a kiss.

Together, they fell back onto the bed, arms entwined, mouths melded together, bodies straining close…stuffed pandas and ponies and monkeys crushed under them.

Jessica giggled as Poo-Poo Panda was lifted out from beneath Matt, and he tossed the stuffed animal in the general direction of the window seat. He kept pushing at the collection, her childhood companions, as he attempted to turn her onto her back, even as she worked at opening his belt.

They really had to slow down one of these days, or else they were going to kill each other.

But not yet.

The old bed creaked on its slats under their combined weight, and the canopy rocked back and forth on its posts as Jessica and Matt struggled to remove each other's clothing, Jessica finally sitting up and straddling him, her blond hair falling into her face as he reached up, cupped her breasts in his hands.

Matt's head was half resting on the plush palomino, Charlie Horse, and Jessica had to bite down hard on her bottom lip to not yell, "Ride 'em, cowboy!" as Matt lifted his hips to hers and she caught his rhythm.

When she'd been rocketed to the moon and beyond, and had collapsed against him, Matt kissed her cheek, her hair, her neck, his breathing coming back under control enough for him to whisper, "Don't look now, but we're being watched from the window seat. And I think a couple of them are jealous."

"They should be," she told him. "That was… wonderful. Are you all right?"

"I've been a lot worse," Matt teased, lightly smacking her bare buttocks even as he nipped gently at her earlobe. "I think we have time for a shower, if you're interested?"

"Are you? I can't promise there isn't still a rubber ducky on the side of the tub."

"We'll blindfold him with a washcloth," he said, easing her off him and then taking her hand, helping her down from the high mattress. He looked at the bed. "It doesn't look so virginal anymore, but it's still too damn narrow."

"Did you hear it creaking?" Jessica asked as she gathered up her scattered clothing and threw him his jeans. She put a hand on one of the posts and gave it a small shake. "We're lucky the canopy didn't come down on top of us."

As if her slight touch had provided the final straw of vibration, the canopy did just that, first rocking slightly before one of the corners slipped free of its post and the entire canopy frame tipped sideways at a drunken angle. Matt's expression was adorable, and fairly dumbfounded.

"Okay, so there's more to raising boys than I thought," Jessica said as she grabbed his hand and pulled him toward the hallway bathroom. "Wipe your feet, don't bounce the ball in the house, put down the lid—and never go near your girlfriend's canopy bed."

What she didn't say was *thank you,* but she would. Matt had helped her reclaim at least her portion of this house, create a new, much happier memory. Maybe, someday, she would feel comfortable in it again.

One hour and one combined shower later, they were on their way to lunch and a small strategy session before driving to the pink stucco building that housed the practice of one Norman Myster, D.M.D., otherwise known as Teddy's lying sack of shit.

Lying sacks of shit seemed to be pulling down some pretty big bucks, because Myster's reception room had been done in pseudo-law-office plush leather and real wood paneling, and he had not one but two receptionists guarding the inner sanctum.

As they'd planned—and over Jessica's protest that he was already in enough trouble—Matt pulled out his wallet and flashed his shield at the receptionist on the right. The dumber-looking of the two well-turned-out dumb blondes.

"Lieutenant Matthew Denby, Philadelphia Homicide, to see the doctor. Go. Fetch."

The blonde blinked, her false eyelashes creating a breeze. "Homicide? He's a *dentist*. We don't kill people here."

"No, you just accept all major credit cards," Jessica said from beside Matt. "Much as I'd love trading makeup secrets, sweetcakes, go tell the good doctor we're waiting."

The receptionist was blinking up at Matt again. "Who's *she?*"

"You want to explain to the doctor that we've been forced to continue this conversation downtown?" Matt bit out, sounding pretty darn scary, Jess thought. Behind them, waiting patients began to murmur anxiously among themselves.

There was something in the way Matt had set his jaw that was all cop. All sexy cop. She'd kissed that jaw just an hour earlier, run the tip of her tongue along its cleanly sculpted lines…

She pulled herself out of her daydream and picked up on Matt's threat. "Or do you want to be a good girl and go tell the doctor we're here?"

"But Norm's just a *dentist,*" the girl persisted, and then shrugged and stood up. "Oh, okay. Follow me."

Jess resisted the urge to hold up her hand to exchange a high-five with Matt, and followed the receptionist beyond the thick teak door, Matt bringing up the rear.

They walked along a wide, thickly carpeted corridor, made two lefts and were finally ushered into an office nearly half the size of Sam Becket's immense living room. There was a brass-and-glass wet bar at one end of the room, behind the putting green. The walls were lined with before-and-after eleven-by-fifteen color photographs of generically pretty young women who had, in their *before* pictures, obviously never once worn makeup or had their hair professionally styled.

"I never saw so many teeth in one place at one time since the last Osmond Family Reunion Tour," Jessica whispered as the receptionist swished her way back out of the room, promising to locate the doctor, who would be in "shortly."

"You don't even know who Donny Osmond is," Matt chided her as he picked up and examined a plaster mold of a set of teeth.

"Sure, I do," she corrected him, being purposely provocative. "He's this middle-aged guy who shows up on *Entertainment Tonight* once in a while, and his sister did a turn on *Dancing with the Stars.* Her whole family was in the audience one night. Very *toothy* people. Oh, and I understand they all sing a bit."

Matt put down the mold. "Funny girl. And they recorded those songs on vinyl records. You ever see one?"

"In a museum somewhere, yes, I think I did," Jessica said, still grinning. "And I once had to *dial* a phone, not just push the speed dial. I have suffered, Matthew Denby, I have seen the past. Not as far back as you have, of course. What did you call your pet dinosaur, by the way?"

He looked across the room at her, his eyelids narrowed. "Ever hear the expression—'Wait till I get you home, young lady?'"

"Promises, promises." She was on her way across the miles of carpet to kiss him when the door opened and Doctor Lying Sack of Shit came bounding in, looking tanned, blow-dried and furious, and sounding like he'd heard his lines before, on some bad TV cop show.

"What's the meaning of this intrusion? I've got patients out there, listening to you threaten my receptionist. *Homicide?* How dare you! I'll have your badge!"

"It's a shield, Doctor, and you'll have to get in line," Matt informed him calmly. It was pretty much also a standard TV-cop-show line, but Matt delivered his with more conviction.

Clearly it was time for Jessica to get into the act. She would play the part of the cable-news reporter.

"Dr. Myster," she said, holding out her hand as she sashayed—yes, *sashayed* was the word—across the plush carpeting. She looked pretty good, she knew that, dressed in clothing she'd pulled from her closet at home after her shower: a remarkably well-fitting short black skirt, a white blouse above a wide red belt and a pair of red heels that a girlfriend of hers had told were called…well, heels like that had a name.

"How *good* of you to see us without an appointment. I'm Jessica Sunshine. *The Sunshine Report?* You've heard of it, I hope? The lieutenant and I are here to ask you a few simple questions, and promise not to take up too much of your valuable time."

The dentist unsnapped another snap on the row that marched from his throat to his shoulder, the baby-blue nylon smock making him look pretty much like he should be shilling tooth-whitener on cable, at midnight. "I know who you are, Ms. Sunshine. You're the daughter of that pushy private detective who murdered poor Melodie Brainard and then shot himself. He was here a couple of weeks ago, you know, threatening me. I guess I'm lucky I'm still alive."

"Yeah, wouldn't want to miss your tee-off time," Matt said, joining Jessica, the three of them now standing a little too close for any of them to feel comfortable. "We're here about one of your patients, Norman. Tarin White."

"You remember the name, don't you, Doctor?" Jessica asked, seething on the inside, smiling on the outside. "I just know you want to cooperate."

"I do not discuss my patients, Lieutenant. There are matters of confidentiality, and so I told your father, Ms. Sunshine."

Clearly it was time for a patented Sunshine Zinger to come whipping in from left field.

"Tarin White is dead, Doctor. Beaten, raped and strangled and left in an alley like so much unwanted garbage," Jessica reminded him, all trace of the approachable blonde gone in a heartbeat. "She could give a flying flip about who knows she had some bridgework."

Dr. Myster backed up a pace and then cut around Matt to position himself—hide himself—behind his massive desk. "We do *not* call what I do *bridgework*. Porcelain veneers are not simple *bridgework*."

"So Tarin White had porcelain veneers," Matt said, approaching the front of the desk even as he took a small spiral notebook from his jacket pocket and pulled a pen out of the other pocket. "I seem to remember something about titanium screws, a bone graft—some fairly intricate and expensive work, Doctor, I'd say. Oh, and according to the medical examiner, highly skilled work."

Myster seemed caught between belligerence and pride. "I will not reveal personal information about a patient, living or deceased. You're wasting your time and, more importantly, mine."

Jessica walked around the side of the desk and perched herself on the corner, crossing her long and, or so she'd been told, terrific legs. "Let's cut to the chase, Doctor. We know you're the dentist who did the work on Tarin. Now we want to know who paid for that work. Because you know what? Tarin White's death is an unsolved homicide, and there's no statute of limitations on homicide. Cooperate, or the lieutenant makes sure this entire office gets papered with legal documents demanding you do. We'll subpoena your records, all of them, just for starters. And the obligatory search warrant that makes a mess of your entire office, of course, and closes you down for a week or more."

She turned her head to look at Matt. "Lieutenant, you'll be sure those papers are served one at a time over the course of several days, just so more of the good doctor's patients get to see a line of cops marching in and out of the office?"

"Sounds like a plan to me," Matt said, and she could see that he was trying hard not to smile.

They were making a pretty good team. Batman and Robin, maybe. She resisted the impulse to swirl an imaginary cape.

"But you know how it could fall out here, Doctor?" Jessica pushed on, pretty sure she had the advantage now. "You didn't *know* your patient was murdered all those years ago, was a part of the Fishtown Strangler serial-rapist-killer case. Not only that, but Teddy Sunshine was never here, you never met him. Until the lieutenant and I walked into this office today, in fact, you had no clue that you could hold a key piece in the puzzle of Tarin White's murder. Of course you wish to cooperate. You're a good citizen, Doctor Myster, aren't you? The name, Doctor. You don't know why we want to know it, you don't want to be involved at all, do you? But you *do* want to be a good citizen. So—who paid for Tarin White's dental work?"

Okay, so, on their way out of the office she did hold up her hand for Matt's high-five. Some things were just too good not to celebrate.

CHAPTER ELEVEN

THEY WERE ALL SITTING around the large granite-topped island in the Becket kitchen, their pizzas already delivered and eaten, although it was only five-thirty. Even Ernesto, who had been told to consider himself a member of the family and had happily agreed to do just that, was there. Mrs. Archer had the night off, and Jessica was busy assembling the ingredients to make a double batch of brownies, "from scratch" as she called it, explaining that a celebration without chocolate technically was not a real celebration.

Matt, if asked, would be willing to put chocolate on his list, but it would come in second to taking Jessica somewhere private and kissing every inch of her body. *Combining* the brownie batter and the somewhere private was also an option. Maybe it was a man thing…

She and Matt had just finished telling everyone what they'd learned at Dr. Myster's office, and the silence in the room remained deafening until, at last, Court Becket spoke.

"Joshua Brainard? *Joshua Brainard* paid for

Tarin White's dental work? Sweet Jesus, what the hell is going on here?"

"Remember our theory?" Matt asked. "We're working with the idea that Tarin White maybe, possibly, somewhere in the realm of probability, could have been the mother of the baby in the Dumpster, right? Timing is off, but not by much, no more than three months, when you consider that the medical examiner's report showed that the baby's body had been frozen for a while before it was dumped, so we can't determine exactly when he was killed."

"I think I hate that part more than anything," Jessica said, sighing. "No wonder it's still the most talked about old murder case in the city."

"I know. So let's go back to the realm of probability. The Tarin as the baby's mother idea is far out, but it was also all we had, so we ran with it, right? We were talking about a living donor for DNA, hoping to find the father of the baby, right? We found Myster's name through Teddy, just as we told you, and now we've got the name of the person who paid for Tarin White's dental work. That doesn't make our friendly mayoral candidate the father of her baby, but it's a start, right?"

"Isn't he cute? He does that a lot when he's thinking out loud," Jessica said, pausing in her search through the kitchen pantry to go press a kiss on Matt's cheek. "Says *right*. But those are really rhetorical questions. The biggies are—how do we get Joshua Brainard to volunteer us some of his DNA? How do we get a sample of the baby's DNA for comparison?"

Matt sort of growled at Jessica, who giggled—still obviously happy with the results of their work this afternoon—and then quickly retreated to the pantry. "As usual, Jess is jumping ahead. At the moment we really don't know what we've got, and if we try going to the DA with the information we got from Myster, the guy will probably have lawyered up by then and say he doesn't know what the hell we're talking about, claim patient confidentiality again, and we're screwed."

Jade held up her bandaged hand. "Whoa, guys, back up. I really want to go back to Teddy, okay? You found the business card we've just seen. But did Dr. Myster tell Teddy about Joshua Brainard? Is that why Teddy was trying to meet with Brainard? Is that why he was visiting the Brainard house, speaking to the wife, trying to get to Brainard through her? The now *dead* wife? How much do you think Teddy told her? You see where I'm going with this, don't you? Motive."

Matt shook his head. "Sorry, Jade, but we can't know the answers to those questions. We have no way of knowing the timeline here, either. Teddy might have smelled a rat, felt that Myster—out of all the dentists he's probably been canvassing for God knows how many years—is actually the one Tarin

White visited for her dental work. But that doesn't mean your father got any further than that before he was killed."

"Of course he did," Jessica protested as she one-handedly cracked eggs into a mixing bowl. "Why else would he have gone after Brainard and his wife?"

"Yes, Matt," Jade said. "I think we can safely assume that Teddy knew, even without having solid proof that he did. But you said that Dr. Myster swore he never told him. Do you think Teddy found out some other way?"

Matt and Court exchanged looks, and Court nodded, then said, "Jade, it's always possible that Teddy went back after hours and took a look at Myster's files."

"Oh, cool!" Jessica said, beating at the chocolate mixture with great energy. "He could do that?"

"No, he couldn't do that," Jade told them, frowning. "Not legally. But I'd say that, yes, he could do it—the mechanics of it, at least. Teddy…he, well, he was very interested in security and how to broach it. He had clients, more than one, who hired him just to test their security systems. He made it through every one of them without detection. He'd ask the client to put something on his desk, a small statue or something, before locking up for the night, and then the next morning there would be Teddy, strolling into the guy's office, the statue in hand."

"Your dad would have been the bomb in my neighborhood," Ernesto said in some awe.

"God, I miss him," Jessica said, leaning against the wall oven after sliding in the pan of brownies. "I wish I could have seen him work."

"And he probably didn't have to break into the actual office," Matt said, wishing he could shut up, because Jessica and Ernesto were enjoying all this just a little too much. "The records on Tarin White were old, and Myster most likely had them stored somewhere off-site, with other old inactive patient folders. It wouldn't take much to find out where, what storage facility. Not the kind of place that's loaded up with high-tech security systems, by the way, if I read Myster right. Big bucks on his office, anything that's for show—but a crappy low-rent storage garage for his old records."

"It sounds like you've given this some thought, Matt," Court said.

Matt shrugged. "Yes, I have. It's what I might have done if I'd been following dead-end leads for a dozen years and finally thought I'd caught a break. I'm not proud of that fact, but I understand why Teddy might have bent the law in this case. Sometimes there's less cop in me than maybe there should be, I guess."

"It's the new shoes," Jessica teased him, leaning on her forearms beside him as they stood behind the center island. "In fact, you hardly look like a cop at all now. What a hunk."

Matt rubbed at the back of his neck, not knowing what to say.

But Ernesto did, or at least thought he did.

"Just like my old Uncle Berto used to say, Lieutenant. *Lo tiene en un puño,*" he said, laughing.

Now Matt felt the back of his neck growing hot, and probably turning red, damn it.

"What? What does that mean?" Jessica asked Ernesto, who had prudently dropped to the floor to pet the adoring Rockne—and be out of range, Matt supposed. Smart-ass kid.

"Ernesto said that you have Matt in your fist, Jess," Court told her. "Or, as we say it, wrapped around your finger."

Jessica stood up, tilted her head to one side as she grinned at Matt. "Well, how about that. Out of the mouths of babes, huh?"

"If we could get back to our discussion now?" Jade asked, and Matt looked at her gratefully. For a grown man, he was pathetically unable to hold his own against Jessica's teasing smile. It worried him. "Because, if none of the rest of you have thought of this, I have. After Teddy visited him, did Dr. Myster call Joshua Brainard and warn him that Teddy had come asking questions?"

Matt had thought of that possibility, but he'd

hoped nobody else would, at least not for a while. Jessica was already too eager to jump off any convenient bridge that might lead to an assumption of theory as fact.

"Damn, Jade," Jessica said, losing her smile. "That would explain a lot, wouldn't it? A Myster-Brainard connection? All those rich country-club guys—they stick together."

"Jessica, that's an assumption of—oh, never mind," Matt said, grabbing up his bottle of beer. "Yes, Myster could have alerted Brainard about Teddy's visit, his questions. But before you put Teddy's service revolver in Joshua Brainard's hand, or the man's hands around his own wife's neck, there's a long road stretching between wishing something might be true and proving it."

"Somebody get me an umbrella," Jessica said, groaning. "The man's raining on my parade again."

She turned to look at Matt. "Seriously, Matthew. It fits. Teddy finds out that Brainard paid for Tarin White's dental work. I won't say that makes them lovers, but it isn't a far guess to think so. Then Brainard finds out Tarin's pregnant, and realizes that fun is fun, but leaving his wife isn't a part of his plans."

"We did consider that maybe the reason the father of that poor baby never came forward was because he was married," Jade said, leaning her elbows on the countertop. "Go on, Jess."

"Yeah, like I wasn't going to, anyway? Brainard wimps out, Tarin has the baby on her own, ends up hooking to make ends meet. In a real twist of coincidence, she becomes a victim of the Fishtown Strangler, and whoever kept her baby for her didn't want the responsibility and one day killed it. Him. The baby. Brainard can't step forward, say maybe he knows the identity of the baby. Well, he could, but he wouldn't. He's not the type. And it would explain that anonymous donor paying for Tarin's plot and headstone. Joshua Brainard, feeling guilty. The dental work is the key to everything, and Teddy found the key."

"Not to forget, Jess—" Jade broke in again. Matt was getting the feeling the sisters were playing a tag-team match, and they were damn good at it. "—that Joshua Brainard's father was a part of the citizen task force formed to help find the Fishtown Strangler. Maybe he did it because he's a good civic-minded citizen and the mayor asked him to, and maybe he did it because his son asked him to—the son feeling just a little guilty that abandoning Tarin left her to support herself by turning tricks."

Court sighed. "Turning tricks, Jade? No wonder the idea of joining the Young Matrons League in Hampton Roads didn't intrigue you."

"It's just an expression, Court," Jade snapped. "Where was I going with this? Oh, okay. We have to go back, find the date the task force was formed. Maybe it wasn't until after Tarin became one of the strangler's victims?"

"Theories, subjective thinking," Matt warned them yet again, looking hopefully at Court, who only smiled and shrugged, clearly a man who had figured out when to fight and when to just sit there and listen. "Nothing that could be proved anywhere."

"Cut that out!" Jessica ordered him as the oven timer dinged. She grabbed a pair of oven mitts and went to rescue the brownies. "We're solving four crimes here, four cold cases you guys in the department couldn't solve. Well, three out of four. Sorry, Jade, but Terrell Johnson's case is a real dead end. Still, we're making *huge* progress. Right here, in Sam's kitchen. I can't freaking believe it, but you're going to have to live with it, Matt."

"Okay, I give up. What else has that squirrelly mind of yours dreamed up between leaving Myster's office and now?"

"I'll ignore that swipe for now, but you'll pay for it later." She dropped the pan on the stove top. "Oh! Oh! What if Joshua Brainard is the Fishtown Strangler, too? Wouldn't that be a shocker? He kills six women, all to cover up killing Tarin, who threatened blackmail or something. Maybe he even murdered his own *son*. Not to mention his own wife—strangled, just like all six Fishtown murders—and then framed and killed Teddy. My God, the man's a monster, Philly's own Joshua the Ripper—and he's about to become the next mayor!"

"What is that now, Jess?" Matt said, unable to stop himself. "Theory six…seven?"

"Another beer? Something stronger? Scotch? Perhaps a double?" Court asked Matt, who was pretty sure he looked ready to explode.

"No, thanks, anyway, Court," Matt said, waiting for Jessica to finish slicing the brownies with a very large sharp kitchen knife. "Jess? If you're ready to be reasonable now?"

She piled hot brownies on a large plate and then licked her fingers one by one. Matt pretended not to notice. "I *am* being reasonable, Matthew. Tell me where anything I just said doesn't add up. I'm listening. Jade? You see the logic in all of it, don't you?"

"Well, I guess I—"

"See?" Jessica interrupted her sister. "Jade sees it. Court, you see it, don't you? Ernesto? You're logical, aren't you? Logistics? That's pretty much like logical, at least. Tell him."

"No hablo inglés, señorita," Ernesto said, getting to his feet. "The little Spanish kid is going to go walk the dog now, *sí?"*

"Chicken!" Jessica called after him, and then rounded on Matt again, so that he nearly choked on his first bite of brownie. "So? Tell me where I'm wrong? Blow holes in my theory. Theories. Go on, I'm waiting."

"All right," Matt said, grabbing a second brownie, because he was pretty sure Jessica wouldn't offer him one. "I admit that, on the face of it, you tell a good story, Jess. Now prove it. Any of it."

She opened her mouth, lifted a finger as if she was about to begin ticking off facts one by one, and then sort of deflated right in front of him. "We don't have any facts. We can't prove anything. We need at least two sources to put anything on the air, and we don't even have one source, do we? I mean, Myster's going to lie like a rug, say he never told us anything—and probably cost you your shield."

"The hell with my shield for the moment. Concentrate on proving your theory."

"We should have hidden a tape recorder in my purse," Jessica said quietly. "That's mistake number one—we should have gotten Myster on tape."

"Illegal to tape the man without his consent, inadmissible in court. Not to mention too late. Go ahead. Got anything else?"

"You're not helping, Matthew," she said, glaring at him. She frowned, deep in thought, and finally said, "We need the DNA. It goes back to that, doesn't it?"

"It does. Although it goes back further than that, Jessica. How do we *get* the DNA?"

Jessica looked at her sister, who had pointed out

that particular problem. "Now you guys are ganging up on me. We…uh…we get the DNA by buying Brainard a cup of coffee or something and then using a pencil or something to carefully pick up the cup once he's done with it, taking it to a lab, getting it tested and typed, or whatever they do to DNA."

"Good," Matt told her, rubbing at his forehead and the beginnings of a headache. "Watch a lot of TV, do you? So we get Brainard's DNA, have it tested in a private lab—because there's no way I can get anybody to order the test, and it would take months to come back through channels even if I could find a way around one small technicality, that technicality being that there's this niggling little rule called probable cause."

"Stop rubbing it in," Jessica said, nibbling on a brownie. She had a swipe of brownie batter on her cheek, and he was itching to lick it off. But they weren't alone. And his gorgeous blond bombshell was hating him at the moment.

"We also have nothing to compare Brainard's DNA *to*. And before you ask, no, I'm not going to break into the lab and steal a sample of the baby's DNA so you can have it tested for comparison—or steal a DNA report, if there is one, just in case you're thinking of that idea. You're cute, but I'm not going to jail for you, sorry. There's more than a couple of really big nasty guys I put there I can think of who'd be too happy to have me as a cell mate."

Jessica was blinking rapidly now, and Matt was pretty certain she was trying not to cry. "Okay. So what *do* we do?"

"Sweetheart, if I had the answer to that, they'd make me king. Sorry. Now, if you'll excuse me, I think I want to go take advantage of Sam's exercise room."

"Feel the need to burn off some excess energy?" Court asked him. "Sam's got a punching bag down there, if that helps."

Matt took another quick look at Jessica, who looked completely crushed, dejected. And he was the one who'd had to rain on her parade. "Yeah. Thanks, Court. Sounds like just what I need."

"Matt?"

He hesitated, looking at Jade. "Yeah?"

"Thank you," Jade said. "We learned something new today. Something important, even if we don't have all the pieces yet or even know where they fit in the puzzle. Teddy would be very proud of you, of both of you."

Matt nodded, unable to think of anything to say, and left the room. He climbed the stairs to his bedroom, fed Mortimer, changed into his old high-top sneakers, a pair of dark blue knit shorts and a gray tank top with Property of U of P Athletic Department barely visible after about one hundred washings, and headed to the exercise room in the basement.

Jade was already there, jogging on a treadmill that

faced the wall and a large flat-screen television set turned to the six-o'clock local news. She moved with a grace that told him this wasn't her first time on a treadmill, her first time working out. She had fantastic posture, a lean runner's body. Night and day, compared to Jessica's lush curves, but very attractive.

"Hi, hope you don't mind," she said, not taking her eyes off the screen. "I'd run outside early in the morning, but it's dark out there. The fancy suburbs don't seem to be big on a lot of streetlights. I don't know the roads around here all that well and don't want to take a fall. It helps, doesn't it—exercise?"

"That's the plan, yeah." *But it's not any more helpful than cold showers,* he thought, although he knew it wouldn't be good to say that to Jade. Matt looked around the room, spying an all-in-one exercise machine and bench, and sat down, reaching up for the handlebars that controlled the weights.

"She'll get over it," Jade said, speeding up her pace as the treadmill began to slowly angle upward a few degrees, running through a programmed routine. "Jessica is very impulsive, quick to get excited, and then can crash in a hurry. But she's resilient and wickedly smart, actually. She'll see our point, and then do her damnedest to find a way around our every argument. With luck, she'll succeed. She doesn't give up easily."

Matt eyed the television screen, where it looked

like an orangutan was trying to sell floor wax. No wonder he didn't watch much television. "She also has a way of making the illogical sound logical. It all could have played out just the way she laid it out, actually. Any one of her scenarios."

"Joshua Brainard a serial rapist and killer? I don't think so. Those guys don't stop until someone stops them, yet there hasn't been another Fishtown Strangler case in a dozen or more years, which has always made me wonder if the guy is dead. And while Brainard might commit two murders in order to cover up one of them, I can't see him kidnapping, raping and strangling six women. That's—if you'll pardon the expression—overkill."

"I know." Matt struggled with something that had bothered him since he'd first read Tarin White's autopsy report. At least Jade was a licensed P.I., not a complete civilian. She might more readily understand where he was going with one of his own theories. "Pardon me for being so blunt here, Jade. The perp used a condom in the rapes, so there's no semen to match when and if we do get a suspect. There were some trace bodily fluids recovered from five of the victims. There's always something, some transfer during intercourse. Hair, fluids, you name it. The bad part is that our perp is also a damn non-secreter."

"A non-secreter? Oh, wait, I've read about that in

one of my reference books. It means you can't get a blood type just from the fluids. That is a bad break."

"Not insurmountable. We could, if we found our guy, at least prove he's a non-secreter. His lawyer would punch huge holes in that, trot out statistics on how many of the male population are non-secreters. But getting back to Tarin, there were no fluids, no hairs, collected in her case, making me think the body had been washed clean before it was dumped."

"That's unusual, isn't it?"

"Not so much now, with all the forensics shows on television. We call them How-To's for Murderers. But back then, yeah, it would be considered unusual."

"Why would the Fishtown Strangler get so fussy with Tarin and not the other victims? That doesn't fit the guy's MO. And there was one more victim, Kayla Morrison, after Tarin, so he wasn't just adding something new to his MO as he went along. So why the difference?"

"There's the big question. I'd love to get hold of the entire casebook, but the medical examiner's preliminary reports on all six victims in Teddy's file suggest that the rape end of the crime didn't go down quite the same for Tarin as it did for the others. I'm thinking he was hinting at some foreign object, but didn't have the facts to support that. Just that the injuries to the genital area might have been postmortem."

"Pardon me for saying this, Matt, but that's insane. Nobody picked up on this?"

"Afraid not. All except for Teddy, I'm thinking, which was why he was zeroing in on Tarin, comparing her to the last victim. The problem is, the victims were just that—the victims, being rolled into the morgue at a rate of nearly one a week. The city was in a panic by the time the third body was discovered. All the concentration of the department was on finding the perp, not investigating a…well, a bunch of dead hookers. They had to have been looked on pretty much as interchangeable victims of type and opportunity, and in everything else, Tarin fit the pattern. So there's that, and the fact that no DA ever had a suspect he was going to go to trial on. I'm sure the forensic discrepancies between Tarin and the rest of the victims would have been discovered then, and alarm bells would have gone off in somebody's head."

"The guy could tie her up, beat her, strangle and kill her—but he couldn't bring himself to actually rape her himself?" Jade grabbed on to one of the support bars as she turned her head to look at Matt. "What does that mean, Matt? A copycat, a guy with something else on his mind besides torture and rape? Then Jess could be right—or at least sort of right?"

"Please, that's between you and me right now, Jade. I've already taken the medical examiner's preliminary report on Tarin White out of the folder and put it in my room. We talked about it, the fact that White had given birth shortly before she was killed, but that's it, that's all Jess really knows. I don't want to have to bail her out of lockup after she goes charging into Brainard's campaign office with lights and cameras to accuse him."

"She wouldn't do... Okay, maybe she would. Let's think about this, Matt. We're working on four cold cases, hoping to connect one of them with Teddy's murder, Melodie Brainard's murder. The Vanishing Bride was all but solved before he died, and Jolie and Sam worked out the rest of it. One down. I'm working the Terrell Johnson murder, and getting nowhere, as Jessica so often reminds me. Teddy had been after Jermayne to go to school, and that's all I've got for why Teddy spoke to the kid in the week before he was killed. Nothing else new or reasonably earth-shattering. With me so far?"

"As far as we've gone, yes," Matt said. "I think we're up to the Fishtown Strangler now."

The base of the treadmill lowered once more and the speed began to decrease. "Which, weird as it seems, is beginning to dovetail into our fourth case, the Baby in the Dumpster."

"Right."

"And within days, maybe a week or two of finding out that Tarin White's dental work was paid for by Joshua Brainard—we can't be sure of the time frame, but I think we can be pretty sure that Teddy knew it was him—both Melodie Brainard and Teddy are dead."

"Which would connect three murders, Jade. Teddy, Melodie Brainard and very possibly Tarin White herself. Move Tarin from column A, Fishtown Strangler, to column B, in with Melodie and Teddy. Right?"

"Okay, let's try that. Keeping the baby out of the picture for now, because that's really farfetched, we still have Tarin White and her connection to Melodie Brainard's husband. Tarin is old news, Melodie and Joshua supposedly had a convenient arrangement that didn't extend to Melodie getting all bent out of shape to learn that he'd had an affair a dozen years ago. But Joshua is running for mayor now. There's no such thing as old news when you're running for office. His campaign would be dead in the water if his association with one of the Fishtown Strangler victims came out. One of the *prostitute* victims."

"Go on, this is fascinating, really," Jessica said from the doorway. Matt watched as she walked into the room, carrying a bowl of popcorn. Caramel popcorn. Still celebrating, obviously. She held the bowl out toward him. "Want some? It's only microwave stuff, but it's nice and warm and pretty good."

Matt recognized a peace offering when he had it up close and personal with his nose. "Sure, thanks."

"Cute shorts. Cute knees. And you're welcome,"

Jessica said, sitting down on a freestanding weight bench. "You're sweating like a pig, Jade. You, too, Matt. I can't imagine why people do that. Exercise, that is." She popped another piece of popcorn into her mouth. "Won't catch me doing it."

"Oh, admit it, you don't work out because you don't want to jiggle the girls. But you'd better rethink that. In twenty years, Jessica Marie, or whenever your metabolism finally turns on you, you'll change your mind. Either that, or we'll have to start *rolling* you everywhere," Jade warned her, the treadmill now slowed to a cool-off phase.

"Or I could be all boney and sweaty now, like you. As for the rest of it, mammary envy does not become you," Jessica shot back, her smile taking the sting out of her words. "Matt? Can you continue with what you were saying? Oh, wait a minute—look. Isn't that Angela Pearson?"

Matt, really, *really* happy for the change of subject, followed Jessica's gesture toward the television screen even as Jade grabbed the remote and pressed the button that had kept the sound muted.

"That's a mug shot! Hey, and now the perp-walk, right down to the orange jumpsuit," Jessica said, walking toward the screen. "Oh, not a good look for you, hon. *God* got you, even if David wouldn't press charges."

Matt leaned to his left to see around Jessica's

body, and listened as the reporter explained that well-known socialite Angela Pearson, estranged wife of David Pearson, had been stopped at four that morning when her vehicle was observed proceeding erratically and at a high rate of speed along Kelly Drive.

"Pearson," said the reporter, "pictured here in her prison garb, has been charged with being drunk and disorderly, driving under the influence, resisting arrest, two counts of assault on an officer and other charges. Because of the severity of the charges, bail has not yet been arranged."

"Drunk? Well, damn," Jessica said, grinning at Matt. "Do you get the feeling good old Angela isn't taking being kicked out of her plush digs all that well? I hope David and his little family are deep in some woods somewhere and nobody can contact him for comment. He's got enough to worry about. Not that I won't ask him about it when I do my interview."

"I thought you liked David Pearson," Matt said, seeing the gleam in Jessica's eye.

"Well, sure. But that doesn't mean he gets off scot-free. The guy had all the backbone of a sponge when his bride, the supposed love of his life, didn't show up for the wedding. You know how long it was before his mother and Angela got him to the altar again? Six months. I don't know how many camping trips that one is going to take to explain to Cathleen."

"But you're going to find out, right?" Matt asked, giving up on the idea of exercising away his tension. "You guys love to pick at scabs, don't you?"

"You guys?" Jessica looked at him through compressed eyelids. "I know the truth, you know. All of it. Everything that Angela had planned for poor Cathleen Hanson. Am I running with that story? No, I'm not. And I won't, because there's a kid involved. I've got ethics."

"Leave David Pearson alone, Jess. Leave all three of them alone. They're yesterday's news."

She looked at Matt as if he'd just grown a second head. "Do you have any idea what I *do?* I'm a journalist. I report the news. I don't make it. Discretion, yes. I use discretion." She waved in the general direction of the television set behind her. "But that's news, buster. The Vanishing Bride was big news when it happened. Okay, not great news, but news. Terrific for the ratings, if you must know, because people may say they don't want to hear this stuff, but they love it, they eat it up. And if people like Angela Pearson and Britney Spears and O. J. Simpson and anybody else want to make idiots out of themselves on a regular basis, hey, let 'em at it. I don't have to like it, but for every hard-hitting exposé on drug use or in-depth three-part series on the crappy state of meat and produce inspection in this country, I have to find a way to draw in the lowest-common-denominator stories that get the viewers drooling. Every story we air can't be Emmy material. Sometimes you just have to pay the bills."

"Marshmallow on the outside, solid steel on the inside," Matt said as Jade turned off the treadmill and stepped off it to grab a towel, drape it across her shoulders. "I think you did warn me, didn't you, Jade?"

Jade shrugged. "Like she said, Matt, it's her job. I can't help thinking back to an earlier discussion we all had. How delighted are you when you have to arrest a battered woman for finally having enough and shooting her rat-bastard of a husband?"

"That's apples and oranges. There is no comparison between the two, *none*." Matt rubbed hard at the back of his neck. "Damn it! Okay, I don't like it. I hate it."

"But it's part of your job, so you do it. The good you do outweighs the times when you'd rather give the woman a medal and maybe a parade," Jessica argued. "I do good things, Matt, I truly believe that. If I have to toss in a puff piece now and then so that my producers let me do those hard-hitting stories, or a sordid story like this Pearson thing? That's the price I pay."

"I couldn't do it," Matt said honestly.

"And I couldn't do what you do," Jessica answered quietly. "Walking into houses to see dead bodies, man's inhumanity to man, on a daily basis? No. I couldn't do it. But that doesn't mean I don't respect what you do."

"I didn't say I didn't respect… Okay, so maybe it sounded that way. If so, I'm sorry, Jess. I really am."

"Forgive him, Jess," Jade whispered none too quietly as she walked past her on her way out of the room. "He forgave you, and you didn't even apologize, except for the popcorn."

Jessica smiled, her head tilted, her expression slightly sheepish and completely adorable. She held out the bowl once more. "Popcorn, Lieutenant, sir?"

Matt chuckled, shaking his head, and reached into the bowl.

The familiar sound of the TV stations *Breaking News* alert had all three of them turning to the television screen once more.

"This just in," the reporter announced, reading from a piece of paper in his hand. "Sources tell us that the *Philadelphia Inquirer* is running a news story in tomorrow morning's edition on mayoral candidate Joshua Brainard, what is being called an important update on the murder of his wife and that murder's possible connection to the well-known murders, still unsolved, that occurred several years ago in the Fishtown section of the city. Please tune in for the eleven-o'clock news and, we hope, a further update."

Jessica stood very still, the bowl still extended, and looked from Matt, to Jade and then back to Matt again. "Wow," she said quietly, a nervous tremor in her voice. "How about that."

"Jessica Marie, *what* did you do?" Jade asked her.

Matt shook his head. "You don't stop, do you? Screw this. I'm out of here."

Jessica shoved the bowl of popcorn into her sister's hands and chased after Matt. "Wait! Matt, come on, wait for me. Let me explain. Teddy was investigating a strangling case and talking to Melodie Brainard, for some reason. Next thing we know, she's strangled. It's all circumstantial, sure, but it was enough to get somebody asking questions, wondering if there's some kind of connection. Come on, Matt—it's done all the time. Jolie got one story out of it already, so why not go for two? Besides, Brainard ratted on you to the mayor about our little visit to his house and got you in trouble with your chief. Payback's a bitch, but that's also the way it works, and Brainard should have known that if he wants to play in the big leagues. Now he does."

Matt hesitated halfway up the staircase and turned to look at her. "You're telling me you did this for *me?* As payback?"

She nodded furiously. "It was my fault that he got to do that to you. You wouldn't have trespassed, except that I went in through the hole in the fence and you followed me. And, okay, I also did it for me. And for Teddy. For all of us. I saw an opening, both literally and figuratively, and I took it."

He continued up the stairs and then slammed

down the hallway and out onto the terrace via the French doors in the living room. He took three quick deep breaths, trying to calm himself before Jessica joined him. "Go. Away."

"No, Matt, I can't do that. And I didn't do anything so terribly wrong. If you'll just listen to me?"

"I did listen to you. My shield is on the line, my career's probably in the crapper, *because* I listened to you. Because I stupidly took you along to Brainard's place, because I took you to bed—no, scratch that. I'm not going to blame you because I'm a horny bastard who can't keep it in his pants."

"Don't be crude. It was…it is more than that."

"Really?" He looked at her in the dim flickering light from an ornamental gas lamp near the door. "I don't think either one of us can be sure of the motives of the other guy."

She put a hand on his arm. "You think I went to bed with you just so I could get your help on the case…cases? You really think I'd do something like that?"

Matt shoved his fingers through his hair. "Christ. I don't know what I think. Teddy wasn't my father. I don't know how far I'd go to try to clear his name, what I'd do if I were in your shoes."

"You're saying I'm thinking only with my emotions?"

He looked at her sharply. "Aren't you?"

She bit her bottom lip, nodded. "I guess…I guess I am. I really screwed up, didn't I?"

Matt felt himself weakening. "Maybe you need to ask yourself before you do anything—what would Christiana do?"

"Christiana? Christiana Amanpour?" Jessica smiled weakly. "She'd gather all the facts first. So would Walter. You're right. I went too far."

"Let me guess," he said, leading her back into the house. "When we read this story in tomorrow's *Inquirer,* you'll be the reporter's unnamed source."

She raised her hand slightly. "Guilty as charged. I was so mad when you told me about your chief coming down on you. I'd already planted the seeds with a reporter friend about the cut in Brainard's fence, about printing an update on the Fishtown Strangler. But then I called him back and really went straight for Brainard's jugular."

"The weird part is that you planted the story before we found out that Brainard paid for Tarin White's dental work. Was that all dumb luck? Maybe I can be generous and chalk at least some of it up to a good reporter's instincts."

"Yeah, let's do that," Jessica said, sighing in relief. "Can I show you something?"

"I don't know. Is it going to start another argument?"

"I hope not. Come up to my room. I had the assistant producer at the station look up some stories we've covered and then cobble together some tape I thought might be interesting. She put them all on a disk for me. There's a player in my room."

Matt wanted to say no. Jessica's bedroom was the last place he should be right now, when part of him wanted to, logically, he thought, get as far away from her as he could, and the other part of him wanted to hold her and never let go.

"Sure, why not?" he said at last, and only then realized that Jessica had been holding her breath as she waited for his answer. *Damn.* "Let me go shower and change, and I'll see you in about a half hour."

CHAPTER TWELVE

JESSICA JUMPED at the sound of the knock on the door, and then settled back against the edge of the bed when Jade, still in her workout clothes, pushed open the door and walked into the room. "Oh. I thought you were Matt."

"Isn't it a little early in the evening to be…you know."

"No," Jessica said, her eyes wide and innocent. "Too early in the evening for what, Jade? Please, explain this to me."

"God, you can be a pain. I thought you'd grow out of it, but you never will. I don't think I'll ever forget the night you started reciting what you'd learned in sex-ed that day. You went alphabetically, remember? By the time you got to clitoris, Teddy was choking on his roast beef and running from the room."

Jessica nodded, smiling at the memory of one of her many less-than-stellar moments as a child. "I was twelve. Schools either have to start kids with this stuff younger or wait until they're older. Twelve?

Twelve just doesn't get it. Everything's a joke when you're twelve. Do you know what? I don't think I ever again had a chance to use clitoris in a sentence—until now, of course. Matt was pretty mad when we were downstairs, wasn't he?"

Jade sat herself down on the striped slipper chair, quick to take to the change of subject. "Do you blame him? He's a professional, Jess, he does this for a living. You should be listening to him, deferring to his judgment. Instead, you're bopping around like you're Lois Lane, saying you're trying to do good, but really trying to grab a front-page scoop on Clark Kent."

"Matt is not Clark Kent."

"No. He's a homicide lieutenant, or he was when you met him. God knows what he'll be doing once you're done *helping* him."

"Helping *us*. We're looking for Teddy's killer, remember?" Jessica said tightly. "And you're right, Matt's a cop. He has to follow the rules. I don't."

"So you're satisfied with what you've done? You're happy?"

"Hell, no," Jessica said, boosting herself up onto the bed to sit with her legs crossed on the bedspread. "I've screwed up royally. Matt's right, I watch too much TV. The problem is, real life doesn't cut to commercial when it gets to the sticky parts, then just pick up later, with the good guys winning and everyone going out for a beer."

"What's this article going to be about tomorrow?"

Jessica shrugged. "Not a lot, nothing really new. Just what Jolie got out the first time, really. That Teddy was working on the Fishtown Strangler murders, talked to Melodie Brainard, and then Melodie ended up being strangled. Nobody's going to mention that she wasn't abducted, beaten and raped before she was strangled. Just the barest nod at the facts, and the rest sort of hinted at, I guess. I'm the reliable unnamed source, only providing the information that Brainard's security fence had been breached, yet the cops never pursued that angle, just pinned everything on Teddy. But now the question has been raised—is the Fishtown Strangler back? Did the police do their job, or were they just bowing to political pressure and the probable next mayor, yadda-yadda. That's the angle that sold my reporter friend—the political favors part. The rest is just gravy, for now."

Jade raised her eyebrows. "In other words, the article will be just enough to have questions asked about his late wife every time Brainard gets near a microphone. He might like that. He gets to play the pity card."

"I hadn't thought of that," Jessica said, sighing. "I really didn't think at all, which should have been my first clue that I shouldn't have done anything."

"And the rest of it?"

"What rest of it?" Jessica asked, looking at her

sister. "Oh. You mean how Matt went all moral indignation on me about David Pearson. I'm not going to apologize for that, Jade. You know what kind of story leads off more local newscasts than any other? Fires. People love to look at burning buildings. After that, it's automobile crashes. And if it's a busload of old folks overturning on the expressway on their way to the casinos, wow, big stuff! People are sick, that's my opinion. But if it gets them to turn the channel to us, we're halfway there. Then we hit them with what really matters."

"Fires and bus crashes don't matter?"

"Yes," Jessica said, rolling her eyes, "they *matter,* Jade. Of course they do. But for the big hook, give me a drunk, blond Hollywood wannabe anytime. Look, tune in one night, okay? Listen for how many times we do mini-recap teasers of juicy upcoming celebrity and goofball stories as we go to commercial breaks. People will wait for most of an hour to see what some starlet was wearing—or not wearing—when she went out partying the night before, and in that time I can give them four, five hard-hitting *real* news stories that, hope against hope, inform them on what's going on in the *real* world."

Jade smiled. "So when you get right down to it, you're a saint. Gosh, I'm so impressed. I'm telling you, Jess, it's an honor to say that I'm your sister."

"Bite me," Jessica said, and then laughed. "And

then go away, because Matt's going to be knocking on that door any minute."

Jade got to her feet, but then hesitated. "You promise me you won't get hurt, Jess, okay? Because, for all you don't want to admit it, you're really vulnerable right now. All three of us are."

Jessica tipped her head, pushed her hair behind her ear. "Even Jolie? You think she and Sam aren't going to make it this time, either?"

"No, I suppose not, not Jolie. She was pretty vulnerable, but she's past that point, I think. She and Sam are solid."

"And you and Court?"

"Are not currently a topic for discussion."

"Gee, color me shocked. Leaving Matt and me, right? We like each other, Jade. We get along. Well, most of the time. What can I say? I needed him, and he appeared. Sometimes that's just how it happens."

"He is older."

"I prefer the word *experienced*."

"All right, experienced. Are you also saying he's the right man at the right time?"

"The jury's still out on that one," Jessica said, avoiding Jade's gaze.

"Think, Jess. Before you go any further, think. Who is he? Mister Right, or Mister Right Now? The wrong man at the right time? Even the right man at the wrong time?"

Jessica looked up, smiling. "Who's on first?"

"Very funny."

"No, it's not. Look, I'll be completely honest here. I don't know what's happening, Jade, I really don't. Maybe Matt is just a man, just a very nice guy who showed up exactly at the moment when I needed a strong man's arms around me. I just hope he sticks around long enough for both of us to figure out where we fit or don't fit into each other's lives. That's all any of us can hope for, isn't it? Jade? Where are you going?"

Her sister smiled, a sad smile, but a smile. "To see what Court's doing, I guess."

"Oh, right. Jade?"

"Hmm…?" she asked, slowly walking toward the door, like an old woman, or a prisoner heading for the gallows.

Love shouldn't be like that, make a person feel like that. Should it?

"Court's the right man. The two of you just need to find the right time."

"I guess. Thanks, Jessica. It's nice having grownup sisters."

As the door closed behind Jade, Jessica fell back against the pillows, wondering how much of who and what they were, all three sisters, was nature, and how much was nurture—or lack of motherly nurture. "What a cop-out," she told herself, sitting up again.

"Nobody's pulling my strings. I make my own way, and I make my own mistakes."

She went into the bathroom to splash some cool water on her face, and was just patting her skin dry when there was another knock on the door.

This time it was Matt, and as she stepped back to let him in, she resisted the impulse to run her fingers through his shower-damp hair, contenting herself with just a secret sniff at the aroma of cologne that helped to point out that he'd taken time to shave for a second time that day. A man who shaves twice in one day has plans for that night, or at least she hoped so.

She followed him and went up on tiptoe to plant a short hard kiss on his mouth. "Friends again?"

He slid his arms around her waist and pulled her closer, dropped a kiss on the end of her nose. "Friends again. Now, what've you got?"

Jessica picked up the disk and popped it out of its plastic jacket. "Sarah Jenkins down at the studio went through the archives, pulling anything I asked for, and a couple of bits she found on her own. The disk arrived via messenger a few hours ago. Clips of funerals, newscasts on the Fishtown Strangler, the first on-camera reactions of Joshua Brainard after his wife's murder—like that. You ready?"

"I suppose. But why are we looking at these clips?"

Jessica rolled her eyes. "Well, Matthew, if I knew that, they'd make me king, wouldn't they," she said, repeating his earlier statement. She grabbed the remote. "Okay, hop up on the bed—it's the best place to see the screen."

"You'll be so much warmer here, little boy, the witch cackled as she was opening the oven door," Matt said, but then climbed onto the bed, stretched out his long legs and arranged some pillows behind him. "Where's the popcorn?"

"All gone. Rockne snarfed it down when I wasn't looking. And to think that a week ago we worried that he was so distraught over Teddy's death that he'd never eat again. Life goes on, huh?"

"It always has," Matt said, slipping his arm around her as she settled back against the pillows and hit the play button on the remote. "We add another scar or two to our collection and keep moving. Never forgetting, but learning how to cope with the pain, the grief, and carrying on."

"That's almost poetry, Lieutenant," Jessica said, wondering if he was remembering his wife, and how he had gotten through that pain and grief. It was time to lighten the mood a little. "A bit long for a T-shirt slogan, but you can work on it. Okay, what's first here? Ah…Terrell Johnson's funeral."

"I thought you said the Scholar Athlete murder case was a dead end."

"Well, yeah, *we* know that. But Jade isn't ready to give up yet." Jessica sat forward, cross-legged, on the bed. "Wow, big funeral, huh? I guess that's to be expected."

They watched the two-minute clip in silence. Terrell's grandmother and kid brother entering the church, a snippet of the pastor's sermon, the mourners coming back down the steps and then the gathering in the cemetery. Young Jermayne's face was the natural target for the cameras, and the sight of his sad eyes, the huge tears running down his soft cheeks, were enough to break anyone's heart. Jessica had to look away for a moment.

"Jesus," Matt said quietly. "That kid looks ripped to shreds. Okay, so Jade's not done looking yet and neither are we. That kid was robbed of his brother, maybe his one chance to have the life his brother wanted for him. Ripples, Jess. One person dead, yes, but a family devastated, maybe destroyed. An entire community questioning, asking the big *why*—why do things like this happen to good kids?"

Jessica paused the action as the camera panned the large congregation of teenagers, probably Terrell's classmates. Young girls sobbed, holding on to each other, tall, too-thin boys wore iron-jawed blank expressions that proved they were trying hard not to break down.

"All these kids are grown now, Matt, maybe married, maybe have kids of their own. Do you think they ever remember what happened to Terrell? Do they send their kids off to school in the morning and wonder if they'll ever see them again? Do they worry about the randomness of violence? Or is Terrell just the kid they raise a glass to at their high-school reunion and then forget about again?"

"As we both agreed, Jess, life goes on, although I doubt it ever did, not in a real sense, for Terrell's grandmother and brother. This is what pushed Teddy, you know—wanting to give those people closure of some sort. Okay, enough of that. What's next?"

Jessica picked up the plastic case and read Sarah's notes. "Next is Tarin White's funeral. Thirty seconds, which doesn't sound like much, but is really a lot." She hit the play button and leaned forward once more, squinting because the funeral had taken place during an October downpour, and the video was nearly black-and-white as it captured the dull gray day.

"Obligatory clergyman," Matt said, sitting up beside her as they watched the camera pan the congregated mourners. "Medical examiner—he retired about five years ago, moved to one of those adults-only places in Sarasota or somewhere. Central-casting funeral director in the black... I don't recognize either of those women, but they have the look."

"The look of what?" Jessica asked, pausing the video again. "Hookers?"

"Sorry. Not too politically correct, huh?"

Jessica studied the frozen picture. Both women

looked tired, the sort of bone-weary that's a lot more than having lived through a couple of late nights in a row or a few hard times. Beneath the makeup, their eyes were as old as the world, and as tired and resigned as those of demoralized prisoners staring out from behind a chain-link fence. "They do have the look, don't they? Nature or nurture, do you suppose?"

"What?"

She shook her head. "Nothing. I was just wondering if we choose our destinies, or if our destinies choose us. Do you think either of those women, when they were Jermayne's age, for instance, was thinking, wow, I want to grow up and be a hooker? How does it happen? I think I'd like to go see Mama Bunny and her, um, her coworkers again. Their stories would make a great hour, don't you think? I mean, we make jokes about these women, we arrest them, we even despise them—but they're still people. Even if the lowlifes that use them see them as consumer goods and not people at all."

"Hookers as consumer goods," Matt repeated. "I'd love a look inside that head of yours, sweetheart. I think there's a couple of extra gears in there the rest of us missed out on. Let's keep going. Okay…the consumer goods…a city worker of some sort…ah, Teddy. We should have known."

Jessica paused the video again, for the camera

had gone in pretty tight on her father's face. He was wearing his old tan trench coat that she remembered from so long ago, and she could see the collar of a flowered Hawaiian shirt. He stood hatless in the rain, his sandy hair plastered to his head. Younger by a good dozen years, so handsome her heart squeezed painfully in her chest. He'd always teased that he was descended from Irish kings.

"Look, Matt. Look at his eyes. They're the same eyes as those women. Old as the ages. Ah, Daddy, I'm so sorry. I never realized…"

Matt rubbed at her back. "Teddy was old school. He lived, ate and slept his job, Jess. It takes a toll."

With his wife gone, with his girls growing up and ready to leave, what else did the man have? And then he got injured on the job, was forced into retirement…playing games as a P.I., maybe only really alive when he was working his cold cases. Poor Teddy.

Jessica bit her bottom lip, then looked at Matt. "Is that how you're going to look in another ten years? All hollowed out like that? Still living alone in some dump that's cheap because you're a cop, watching TV in your plain vanilla living room, talking to your current Mortimer, trying to remember the color of Mary's eyes?"

"No," he said simply, his jaw set. "It's not."

Jessica knew when to leave something alone—at

least most of the time. She hit the play button again, and then just as quickly paused the video again. "Joshua Brainard. *Hell*-o."

"And Clifford Brainard, his father, standing beside him, along with a couple of other stuffed shirts. Probably the whole Citizens Task Force, there for the photo op. We can't read too much into this, Jess."

"Maybe you can't, but I can. Why else would Joshua be there?"

"To support his father? Hold the damn umbrella over his head? How the hell should I know? And you don't know, either. But I'll admit this much, it is interesting to see our mayoral candidate at Tarin White's funeral." He looked into Jessica's face. "Uh-oh. I'm beginning to recognize that expression. You're going to pass this bit of video to one of your nightly news guys at the station, aren't you?"

"Do bears…well, you know," Jessica said, those extra gears in her head spinning at warp speed. "Hey, it's enough to keep the story going for one more news cycle at least. Next?"

Next up was the tenth anniversary memorial service for the unidentified baby murdered and tossed into a Dumpster. The service had been held at one of the larger downtown churches, and the speakers spoke to a packed house. Nobody could forget that poor nameless child.

This time Jessica was prepared to see Teddy's

face, but he never appeared on the video. But once again Clifford and Joshua Brainard did.

"No big deal here, either, Jess," Matt warned her. "Brainard the younger has been running for mayor for two years now, maybe all of his life. He had to show his pretty, professionally solemn face at a ceremony like this one. His dad doesn't look too hot, does he? Aged a lot in ten years. I remember that he had some heart problem, or maybe a stroke, a couple of months after that last clip we saw. That's when he stepped down from the family business and really began pushing his fair-haired son into public service."

"Uh-huh," Jessica said, her mind already on the next clip Sarah had included. "Here's Joshua Brainard after his wife was found dead. And, hey, no surprise, there's his daddy, standing right beside him. Let me take it off mute."

The news anchor's voice was heard while the cameras stayed on Joshua Brainard, who looked sad and appealing and just the all-American boy who would persevere no matter the odds, keep on keeping on, stiff upper lip—no, that was British. "He may be the grieving widower," Jessica said, "but he *looks* like the mayoral candidate."

"I understand the police have a suspect," Joshua Brainard was saying into the camera now, "but I don't wish to comment one way or another on that, except to say that this man, this Theodore Sunshine, has been harassing poor Melodie for a few weeks now, and she was very reluctant to even speak of the man. Thank you…I…I need to go…make arrangements. Excuse me…"

Jessica watched as the elder Brainard put himself between his son and the cameras, his arm around Joshua's shoulders as he guided him back toward the Brainard residence.

"Where does the old man live?" she asked Matt as she paused the video again.

"Not there, if that's what you're thinking. He used to. The house has been in the family for a long time. He moved out when Joshua got married, gave them the place and bought himself the top floor of some building on Market Street. Why?"

Jessica shrugged. "I don't know. He just seems to always *be* there. Like he and his son are joined at the hip or something. If Joshua had anything to do with Tarin White's death, his father knows. Count on it."

"And the same for the wife's death, Teddy's death. I know," Matt said, looking at the television screen. "And I also know you're thinking he looks like an easy target. But we can't touch him, Jess. He's old, but he's powerful, and he's not in the best of health, either. You go storming in on him, demanding answers, accusing his son of anything, and the guy could have a coronary. We've already got enough problems without killing an old man."

"Teddy didn't get the chance to live to be an old man," Jessica said, and hit the mute and play buttons one last time. All the rest had been buildup. They'd caught a few bits of information she hadn't counted on, but this next clip was the entire reason she'd asked Matt to watch the videos with her.

She had to make him *understand*.

Again the local station feed had been uninspired, starting at the church, with she and Jolie and Jade trooping up the steps, then down the steps, the focus on Jolie's sad beautiful face as the three of them walked behind the casket, Jolie holding on to Rockne's leash. The wider shot showed Jade, looking closed-in and solitary even with Court's arm around her waist, and Jessica's own face, her expression mulish, defiant. Sisters, yes, but definitely not as alike as peas in a pod.

"Put the sound on?"

"No way. I've already heard the idiot, all the crap about Teddy's funeral the day after Melodie Brainard's putting the end to the sad story, if not the questions about how a man so decorated by the Philadelphia Police Department could have fallen so far, become a murderer. Bastards. Okay, we're at the cemetery."

Jessica watched as the mob of paparazzi were shown being held back none too well by a few rent-a-cops as Teddy's casket was carried to the grave site by employees of the funeral home. "You see that?

Everyone was warned to stay away—there could be no show of unity with a disgraced fallen colleague and friend, orders that came down from the top, I found out."

"Yeah. I got the memo none of us supposedly got."

"Sickening. No pals and former comrades-in-arms carrying their friend to his final rest on their shoulders. No flag on the casket. No honor guard. No salute. Nothing, Matt. He put in his time, did a damn good job, had to retire because he was injured in the line of duty—and this is what he gets? This is what kills me, Matt, what breaks me up inside, smashes me into tiny jagged pieces."

"You wanted a cop's funeral."

"Damn straight, I did. I still do," she said, angrily wiping tears from her cheeks with the backs of her hands. She'd known what she'd see, had prepared herself—but it still had the power to hit her like a fist to the stomach.

She closed her eyes, envisioning the scene. "I want a do-over when the truth comes out, Matt. I want a thousand cops in their dress blues and those black bands strapped across their shields, coming from all across the tri-state area to pay tribute to Teddy. I want the flag folded with all that heartbreaking solemn ceremony and given to Jade as the oldest daughter. The sharp crack of a rifle salute that makes you jump even when you know it's coming. I want taps played,

I want some guy in a kilt working the bagpipes as he walks off over the next hill, taking the sweet, haunting, mournful melody of "Amazing Grace" with him. I want a damn *mist* on the ground, swallowing up the piper as he walks away, disappears."

She hit Stop on the remote and then clenched her hands into fists. "I want the wake, the toasts, the stories, the laughter that drives away the tears. It's what Teddy wanted and it's what I want, what all three of us want. And it's damn well what we're going to get. We're not doing this for revenge, Matt. I'm not doing it for glory, or ratings, or even for ego. We're doing it for Teddy, because he *deserves* the best send-off we can give him." She turned to look at Matt, her composure hanging by a slim shredding thread. "Please understand that."

"Come here," Matt said softly, holding out his arms to her.

She resisted for a moment, wishing she had more control over her emotions, but then threw herself at him, burying her head against his shoulder as she let loose a torrent of tears she thought had all been shed in the first hours after she'd gotten Jade's call.

She'd cried those tears alone.

But now Matt was here with her.

Now she could let down her guard, allow herself to feel, when she had told herself that she wasn't permitted that luxury when she had work to do.

Now, safe in his arms, she knew who Lieutenant Matthew Denby was.

He was the right man at the right time.

MATT SHIFTED slightly on the bed, his right arm having gone partially numb beneath the weight of Jessica's head as she slept on, her body curled against his.

He squinted at the clock on the DVD machine across the room. Half-past six. The sun was already lightening the sky.

He hadn't spent the night with a woman since Mary. He hadn't slept with a woman in his arms since Mary.

He hadn't been to bed with a woman since Mary and even considered sticking around to spend the night, talk, have breakfast together.

And he sure as hell hadn't spent time in bed with a woman since Mary without sex being the only reason he was there in the first place.

So what was he still doing here, with Jessica warm and soft and trusting, lying next to him?

Poor kid, she'd really cried her heart out. Probably a good thing, a necessary thing. And when, exhausted, she'd begun to drift into sleep, he'd moved to leave her, only to have her grab on to him again. Had she even known she'd done that?

Probably not. He could have gone. Draped a cover over her and left her to sleep alone.

He also could have cut off his right arm and beaten himself over his own stupid head with it. And he could mentally call her kid until the sky grew dark again, and she'd still be the very real *woman* he couldn't seem to get out of his mind.

Matt had been living alone for nearly twenty years, dependent on and answerable to only himself, nobody but a succession of big-eyed fish dependent on him—and if he didn't like it, at least he was used to the routine.

He didn't want to be *involved,* damn it. He had never planned to be involved. He'd had questions of his own about Teddy's death, Melodie Brainard's death, and the Beckets and the Sunshine sisters had offered him an in, which he'd taken. That was all that was going to happen. He needed involvement with Jessica Sunshine like Mortimer needed a pair of sneakers.

Which, of course, explained why he was lying in this bed...

"Jess? Jessica?" he whispered close to her ear. "It's morning. Jess? Come on, honey, wake up."

"No, don't want to," she mumbled back at him, snuggling even closer, as if seeking his warmth. And then, as he watched her sleep-flushed face, her eyes popped open wide. "Morning? It's *morning?*"

"Whoa, easy," he warned, grabbing her as she jackknifed into a sitting position. "All the blood's going to drop to the bottom of your heart, or something like that. Give yourself a minute to wake up."

"Can't," she said, avoiding his eyes as she pushed her fingers through her masses of sleek blond hair. "Newspaper's probably already here, remember?" And then she finally looked at him. "I'm sorry," she said sheepishly. "I really took advantage of you last night, didn't I, going all girly and weepy on you like that? I'll bet my eyes are all red and puffy, huh? Not a good look for me, I know. You didn't have to stay with me."

Matt sat up, rubbing at his arm, which was now tingling as the nerves came awake once more. Clearly it was a new day, and Jessica's defenses were back in place. It was time once again for her to play the smart but slightly wacky blonde and for him to play her casual lover. "Now she tells me. But that's all right. You can make it up to me now, if you want to? I did wake up with you draped all over me, you know. I'm not that old, and, according to certain physical signals currently being sent out by my baser self, I'm not dead."

"Funny. Crude, but funny." Jessica leaned across the bed and kissed his cheek. "Sorry, hot stuff, but I don't think I'm much of a morning person. What with nature and my empty belly calling, and my mouth feeling like somebody died in there, and all that icky stuff. But I'll take a rain check?"

"I'll have my libido pencil you in for sometime tonight," Matt told her, and then covered a yawn with his hand. "Remind me never to fall asleep again with my shoes on. Now that you've mentioned it, I'm feeling pretty grungy myself."

"When did I say I was grungy, Lieutenant?" Jessica countered, already opening drawers in the dresser and pulling out some definitely interesting-looking lacy things. "I, sir, am perfection at all times, and was only fishing for compliments. You, however, need a shave."

Matt rubbed at his chin. "True. Jess?"

She still had her back to him. "Hmm?"

"You okay?"

She nodded. "Thanks to you, yes."

He got to his feet. "Good." There was nothing else to say, so he repeated himself. "That's good. See you at breakfast?"

"Sounds like a plan," Jessica said, still with her back to him.

He was going to simply walk past her and leave the room. That would be the smart thing to do, and probably what she wanted him to do. But he couldn't do it. He walked over to her, pushed her hair out of the way and pressed a kiss to the back of her neck. "I like waking up with you beside me, Jessica Sunshine," he whispered. "I like it very much."

Then he left. While he still could.

CHAPTER THIRTEEN

OKAY, SO THE HEADLINE was below the fold on page two, but at least the story was in there: *New Questions in Brainard Murder Case.*

Jessica nibbled on her second slice of whole-wheat toast, trying to pretend it was an apple Danish, which wasn't working well at all. "I guess we take what we can take, huh?" she asked Jade and Court, who had their heads together as they read the story. "I mean, it's in there, right?"

"It's a very good story, Jessica," Jade said, sitting back in her chair. "Your eyes are a little puffy. Didn't you sleep well?"

"Well enough, I guess," Jessica said, ducking the real question, which probably ran along the lines of *Did you sleep alone?*

Jessica was pretty sure Jade had, because Court wasn't exactly looking like the cat that got the canary, or whatever that old saying was. In fact, he looked anything but happy. "Court? Anything wrong?"

"Pardon me? Oh, no. Nothing's wrong. I had an

e-mail from Morgan Eastwood this morning, that's all. She's in the States. Somewhere in Michigan. It turns out there definitely are a lot more Beckets still floating around out there than either of us knew. Including a couple in Hampton Roads, if you can believe that one. I play golf with one of them, as a matter of fact. Rob Greenawalt, a white-haired old guy who was a hell of a defense attorney before he retired, and whose wife—third one—isn't much older than you, Jess." He shook his head. "It's a strange world."

"How do you misplace a relative?" Jessica asked, frowning at her wheat toast, because she was actually beginning to acquire a taste for it. The world could be nothing but downhill and bran flakes, if that could happen.

"Good question," Court told her, smiling. "Morgan included some back story in her e-mail. Rob's part of the Becket family goes back to one of the original orphan sons, Spencer, and his wife, Mariah. They emigrated with the patriarch, Ainsley, the only true daughter, Cassandra, and her husband, Courtland—another of the orphans—and the guy I was named after. Clear?"

"Vaguely," Jessica said, taking mental notes again. "Go on."

"There's not much more, at least not yet. Morgan says she can trace both branches through the early

1900s, and then there was some family falling-out over a broken engagement between the families. I think the guy in the picture was the bad guy—my relative. Contact was cut off, several in both families died in the flu epidemic in, what, 1916, 1917? More decided to give up farming and moved to California sometime during the Great Depression. And that's all she wrote—Morgan, that is."

"Gee, your very own Hatfield and the McCoys. And Morgan found more Becket descendants in Michigan?"

"And in England. We're lucky, really. With all the genealogy sites on the Internet, we've got sources we wouldn't have had forty years ago. But it's strange. A family made up of so many strangers, not connected by blood. Yet still family. Look at Sam and me. We'd never consider ourselves anything less than cousins, even if I'm the only one left with Becket blood. We're still connected."

"And each of you still has a share in the Empress," Jessica reminded him. "When we find it, of course. How many ways are you going to have to split this fortune, do you think?"

"They're not going to find any priceless emerald, Jessica," Jade said at last. "It's probably just like Sam said it could be. An old legend, passed from generation to generation, and embroidered until there's not a bit of truth left in it. A cursed stone? Hidden away until its bad luck has worn off? That's a fairy tale, and not a very good one."

"Ah, ever the pragmatic one, Jade," Jessica said as she watched Matt enter the room and go directly to the buffet, waving, instead of saying hello, and not interrupting the conversation. "Ainsley Becket was a big bad pirate, remember? Why couldn't he have a big bad uncut emerald worth millions?"

"I'd like you all to see Becket Hall," Court told them as he poured more coffee into his cup, and then Jade's. "The man was a genius. The defenses he built into that place? They could have held off an army even while being attacked from the sea. And there isn't an inch of the place that isn't filled with antiques Sam is going to drool over. But, for as well as privateering and piracy paid, Ainsley paid a high price. They all did. Morgan's great-grandfather compiled a history of those bad old days, and when she's had copies made, she's going to give them to Sam and me."

"We can trace the Sunshines back to the Auld Sod, to about the time of the potato famine," Jade told Court and Matt, who was now sitting beside Jessica and cutting into a thick slice of ham. "According to Teddy, the English took all our land and titles, cut down all our trees and shipped them back to England, married the prettiest daughters, defiled the rest and then called us dirty lazy lugs. Our great-great-grandmother and her sisters landed at Ellis Island and became housemaids in Manhattan, and our great-great-grandfather helped dig the tunnels for the subway system. No emeralds for the Sunshine family. Just the memories of an Emerald Isle."

"And some great stories," Jessica added, leaning her chin in her hand as she propped her elbow on the table. "Uncle Shamus was a thief, and a damn good one. Teddy said the joke his grandfather told was that Shamus was such a dedicated thief that, if you threw a halter of snow on his grave, he would have jumped up and gone off to steal a horse. Aunt Morag was the toast of the Dublin stage for a while, until some English earl or something convinced her to go to London with him, where he dumped her, and she ended up becoming a wardess in a Magdalen House."

She turned her head to smile at Matt. "That's a pretty name for a house for repentant prostitutes. I guess that's why I have a soft spot for Mama Bunny, huh? Maybe it's in the blood."

"Jessica Marie," Jade said wearily, "have another bite of toast, why don't you? A *big* bite."

The cell phone in Jessica's pocket began to vibrate and she pulled it out, looked at the number: private caller. "I guess we've got a slow starter in the nutcase derby. I haven't had a call on this phone in a couple of days."

"Give me that," Jade said, reaching across the

table and grabbing the phone. "There. Just let it go to voice mail."

"I'd answer it," Matt said—his first words since joining them. "The mention on the news last night, the newspaper article this morning? It's probably just another nut shaken from the tree, but the way things have been going around here, anything's possible."

"I suppose you're right," Jade said. She pushed the button and put the phone to her ear. "Sunshine Hot Line," she said, making a face at Jessica, who merely smiled, because the name had been her idea. "No, this is *not* Jolie Sunshine." She frowned at the phone. "I know my sister said that you could talk to any one of us, but—hold on, please." She looked at Jessica, who had been waving her arms above her head. "What?"

"Give me the phone," Jessica said. "I can pretend I'm Jolie."

"No you can't. You don't sound anything like Jolie."

"Wanna bet? Come on, Jade, give me the phone. It'll be fun."

"*Fun.* You call this *fun?* Oh, all right." Jade held out the phone and Jessica snatched it even as she got to her feet, began to pace the carpet behind Matt's chair.

"Hell-o, Jolie Sunshine here. How may I help you?" she said, lowering her voice a half-octave, careful to keep her top lip from moving as she formed each word. Jolie had learned how to do that by practicing in front of the bathroom mirror—as men never moved their top lip when they spoke, only women. Which was why women got those little wrinkles around their upper lips, and men didn't. When Jolie had practiced, Jessica had sat on the downed toilet seat, holding her Strawberry Shortcake hand mirror, and practiced with her.

"I love your movies, Ms. Sunshine," the female voice said through the phone. "You're a very good actress."

"Actor," Jessica corrected. "We all prefer to be called actors. But thank you so much. Go on."

"Yes, well, I don't think you could be such a good actress, um, actor, if you weren't really as good a person as you play in your movies, you know? That's why I wanted to talk to you, and tell you what I know. I don't know who this Jade person is—except that she's your sister, I know that—and Jessica Sunshine is…well, I know she's your sister and all, too, but she's a little…weird."

Jessica held the phone away from her ear and looked at it for a moment, then brought it close once more. "Jessica has always been a little strange. We understand it's because of her IQ. Genius range, you understand. Don't let the blond hair fool you. What did you want to tell Jo—tell me?"

"Well, you know, I don't like to carry tales, you know…but, well, I work in this salon, see? Shampoo girl? And I sweep up the cut hair, wash the towels, you know? I graduate next year, because I have to work in the day and go to school at night. Nobody notices us, like we're invisible, Jolie, like we don't have ears, you know? So we hear a lot the clients think only their operator is hearing. You wouldn't believe some of the wild stuff women tell their operators. You wouldn't believe how many want your haircut, too, or some other movie star. Loretta—she's one of the operators—she goes nuts when the patrons do that, says she's a beautician, not a miracle worker. Oh! Forget I said Loretta, okay?"

Jessica made a mental note to bring a book to her next salon appointment and never open her mouth. "Already forgotten. I understand that you want to remain anonymous," she said as she made motions with her free hand, scribbling in midair as she asked for pen and paper. "But I can imagine you do hear a lot of very private information. That is why you've called me, isn't it? Why don't you tell me what you heard?"

Matt had opened his small spiral notebook and placed it and his pen on the table. She switched the phone to her left ear and grabbed the pen, to write: *a live one!*

"Hello?" Jessica winced, because she wasn't getting an answer. "Hello? Are you still there?"

"Yes…but I shouldn't do this. People deserve their privacy, even dead people."

Jessica put two and two together and came up

with: "You're talking about Melodie Brainard, aren't you? Please, if you have any information, tell me. My father didn't kill her. Don't let the real murderer go free. Not if you know something that can help us. Hello? *Hello!*"

"She…she came in a couple of weeks ago. Four, five days before she died? She's been coming in for years. I shampooed her. We've got these really bright lights at the shampoo bar, you know, up in the ceiling? If those women knew how bad they look under those lights, man, they'd have fits. Big pores, wrinkles—it can get ugly! So I could see where Mrs. Brainard had tried to hide some bruises on her cheek and…and behind her one ear. On her neck, sort of, you know? Good makeup job, but I could see past it. And she winced when I had to lift her a little to soap up the back of her head."

"Somebody had hit her?" Jessica prompted even as she was scribbling like mad on the notepad. *Melodie… marks on neck…bruises…three weeks ago?*

"She didn't say anything to me, but you don't need to be a genius like your sister to know when somebody's been batted around, you know? And then I heard her telling Lor, telling her operator that if he touched her again she was going to burn his ass, and she didn't give a flying fuck—sorry, that's what she said—about being the mayor's wife, that nothing was worth it. What *it* was I don't know, you know?"

"Can we meet somewhere?" Jessica asked, her mind going a million miles an hour. Get the girl, talk to the girl, get the name of the salon, get to Loretta—

"No! No, I couldn't do that! I…I've got to go."

"Wait, wait! Give me a sec here, okay? Don't hang up!" Jessica couldn't afford to have the woman hang up the phone. She madly searched for a soft spot and then decided she'd found one. "I'm…I'm out here in Hollywood right now, did you know that? It's true. My sister patched this call through to me—who understands these new phones, huh? But you know what? I could arrange for a jet to pick you up at the Philadelphia airport and bring you out to me. Would you like that? Would you like to stay with me for a few days? Either in a hotel, or with me at my place. I really want to talk to you some more, maybe ask you a few more questions, see if you can remember anything else Melodie Brainard might have said since she's been a client at your salon? And…uh…" she made a face at Matt "—and I could take you on a tour of the studio, even the…the hair and makeup department. You'd like that, wouldn't you?"

Five minutes later, with Jade just hanging up another phone after saying goodbye to Jolie, Jessica at last ended the call and collapsed into her chair beside Matt. "My *God*. I've never talked so fast in my life. But we've got her. Court," she said, looking to him as Matt rubbed the tight spot between her shoulder blades, "thank you so much. Do I want to know how much it costs to get your company jet from here to Hollywood?"

"Probably not," he said, slipping his own cell phone into his pocket. "Besides, it's already out there, with Sam and Jolie. I rented a small jet and crew. They'll be waiting for our mystery guest when she arrives at the terminal."

"So you don't think Cindy Crawford is her real name?" Jessica asked, smiling. "Yeah, well, she has to show ID to get to the plane, so we'll get her real name soon enough. Jade, what did Jolie say? She's okay with this?"

Jade smiled. "Is she okay with it? Are you kidding? The last time I heard her squeal like that she was about ten years old, and I'd accidentally slammed the car door on her fingers. Jess, I apologize. I still can't really believe it, but your plan worked."

Jessica jabbed Matt with her elbow. "Did you hear that? My plan worked. And she didn't even qualify that by saying that my idiot plan worked."

"A one-in-a-million shot," Matt said, still rubbing her back, which Jessica knew she could get very used to having him do on a regular basis. "But, yeah, Jess, good work, sweetheart. You should be on our hostage-negotiation team. You could have talked Al Pacino out of the bank in *Dog Day Afternoon*."

"What?" Jessica asked, not making the connection.

"Old movie. Forget it."

"If there wasn't a role for a leading lady, Jolie didn't force us all to watch it a dozen times. But if you like it, maybe it's on DVD? I'll make brownies?" God, she was babbling. She was so *high* on her success. Almost giddy. She shot her fists into the air. "We've got him! We've got our toothy mayoral candidate all ready for us to nail his hide to the barn door, or to the City Hall doors. We'll nail him somewhere."

"Jessica, calm down," Jade said, leaning her elbows on the table. "We still don't have anything solid, just this girl's story, which she might have embroidered a bit to make herself feel important. Jolie and Sam are going to have to listen to her, ask her questions and then decide if we've got anything at all. We're a long way from proving Joshua Brainard killed his wife."

"And Teddy. If he killed his wife, he killed Teddy," Jessica said tightly. "That's the real biggie. That's the one I really want."

"That's what we all want, Jess." Jade got to her feet. "Now, I've got an appointment for one last look at my hand before the doctor releases me. No, Court, just stay there. I don't need you to go with me. I want Jessica to go with me. Jess?"

She's going to grill me about Matt, turn me inside out for information, and then not tell me a damn thing about her and Court. The hell she is! "Sure,"

Jessica said brightly, getting to her feet. "We haven't had a girl-time for a while. You boys be good, we'll be back in a... Jade? When will we be back?"

"Two hours, unless you want to grab an early lunch when we're done?"

"Four hours," Jessica said, grinning at Matt. "I'm still kicking myself about that purse I put back down on the counter at Neiman Marcus the other day. There's nothing worse than shopper's regret. You two play nice together. Maybe take Ernesto and Rockne for a walk."

"Which one do we put on the leash?" Matt asked her as Ernesto wandered into the room, mumbling *Excuse me* to the doorjamb he clipped with his shoulder as he kept his eyes on the hand calculator he was working with. "I don't know if he's ready for Penn State, or if it's a matter of Penn State not being ready for him."

Jessica laughed, and rubbed at Ernesto's head as the boy sat down, still poking at the calculator's keys. "Yes, well, young man," she said to Matt, "you brought him home, now it's your job to feed and care for him."

"Here, *amigo*," Matt said, shoving the last slice of Jessica's toast in front of the teen. "Eat. Grow strong, so that you may fly free, leave the nest."

Ernesto finally looked up from the keypad. "You people are all a little nuts. You do know that, right? Especially the guy on the phone a couple of minutes ago."

The rest of them exchanged looks. "Wait a minute," Jessica said. "I was on the one cell with our mystery caller. Court, you were on yours with the airport. Jade, you were on your new one with Jolie. Did the house phone ring?"

"I answered it in the living room," Ernesto said. "I was working on a hypothetical problem I made up—that's why they call them hypothetical problems—and forgot I wasn't at home and it wasn't my phone. But it wasn't anything important. The guy didn't ask for anyone or even give me a chance to get any of you, but just did one of those dumb telephone prank jokes and hung up. You know, like, hello, is your re-frigerator running? And you say yes, and then he says, well, then, you'd better go catch it. Dumb, like that."

"And this joke was…?" Jessica asked, longing to rip the complicated calculator out of Ernesto's hands and send it winging through the nearest window. The kid might be a genius, but she'd heard of lots of geniuses who didn't have the common sense to come in out of the rain. For instance: Sam Becket had an unlisted number, so what were the odds of him getting a prank call? "Come on, Ernesto, what was so funny?"

"It wasn't funny. It was just lame." Ernesto put down his new toy and looked at Matt. "Let me get it straight in my head, okay? He kind of took me off guard, his voice all low and *woo-woo,* and like he was trying to scare me. Just some stupid kid playing a joke."

"Ernesto, don't make me hurt you," Jessica said, her fingertips now digging into his slim shoulders. "Spit it out."

"Hey! Okay, *señorita,* okay, hands off the merchandise. He said—and this is a direct quote—'Smart people know when to quit. Do you know when to quit?' That's it, that's all. Stupid. Of course smart people know when to quit. I'm a smart people—person. You quit while you're ahead, right? But like I said, he hung up before I could give him the answer."

Jessica bit her bottom lip as Matt looked up at her, as he slowly got to his feet and headed for the phone on a table in the corner, his expression unreadable except for the white line around his mouth. "Hang on another minute," he said evenly. "I'll drive you to the doctor. And because I'm a glutton for punishment, to the King of Prussia Mall, too. Right after I check the caller ID, although I doubt that's going to do any good."

"You're going to call the kid back and go all postal on him, wave your badge around? All right, Lieutenant!" Ernesto said, getting to his feet. "Just hit star-something, and you redial the guy. But you probably know that, huh?"

Everyone watched Matt as he pushed in some

numbers, and then said nothing while they waited. He finally put down the receiver. "It just rings. Not a pay phone—nobody's dumb enough to do that anymore. Probably a throwaway cell that's already in three pieces in some trash can. We could try to tri-angulate where he called from, using cell towers, except that I can't go to the department with this, either—which is beginning to drive me a little nuts, in case anyone cares. Ready, ladies?"

"I'll go along," Court said, also getting to his feet. "I was thinking Ernesto might like a nice leather case for that toy of his. We've all been working hard the last week or so. Ernesto, you can go with us. We'll shop, we'll have lunch somewhere. We'll make it a party, a day off for everybody. Let me just go use the house phone to call down to the gate, to tell the Bear Man we'll be taking Sam's SUV."

Jessica and Matt exchanged knowing looks. To tell the Bear Man about the threatening phone call and to warn him to bump up his vigilance. That was what Court had really meant.

Jade looked ready to protest, but Jessica caught her eye and quickly shook her head, hoping to keep Ernesto from realizing the importance, the threat, in what he'd just told them. Besides, they *were* smart people—she'd like to believe they were smart people, prudent people—and it didn't take a math genius to know there was safety in numbers.

"WHY ARE YOU wearing the coat, Matt?" Ernesto asked as they stood in front of a display of calculators in a store that pretty much intimidated Matt, who still approached his microwave with the sure knowledge that the damn thing was out to get him. "You packing?"

"Yeah, I'm packing. I'm a real bad guy," Matt said, rolling his eyes. "But you don't need to shout it out for all the other customers. Come on, pick one of these things and let's go back to the food court."

"I'm doing it, I'm doing it. But I'm kind of going back and forth between the Excel-based and this baby here. Calculus. I love calculus."

Matt rubbed at the back of his neck. "Uh-huh. And I get all hot and bothered about my TV remote. What are you going to do with this logistics degree, anyway? Manage inventory somewhere, right?"

Ernesto picked up another small calculator crammed with buttons that might, who knew, trigger a world collapse if pushed in the correct sequence. "That's just a part of it. I'm aiming for the FBI. The OSB, actually, for the RDL unit—the RDLU."

"A couple more letters, pal, and you'll have the whole alphabet. What the hell are you talking about? And give it to me slow."

Ernesto finally chose a handheld that could only

be considered a handheld if you had a really big hand, and they walked over to the checkout counter.

"The FBI is the Federal Bureau of—"

"Not that slow. I know I'm just a dumb cop, but give me some credit here."

Ernesto grinned. "Sorry. OSB means Operations Support Branch, okay? They do some pretty neat stuff, like crisis negotiation, crisis management and logistics. Actually, rapid deployment logistics—the RDLU."

"Okay, I think I'm getting it. You can speed up now."

"There's hope for you yet, *amigo*. The RDLU is pretty new, like about ten years now. When our embassies in Kenya and Tanzania were bombed? That's when the FBI figured out pretty quick that we needed a better way of managing troop and supply delivery, important inventories, everything we'd need for a *rapid deployment,* the RD bit. Plus, we also calculate budgets, so we know ahead of time how much money we'll need for the troops, equipment, other support. Got it now?"

"Got it. And here I thought you'd be in charge of not ordering enough of the hottest Christmas toys for Wal-Mart. You amaze me, Ernesto."

"I'm a pretty amazing guy. Hey, thanks again, *amigo.*"

"Don't worry about it. Think of it as my contribution to the war effort."

Matt paid for the calculator and they headed back

out into the concourse, on their way to joining the others in the food court. As they walked, he shifted his eyes from side to side, on the lookout for strange-looking characters, which was pretty much a self-defeating exercise in a crowded shopping mall.

"Matt?"

"Yeah, kid?"

"I leave for Penn State in a little over a week."

"I know. I've been marking off the days on my calendar."

"Cut that out," Ernesto said, grinning. "I know you like me. Unless you think I'm, like, a chaperon? You know, for you and Miss Jessica?"

Matt lost a step, then picked up the pace once more. "Are you going somewhere with this? Because if I'm about to get advice for the lovelorn from any-one, sorry, but it wouldn't be an eighteen-year-old kid wearing a *Chicks Compute Me* T-shirt, okay?"

"No, I guess not. Besides, I think you're pretty… smooth, you know?"

"You think I'm *smooth?* Want another calculator, kiddo?" Matt asked Ernesto, rubbing the top of the boy's head. "Take two, they're small."

"Cut that out," Ernesto complained, pushing at his hair. "Why does everybody do that to me? I'm not Rockne. Jeez. No, Matt, I want to ask you something, okay? Something important."

"Fire away," Matt said, watching as three sullen-faced teens saw him, made eye contact with him, stopped in their tracks and then quickly turned into an open doorway—although what the boys would buy in a women's shoe store, he couldn't know. It was like, Matt thought, he was wearing a slogan T-shirt of his own, one only the bad guys could see: C-O-P!

"Okay," Ernesto said, nodding furiously as they walked into the large food-court area and began searching for Jessica and Jade and Court in the noon-time crowd. "Here's the thing. I'm going to college now. University, actually. Living in a dorm, all that stuff. There will be parties…things going on. And I—this is hard—and I've never had a date, you know? I've never even kissed a girl, except for my cousin Lupe, and that was *not* fun. We were maybe eight or nine, and she tackled me."

"I see. No, I don't. You don't want me to tell you about the birds and the bees, Ernesto, do you? And please say no."

The kid was turning bright red. "No, I know *that.* I just want to know…know about girls, you know? You're doing okay with Miss Jessica. I see how she looks at you. Like now, see? See her looking at you? Never mind, she looked away. So—how do I get a girl to look at me like that?"

"How was she looking at me?" Matt asked, holding Ernesto back as he moved to walk to the table. "Come on, give."

"I don't know," Ernesto protested. "I told you, I don't know anything about girls. She was…okay, she was looking at you like you were a raspberry-ripple double-scoop cone, and she wanted to…to lick you."

Matt smiled, biting his bottom lip. "Really? Double-scoop?"

"You're useless," Ernesto said with a sigh. "I must have been crazy to even ask you. You didn't find *her,* she found *you*. And you don't know what to do with her any more than I'd know what to do with a girl if I ever got one. Come on, it looks like they bought pizza."

Matt slipped into the chair beside Jessica and reached for a slice with pepperoni and sausage toppings. "Ernesto and I had a little talk while we were shopping. A very interesting talk"

"*Amigo*—no!"

"Oh?" Jessica asked, looking at Ernesto. "Did you remember something else about the crank call?"

"No, afraid not," Matt said, and let Ernesto off the hook. "He told me what he plans to do with his logistics degree. He's going to join the FBI and save the world."

"Really?" Jessica reached across the table to squeeze the teen's hand. "I think that's wonderful, Ernesto. I'm so proud of you. Jade, Court—isn't that terrific!"

Ernesto melted, sort of like a puppy that had just been praised for peeing outside. Matt was surprised the kid didn't drop to the floor and turn on his back so Jessica could rub his tummy.

Court began asking Ernesto questions, and while the two of them talked acronyms and how Court's friend had once gotten him in for a civilian's tour of the FBI Academy in Quantico, Virginia, Jade caught Matt's attention.

"Jermayne Johnson works at a car wash not too far from here, Matt," Jade said quietly. "I think Sam's SUV needs a wash, don't you? Even a good vacuuming—the whole package. It's the least we can do for him, using his house, his cars."

Matt looked at Court, who was now talking about the joys of Virginia, and then to Jessica, who had that damn mischievous gleam in her eye again. Clearly she and Jade had already discussed this and decided they'd found a way around Court's sure objections to taking another run at Jermayne.

He got a quick mental flash of the younger Jermayne as seen at his brother's funeral. Little boy. Big eyes. Big tears.

"Pretend I fought you on this for ten minutes before I caved, okay?" he said at last, and Jessica leaned into his side as she planted a kiss on his cheek.

"Ah, I'd wondered about the coat. You're packing. Right here, in the middle of the mall," she whispered, nearly as giddy as Ernesto had been. "Very dangerous, very sexy."

Matt edged away from her. She wasn't frightened. She was enjoying herself. He should let Ernesto in on the secret—no man understands women. "Yeah, I'm a real bad guy…"

CHAPTER FOURTEEN

"Where's Jade?"

Damn, he'd noticed.

Jessica inserted one last quarter in the vending machine and pushed C-6, not answering Court until her soda plunked to the bottom of the machine. Even then, she pretended she was having trouble getting it out of the slot. Every second she could give Jade...

"I think she went to the ladies' room. Which, in a place like this, you've got to be *really* desperate to do," she said, unscrewing the cap even as she rolled her eyes in mock horror. She took a long drink, trying not to gag when she realized she'd hit the diet-soda button by mistake. "Was that an important call?"

Court had excused himself to go outside the carwash waiting room to take the call five minutes earlier. Which was when Jade had made her break for it. Matt had gone with her, to keep his distance, but cover her back.

Court slid the cell phone back into his pocket.

"That depends on your definition of important. It wasn't about Joshua Brainard, if that's what you mean. Just a problem about seating for a conference wrap-up banquet next Saturday. Or, I should say, *two* conference banquets somehow scheduled for the same ballroom at the same time. One of them is now a luncheon banquet, and it would appear their chicken divan is now filet mignon, at my expense."

"Sounds like you handled that pretty well. Do you need to go back to Virginia soon? You know, Court, it's pretty terrific of you to be here, with Jade. She really needs you."

"It's nice that one of you thinks that."

"Ah, Court, I'm sorry. She's my big sister, and I love her, but she's kind of out of whack right now, you know? She's convinced that solving one of these cases will clear Teddy."

"But solving even all the cases won't bring him back," Court said. "She knows that. Rationally, intellectually, she knows that. But it's still going to hit her like a ton of bricks when it happens. That's when she's going to finally have time to realize that he's gone, her home is half burned down, her business is probably past repairing. You and Jolie, you both have full lives. Jade had Teddy."

"And you," Jessica said, wanting to hug him. "She's got you."

He managed a grin. "Yes, that's me, the actual

Court of last resort. I think that's how she believes I'd see it, anyway."

"Any *Court* in a storm?" Jessica quipped, trying for a joke. A really lame joke. "I'm sorry. But I think I see where you're going here. She loves you, but she wants to come to you without looking as if you're… well, that you're a convenient place to run. And what do you think? Do you think that's all you are to her?"

Court pulled two dollar bills from his pocket and slid them one by one into the soda machine. Now it seemed to be his turn to wait for the machine to work, wait for the plunk of the bottle, delay some more while retrieving it and his change, opening the bottle, taking a long drink. Men were so transparent. Women, too, maybe.

"Sometimes I wonder if that's how she saw me the first time around," he said at last, looking at Jessica with some intensity. "Like some big dramatic stab at independence, at breaking away, living her own life. Which, as we both know, didn't last past one call from Teddy, asking for her help."

Jessica was genuinely shocked. "I…I never saw it that way. You guys met through Sam, clicked, and the next thing we knew you were calling from Vegas to say that you were married. I thought it was romantic. Don't you think you're reading too much into this?"

"Probably. I've had a lot of time to think in this past year. Fourteen months, three weeks, five days—

not that I'm counting," he said, his smile breaking Jessica's heart.

"You love her so much," Jessica said, longing to hug him. The big bad hotel magnate; he was handsome, intelligent, rich, sophisticated, all that good stuff. But when it came to Jade, he was completely insecure, off balance—just a regular guy.

"I love her as much as it's possible to love anyone, I guess. Which is probably why I reacted like an idiot when she was shot at, and gave her that ultimatum. The job or me. What I didn't realize was that Jade heard that demand as *Teddy* or me. I was the loser the moment I opened my mouth."

"Little Mama," Jessica said, blinking back sudden tears. "When our mother left for that last time—and for years before she took her final hike—Jade elected herself our protector. And not just us, but Teddy, too. And being Jade, she took her responsibilities very seriously. I didn't see it back then, and I'm sure Jolie didn't, either, but we all took terrible advantage of Jade. We were the grasshoppers, and she was the ant."

"You and Jolie were kids. Teddy was the adult. *He* should have put a stop to it. *He* stole Jade's childhood. He and your mother both. I liked Teddy, I really did. But I can't forgive him for that."

Jessica's head shot up, her temper rising as she was ready to defend her father, just the way all three of them had always defended him, right or wrong.

And then she sighed, the fight draining out of her. "I know. You're right." She walked over to the railing and the glass wall, looking at it without really seeing another car go down the tracks inside the car wash. "It's not just nature or nurture, is it, Court? It's expectations, fitting into the roles somebody else has cast for us. Jessica, the baby. Jolie, the dreamer. Jade—the responsible one."

"And Teddy, with his broken heart, his bigger-than-life smiles and his dark moods and his Hawaiian shirts," Court added, joining her at the window.

Jessica turned around, rested her back against the railing. "My mother's no saint, Court, and never was. Maybe she shouldn't have married a cop who lived his job 24/7 and left her alone too much. Maybe she shouldn't have had kids." She tilted her head to look up at Court. "And maybe there's two sides to every sad story. Wow. Revelations in the middle of a car wash. It's kind of scary."

Court put his arm around her shoulders and gave her a quick hug. "Not to get all drippy and sentimental here, but I think Jade did a pretty damn good job raising you and Jolie. The three of you stick together, and that's terrific. Now…where is she? Did we give her enough time to talk to Jermayne?"

Jessica stepped away from him, astonished. "You *knew?*"

"Jess, I've known since Jade first asked you to go

with her to the hospital burn clinic, instead of me. Jade and I went back to the house yesterday, to pick up the mail and empty out the refrigerator, throw away any moldy bread, that sort of thing, and found a check to a technical school in Teddy's bank statement. He wasn't just pushing at Jermayne, he'd actually enrolled him in an associate's degree program that starts in September. She had to make another run at him after seeing that canceled check. It's what Teddy wanted Jermayne to do."

"Ergo, it's what Jade wants Jermayne to do. Jermayne was such a cute kid," Jessica told Court as they walked down the car-wash line and out into the sunshine. "Matt and I watched tape of Terrell's funeral. So, so sad."

"Matt?" Court said as they joined him in a patch of shade next to the building. "How's it going?"

"Pretty good. They're just finishing up now. And no, Jess, they aren't polishing the gas and brake pedals."

"Very funny. The jig's up, Matt, he knows," Jessica told him. "Where's Jade?"

"Just around the corner of the building. I'm giving them some privacy. Jermayne made me as a cop, that's definite, so I figured I'd keep my distance, give him some space. But may I say, he's not that sad little boy anymore."

"Big, bad, Jermayne?" Jessica asked, peering toward the corner of the building.

"I've seen guys who spent five years in the joint, lifting weights in the yard every day, that would look pretty puny beside him," Matt said. "But the eyes? They're the same. Old, maybe even haunted, if I'm allowed to get poetic here."

"Scarred for life by his brother's death," Jessica said, nodding her head. "Those ripples you talked about."

"Maybe. He looked ready to run the moment he saw me. Like I was coming to get him or something. And maybe I'm reading too much into it, but the kid seems a little squirrelly to me. He might be into something illegal, just like he was when he was a kid."

Court stepped forward a pace. "Matt? If you see it, would Teddy have gotten the same feeling?"

"Teddy? Probably. Sure. Sure, he would. Teddy was on the job for a long time. Damn, wait a minute. I think I see where you're going here, Court. The Scholar Athlete case may be a big dead end, but there might be something new about Jermayne that Teddy was looking into before he was killed. And Jermayne's a big boy. Strong. Plenty strong enough to wrestle a gun away from an older man, a drunk man, and turn it on him. Is that where you're going with this, Court?"

"I hadn't gotten quite that far, but yes, I suppose so."

Jessica looked from Matt, to Court, and back to Matt again. "Jermayne as a *suspect?* Don't even say that, guys. We can't tell the players without a scorecard as it is. That would mean somebody killed Melodie Brainard, and somebody else killed Teddy for some totally unrelated reason. That the two died the same night was strictly coincidental. We'd be looking for two killers, not one. Besides, it would break Jade's heart."

"It wouldn't have made Teddy feel all warm and fuzzy, either, to think all his hard work with Jermayne had ended with the kid going bad, anyway," Matt pointed out. "Come on. She's been alone with him for a good five minutes."

But just as they headed for the corner of the building, Jade appeared, walking with her head down.

"Jade?" Jessica asked, immediately concerned. "Where's Jermayne?"

"He took off," Jade answered, lifting her head, her expression tight, as if she was hanging on to her control by a thin thread. "But he did take the papers with him, the forms we found that he still has to fill out. I was afraid he'd rip them up right in front of me, but he didn't. He…he held them like he was holding a baby…like they were precious to him. And then he told me he wasn't going to go to school, and that I should just forget about him. That it was *too late*."

Jessica looked at Matt. "He *is* into something, isn't he? What else could that mean—*too late?*"

"It could simply mean he screwed up all through high school and now he thinks he can't cut it," Matt told her as he tipped the employee standing next to the SUV and they all climbed into the vehicle. "It could also mean he's ganged-up and supplementing his great salary here at the car wash with a little dope-running on the side. How the hell do I know? Listen, I have a friend in the local precinct. I'll ask him to do some checking. But that's all we're going to do, got it? We've got enough to handle with Joshua Brainard."

"I agree," Court said as he strapped on his seat belt. "I know this is upsetting to you, Jade, but not every story has a happy ending."

"I know," she said as Matt started the SUV and headed toward the exit.

"Wait!" Jessica was already unbuckling her seat belt. "Where's Ernesto?"

Matt applied the brakes, threw the transmission into Park, leaving the engine and the air-conditioning running. "Oh, for crying out loud. And you wonder why I only have Mortimer? Stay here, I'll go find him."

He slammed the car door on Jessica's giggles and headed back into the car wash, finally running Ernesto down in the stockroom behind the refreshment area, following the sound of a radio tuned to an all-news station.

"And here, see," Ernesto was saying to an older balding man wearing a bemused expression, "here's where you're really overinventoried, Frankie. How many people really go for the wheel protectorant?

Maybe one in twelve, fourteen customers? Look, this bottle has an expiry date on it—wow, I didn't know this kind of stuff could expire, did you? It's not like you drink it, right, *amigo?* Anyway, if you just follow these notes I've made for you, you'll have a much better idea of the inventory you have on hand, and the lead time you need to make sure you don't run out of the quicky-wax again, okay?"

"Ernesto."

The boy turned around, his smile wide. "Yeah? Are we ready to go? We couldn't get the quicky-wax. Frankie here was out of it. So I was just explaining to him how to—"

Matt waved a hand at him. "Shut it, Ernesto," he said, walking over to the radio shoved on a leaning shelf on the wall and turning up the volume.

"…just beginning a question-and-answer segment with the local press after his speech," the news reader intoned. "Joshua Brainard is said to be accompanying his father to Thomas Jefferson hospital via ambulance, where we hope shortly to hear a statement on Clifford Brainard's condition. To repeat. This just in—mayoral candidate Joshua Brainard's father, Clifford Brainard, a long-time fixture in Philadelphia's political, business and social worlds, collapsed about five minutes ago at an outdoor rally for—"

"Come on, let's go," Matt told Ernesto. "We'll listen to this again in the car."

"Okay. It's 1060 AM. You give them twenty-two minutes, and they'll hand you the world, or something like that. The story will be back on pretty soon. This is bad, isn't it?"

"It's not too fuc—yeah, it's bad," Matt said as they walked into the sunshine once more. Out of habit, he looked left and right, and that was when he saw him. Their not-so-good friend and Joshua Brainard's muscle, Leslie, red-faced, fists clenched and coming across the macadam toward him like a freight train. Matt couldn't be sure, but he'd be willing to lay odds that Leslie had been tailing them all morning, and had been sitting nearby in his car, the radio tuned to 1060.

One thing was certain. Leslie was not a happy man. Matt was pretty sure he'd be forced to pull his piece if he didn't get everyone out of here, now.

"Move it!" Matt grabbed Ernesto's elbow and ran him to the car, opening the back door and—grabbing the kid by the back of his shirt and his belt—tossing him inside like a sack of potatoes, right on top of Jade, before hopping into the front seat and laying rubber out of the parking lot.

"Clifford Brainard could be dead or dying. Turn on the radio. AM, not FM. 1060," he ordered Jessica as he looked over his shoulder, to see Leslie running toward a black SUV. Matt repeated the license number, twice, to be sure he'd remember it. Then he swerved into the turning lane and made a quick left onto the expressway ramp. He needed to put some space between the women and Ernesto and the angry Leslie. "And then hold on."

A torrent of Spanish that would have impressed Matt at any other time was coming from the backseat. A quick look in the rearview mirror showed that Ernesto was still sort of flying around the car, trying to seat himself between Court and Jade. "You okay back there?"

"We're managing. Ernesto, please move your foot. Here's your seat belt, strap in," Court said calmly. "Matt? Who's our new friend?"

"Joshua Brainard's bodyguard. Or maybe his daddy's employee, on loan for the duration. Who knows? Jess and I met him socially the other night. Damn it!" he said, pounding his fist twice on the steering wheel. "I can't believe I didn't pick up on him following us. Where the hell was my head?"

"My calculator!" Ernesto shouted in a panic. "Where's my new calculator? Lieutenant, we have to go back! I forgot my new—oh, *gracias,* Señorita Sunshine. Never mind. Got it. I guess you can just keep driving *como un hombre loco* and kill us all."

"Ernesto, be quiet," Jessica said, peering into the side-view mirror outside the passenger door. "Which one is he?"

"Black Chrysler SUV, three cars back," Matt said, slipping into the right lane and then back into the middle lane, in front of a furniture truck he hoped would block his next move until it was too late for Leslie to respond. "Get ready, everybody. I'm going to take the Zoo exit at Girard at the last possible second. And here we go!"

He cut off a tow truck as he accelerated across the right lane and onto the exit ramp, and then swore under his breath when Leslie was able to slide through traffic and follow. He was only two cars behind them now, and it looked as if everyone in Pennsylvania had decided today would be a great day to visit the zoo; there were cars and yellow buses everywhere. They'd soon be in a total gridlock.

"So much for bright ideas. Sweetheart, fish my cell phone out of my pocket, okay?"

"Got it," Jessica said, flipping it open. "Now what?"

"Hit 9-1-1, and hand me the phone."

As soon as the operator answered, Matt rattled off his name, rank and shield number, following it with the SUV's license number and requesting officer assistance. "I've got a minor in my vehicle with me. Four civilians, total, besides being completely jammed-up in traffic, so you guys have to handle it. No, I'm not one hundred percent positive he's the Schoolyard Flasher. But he damn well looks like our guy, fits the flyer we all got. Hey, we're at the zoo, and I'm off duty. The area is freaking crawling with kids. You want to wait around? Or do you want to grab this guy, ask why he's going to the zoo alone, ask him if he's going to go see the monkeys or if he's planning to spank his own in front of a bunch of little kids? That's what I thought. Yeah, I'll try to stay on the line. Signal's not too good here, though, so you might lose me."

He flipped the phone shut and turned to look at Court. "We've got three black-and-whites within two minutes of here. Doors locked?"

"That was brilliant, Lieutenant. You're a very good liar, and the monkey-spanking line was absolutely inspired. Do you really think he'll get out of his car and come after us?" Jessica asked. "Right out here in the open?"

"No, I doubt it," Matt said, checking his side-view mirror. "He'd wait until we're out of this traffic. But he's not going away, that's for sure. That is one pissed-off mountain of muscles back there. Nice to see employee loyalty, I guess."

"Well, we are stopped dead, Matthew," Jessica said unnecessarily. "You could just get out of the car, go back there and ask him what he wants. You do have a gun."

"And if I have to shoot him, I'll have a whole shitload of paperwork I don't want to do. Sorry, I should watch my language. And have you happened to notice, Jess, the cars all around us? The kids in the cars all around us?"

"Oh. Right. I'm sorry. I guess I got sort of carried away. How *dare* he chase us like this? How dare he follow us in the first place?" She swiveled in her seat to look back at Jade and Court. "You know what this means, everybody? That Leslie was sent to follow us, watch what we're doing? It means we're getting really, really close. Why, I'll bet it was Leslie who made that phone call to the house this morning. Sure, it was. It has to have been him. Why, that—"

"Ernesto in the backseat," Matt whispered, putting his hand on her thigh. He could have clapped it over her mouth, but they weren't alone in the car.

"That's okay, *amigo,*" Ernesto said happily enough. "Ernesto in the backseat has already figured out we're in some deep sh—stuff. Hey, look, here come the good guys!"

Matt watched as a pair of squad cars advanced from the direction of the zoo, the traffic in that direction very light. They mounted the curb to park on the grass, and got out, four uniformed officers in total, and approached the black SUV from both sides, their hands on their holsters as they ordered Leslie out of his vehicle.

"Philadelphia's finest in action," Matt said, not without pride as the traffic began to move again and he spied a side road that led away from the zoo. "A real thing of beauty. Too bad we're going to have to miss it."

He pulled up and over the curb, then onto the side road. "Time to go home."

"What's going to happen to you when they figure out that Leslie isn't their guy?"

"Hey, anybody can make an honest mistake," Matt said, knowing he'd pay for this one, big time, at some point. "And I don't think Leslie will be advertising that he works for the Brainards. I'll be fine—as long as we crack the case."

"Which case?" Jessica asked him, laying her hand on his knee.

"Pick one. Any one at all. And soon…"

BY THE TIME they'd driven back to Sam's house they'd heard the story of Clifford Brainard's collapse three times.

Joshua Brainard had spoken at some outdoor youth rally, delivering his regular stump speech, and then had tried to leave the podium without taking any questions from the press. Audio from the rally, played on the various radio stations Jessica had tuned to as Matt wove their way back to Sam's house, picked up the shouted questions about Melodie Brainard, about the possibility that the Fishtown Strangler was back again, about "this cop who took the fall for your wife's murder. You still believe that, Mr. Brainard?"

Joshua Brainard had begun to answer one of the

questions, saying that he had full faith in the Philadelphia Police Department, when suddenly a woman's scream cut through the air. Joshua Brainard had yelled, "Dad! Oh, no—Dad!"

The fourth time they'd listened to the audio, it accompanied a video feed and they were all sitting around the kitchen island, watching Mrs. Archer's flat screen.

"That's a good eight-point bump in the polls right there, in that one soundbite," Jessica said, her chin in her hand. "*Oh, no—Dad.* First his wife, and now his father. The guy's a shoo-in this November unless we stop him."

"Being around the news the way you are has made you cynical, Jessica Marie," Jade said, sighing.

"Oh, I haven't even started being cynical, Jade. How about this one? What are the odds Daddy Clifford is released from the hospital before dinner tonight?"

Matt put down his longneck beer. "You think that collapse just as the reporters were zeroing in on Joshua was a little too convenient?"

"Don't you?"

"Yes, but I wasn't going to say it. And here I was worried you girls would be kicking yourselves for beating up on a frail old man, maybe causing a stroke, even his death."

"Nope, not happening," Jessica said brightly. "Because I'm not buying it, Matt, and I'm glad you aren't, either. That collapse was like something out of a bad soap opera."

"You're a ghoul, Jessica," Jade said. "But I think you might be right. That faint, or whatever it was, certainly couldn't have come at a better time."

"Backing up your theory that whatever Joshua Brainard knows, Clifford Brainard knows. That he's been covering up for his fair-haired boy for as far back as Tarin White, probably for all of Joshua's life."

"Right," Jessica said. "Kind of like those stories that one of Queen Victoria's sons was Jack the Ripper. Joshua's an only child, only son, the hope of his proud papa, the heir to the throne, the old guy's legacy, the reason he worked so hard his whole life—all that horse hockey. Of course he'd protect his little sonny boy, no matter what it took. We've got him!"

Matt took another swig from the beer bottle, knowing he was about to send another downpour heading toward Jessica's parade. "No, we don't. We've got a scenario. More than one scenario. First, that Tarin White and Joshua Brainard were lovers, and Teddy made the connection and asked Melodie Brainard about it—leading to her murder and his apparent suicide."

"Because Melodie wasn't as sophisticated about their marriage as Joshua puts on, and she called Joshua on it. He slapped her around, and she threatened to go to the press. She told Loretta, remember—

she wasn't going to take it anymore. The operative *it* factor, in this case, being either the little dollies on the side or the slapping around—or both. Ergo, she had to be silenced, and the next thing you know, she's dead—even dead in a way that gives Joshua a bump in the polls. I like that scenario," Jessica said with some satisfaction.

"Good for you," Matt said, feeling suddenly weary. "We've also got the idea that Joshua Brainard killed Tarin White all those years ago, for whatever reason, and made it look like the work of the Fishtown Strangler. We've even got the scenario that his dad helped him by joining the Citizens Task Force and feeding his son the killer's MO, so that he could copy it—and then make sure no suspicion ever came near his son."

"We still have to check on those dates," Jade interrupted. "Which came first—the chicken or the egg? The task force, or Tarin's murder?"

Court put a fresh bottle of beer in front of Matt. "Let's not forget the idea that Joshua Brainard actually is the Fishtown Strangler and killed *all* of those women, either to mask his murder of Tarin White, or because he's one very sick bastard. That was one of the theories, wasn't it? The Joshua the Ripper theory, as I remember it?"

Matt's smile was crooked and rather resigned. "Yup, I remember that one. Theory number twenty-two or something like that. Now comes the sticky part—prove it. Prove any single one of those theories."

Jessica stuck out her chin, looking mulish. "Oh, no, you don't, Matt. Not again. I've decided that we don't have to prove it. I play hunches, unwind scenarios and wait for Joshua Brainard to trip himself up. As long as it doesn't take too long, that is—which is why we're going to help him along with that."

"Planted newspaper stories are one thing, sweetheart. But you can't take hunches to court," Matt reminded her, feeling pretty sure this was ground they'd covered before and would probably have to cover again.

"Fight nice, kiddies," Jade said, pushing off the stool. "I'm going to go play around on the Internet for a while to see if I can find anything else on the Citizens Task Force. Jessica? What are we going to do for dinner tonight? Mrs. Archer has the weekend off."

"I already checked out the fridge and freezer. I was thinking about some balsamic chicken, some penne pasta with chunky marinara sauce, and fresh sautéed spinach with garlic. Sound good?"

"You had me right up to the spinach part," Matt admitted, picking up his beer bottle in preparation for going outside to call in to the precinct to ask if his suspect had panned out. If you're going to play the game, you've got to play it all the way through to the end.

"Are you going down to the gatehouse to talk to the Bear Man?" Court asked, following him out of the kitchen.

"No, but that's a good idea. Give him a description of Leslie's SUV and tell him to keep an eye out for it. How are you doing, Court?"

"Hanging in. As a visitor to your fair city, may I say you certainly know how to show a tourist an interesting afternoon," Court told him, smiling. "How are you doing?"

"I think I passed crazy and am edging up on complete lunacy. I could have brushed away all those damn scenarios they were spouting back there, up until the moment I saw Leslie barreling across the parking lot at me with murder in his eyes. That was a mistake on their part, putting a tail on us. A big mistake, right up there with that one last bank robbery that always gets you caught, even if Leslie was supposed to stay out of sight, and would have, if he hadn't heard the news flash about the old man. The damn thing is that I should go back to work by the middle of next week, if only to see if I still have a job. We've got to get this wrapped up, Court. Soon."

"And you think we can do that?"

"I think," Matt said, sliding out of his jacket to expose the shoulder harness and his service revolver, "either we do, or those two in the kitchen are going to do it for us. And, Court, I wouldn't be honest if I didn't tell you that that scenario scares the living hell out of me."

CHAPTER FIFTEEN

"I TOLD YOU that you'd like it if you'd just try it," Jessica said triumphantly as she hopped up onto the side of the bed in Matt's room and watched him unstrap his weapon's holster.

He shot her a dirty look. "I ate it. I didn't say I liked it."

Jessica grinned. "Really? Then why did you eat it, Matthew? Once you're a grown-up, you don't have to eat all your veggies if you don't want to. It's a perk grown-ups get to keep us from remembering we're closer to the grave. Ergo, you liked the spinach."

"It wasn't all that bad," Matt mumbled as he pulled his T-shirt free of his waistband. "I'm going to take a shower. Go away."

Jessica stayed where she was. "Do you really want to go back downstairs and talk about the cases again tonight? Personally, I think we need a break."

"We *do* need a break, sweetheart, which is why we have to keep talking," Matt said, and Jessica made a face at him. He grinned at her. "Not what you meant, huh?"

"Not even close." Jessica sighed and slid down off the high mattress. "Okay, I'll go away. You go soak your head."

"I'm not going to go— When you're good, Jessica, you're good. And when you're bad, you're… impossible."

She dropped into a curtsy, holding out an imaginary ball gown. "Thank you, kind sir. I do try. Did you feed Mortimer tonight?"

"Damn," Matt said, hesitating as he headed toward the ensuite bathroom. "First Ernesto and now the fish. Next time I get a pet rock—and then I'll probably forget where I put it."

"And you won't be able to call its name or whistle it to heel," Jessica said as she opened the can of fish flakes and sprinkled a pinch over Mortimer's bowl. She could feel Matt's gaze on her and turned to smile at him. "I thought you said you were going to take a shower."

"I liked the spinach," he said quietly. "Actually, it was pretty terrific."

"And?" she pushed him, suppressing her delight at how angry he sounded to have to admit such a thing. He was going to thank her now, she was sure of it. Victory, it certainly was sweet. "Matt? Don't you have something else to say to me?"

"Sure. I'll tell you something else. I liked the damn spinach, okay? And if you must know, that really pisses me off," he shot back at her, and then disappeared into the bathroom, leaving her to stare, openmouthed, at the closed door.

"Oh, your daddy's definitely going to have to pay for that one," Jessica muttered to Mortimer, who continued to swim in circles in his bowl, his little fishy mind cleared of its memory every two seconds, so that he was constantly charting new territory.

Jessica looked at the door to the hallway. She lifted one eyebrow assessingly. Came to a decision. Crossed the room to turn the lock on the door. Turned once more, to stare at the closed door to the bathroom.

She listened to the sound of the shower. Sam's many bathrooms and their very unique tubs and showers had fascinated her, and she'd taken the time to look at them all. If she remembered correctly—and she knew she did—just walking into Matt's shower was like embarking on an adventure.

There was actually a travertine tile corridor leading into the shower, a six- or eight-foot-long hallway that then turned, went another three feet or so and turned again into the actual shower. No glass doors, no shower curtain; none were needed. It was like walking into the huge shower room in high school, except that it was beautiful and deliciously private. A…a grotto of earthly delights.

It also, she remembered, beginning to tingle in a few delicious places, had not only a huge rain showerhead, but also pulsing jets on the sidewalls, maybe six of them, as well as a handheld showerhead; all that could be adjusted as to the strength of flow and the tempo of the pulsing, all that could be aimed to hit at a person's legs, belly and chest, back and shoulders.

Or anywhere else interesting a person could think of.

Yes, the shower Matt was probably standing in now, unimaginatively doing nothing more than soaping up before rinsing down again, was actually a whole new world of opportunity for someone with an imagination. It was the kind of shower an advertiser would call more than a shower, more of an experience.

Jessica decided she probably was up to a few new experiences.

She lifted her chin.

She smiled.

And then she started across the room, already unbuttoning her blouse.

She kicked away her underpants as she entered the subtly lit tiled corridor, the sound of Matt's voice drawing her along. She had to bite her bottom lip to keep from giggling as she realized that he was actually singing a Pink song—one with more than one naughty word in it, too. And he tried to tell her he was too old for her? Ha!

Turning the final corner, she saw him standing with his back to her, massaging shampoo into his scalp.

So cute.

And such a great ass.

She padded up to him as he had his hands raised, pressing herself against his sleek wet back as she reached around him and, she thought, grinning, literally caught him by surprise.

"Hi, sailor."

"What the—? Jess! Damn it, now I've got soap in my—damn it!"

He stepped forward, Jessica stepping with him into the dizzying torrents of warm water coming at them from the rain shower, from the jets. He raised his face to rinse the soap from his hair and eyes even as he grabbed at her hands and tried to push her away.

Or at least that was what she thought he was going to do.

Instead, he covered her right hand with his own as he took hold of her left hand, bringing it between them.

She watched, blinking, fascinated, as he slid both their hands down her water-slick belly even as she felt his physical response, quick and hard.

"You started this," he said, his hand sliding lower, finding her, cupping her intimately. Her knees buckled slightly as he slowly turned to face her. "Steady. You don't want to lose your balance."

"So much…so much for me being the…*ahh, yes*…the aggressor…"

JESSICA WAS BENT almost in half in front of the bathroom vanity as she operated the hair dryer while scrubbing at her wet hair.

"Here, let me do that," Matt said as he took the hair dryer from her even while knowing such a personal service was as alien to him as making love in a state-of-the-art shower had been to him an hour earlier.

She dropped her hands onto her thighs and let him work.

Her hair was like silk between his fingers. Shiny, lightly golden, increasingly thick and warm as the dryer did its work.

He felt so good. Their casual intimacy in such a mundane setting, after the highly erotic passion they'd brought to each other, was so damn easy…so damn *domestic*.

Cripes. What in *hell* did he think he was he doing?

"Okay, thank you, that should be good enough," Jessica said, straightening as she took the dryer from him, now directing the flow at the top and sides of her hair as she smoothed it back away from her face. "Don't worry, it only looks like a fright wig until I've combed through it. That's the beauty of a good haircut—it all goes where it's supposed to go. See? Matt? What's wrong?"

He shook his head. "Nothing," he said, still staring at her. "Jess?"

She turned off the hair dryer, took a few swipes at

her hair with a wide-toothed comb and smiled at him, her makeup-free face young, a squeaky-clean shine on her cheeks and the tip of her nose. God. She was the most beautiful woman in the world.

"Matt?" she prompted, her expression concerned. "You wanted to say something?"

He took her hand and led her back into the bedroom. He turned her to face him, put his hands on her shoulders. "What are we doing here, Jess?" he asked her. "Not the cases. You and me. What are we doing here?"

She lowered her eyelids and then looked up at him again. "I was hoping *you* knew," she said before wincing at her attempt to lighten the suddenly tense mood. She stepped into his arms, sliding her hands around his waist, resting her cheek against his chest. Reflexively, he slid his arms fully around her. "Yes, like that. I don't know what we're doing, Matt. I just know that I like it here, with your arms around me."

Matt rested his chin on the top of her fragrant hair. "Yeah. That probably sums it up for me, too. I like having you here, with my arms around you. Do you mind if I tell you that it also scares the living hell out of me?"

He felt her shoulders move as she laughed softly. "Oh, good, I'm not alone. I'm also afraid that the way you feel is scaring the living hell out of you."

"You're impossible," he said, gently pushing her away as he smiled down at her upturned face.

"That's what they all tell me. But seriously, Matt, I do think we're…that we're going somewhere. Or that we could, if we both wanted to. And, hey, lucky for me. I already know that I…that I want to."

Matt felt a slight uptick in the terror factor, that old fight-or-flight juice kicking in.

And Jessica saw it in his eyes, damn it.

"Never mind," she said, her grin widening as she disengaged herself and stepped away from him completely. "Come on, let's go downstairs and talk the cases to death again, because that's what we have to do. Jade and Court are probably wondering where we are. Ernesto, not so much."

He grabbed at her wrist. "Jessica, wait. There's something I want you to understand. It's…it's been a lot of years since I've felt like this."

"Since Mary," Jessica said, nodding her head.

"Yes, all right, since Mary," Matt conceded. "I'm…I'm having some trouble getting used to the idea of having anyone care about me…about what it means for me to care about somebody else as much as I care about…"

"Me. You care about me," Jessica said. "Go on, Matt, say it. It won't hurt to say it. Honest."

"All right, I'll *say* it." Damn, the words had all but exploded from his mouth, as if he was angry, and maybe he was. He didn't know what he was feeling. "I care about you, Jess. You drive me crazy, your logic is somewhere out in left field half the time, I don't always agree with what you do for a living. I get so mad at you—and I have trouble remembering why I thought my life was exactly the way I wanted it to be before you slammed into it."

"And liking the spinach—that pisses you off?"

Matt rubbed hard at the back of his neck. "Yeah. Okay. Yeah. It pisses me off. I'm not right for you, Jess. I'm too old and set in my ways, I've lived alone for too long…"

She reached out, took his hand. "Let's go downstairs. I think there's still some brownies left in the kitchen."

Would she ever stop surprising him? "That's it? We're done talking?"

Jessica went up on tiptoe and kissed his cheek. "I can't talk you into or out of whatever you're thinking or feeling, Matt. You have to do that by yourself. You can't help it that I've fallen in love with you. It's not your fault."

Did she just say that she was in love with him? Matt opened his mouth to say something, what, he didn't know, when the cell phone in his pocket began to ring. "Damn."

"Answer it, Matt," Jessica said, noticing that she'd buttoned her blouse incorrectly and beginning to unbutton it to fix it. "It might be something about Leslie. Maybe he's going to confess to being the Schoolyard Flasher and make our lives easier?"

"Like that's going to happen. I'm not that lucky," Matt said, flipping open the phone. "Denby here."

He listened for a few moments before interrupting the caller to say, "Hold on a sec, Billy-boy, you kind of took me off guard here. Let me get my notebook so I can write this down." He grinned at Jessica, planting a quick, hard kiss on her mouth before pulling her close so that they could both listen. "You can go ahead now, Bill. Give it to me again from the top…"

"I STILL DON'T believe this is happening," Jessica said as they passed the guardhouse and entered the grounds of the Graterford Correctional Institution, which also happened to be Pennsylvania's largest maximum-security prison. "Worse, I'm still trying to figure out if this is a good thing or a bad thing. You know, in how it relates to the different scenarios we've been hashing over about Joshua Brainard. What do you think, Matt?"

"I think we were all up until after two last night, that I had to be at the station at six to fight through all the necessary paperwork, that we've been on the road twice as long as we should have been thanks to those stupid online directions that got us here by way of China, the whole time surrounded by idiots who got their drivers' licenses out of the same damn vending machine. And all for what could prove to be nothing but some con trying to jack us off. Oh, yeah, and I think that if I find out that the guy is lying, I may just have to rip out his throat. Good enough for you?"

"You're not really much of a morning person, are you," Jessica said, grinning. She held up the thermos she'd filled before they left on the thirty-mile trip. "One more cup of coffee?"

"One more cup of coffee, and I could have *flown* here with you strapped to my back," Matt said as he parked the Jeep in the area designated for authorized visitors. "Now remember, Jess, I had to pull every favor anyone ever owed me to get you permission to be here like the bastard demanded, so behave. I repeat. Be. Have."

"Got it," Jessica said, her heart pounding as she unbuckled her seat belt and followed Matt into an ugly stone building that probably hadn't been renovated since it was built in 1929—she'd Googled the prison on Jade's laptop at the same time she'd checked for driving directions. Wikipedia proved helpful on the basic facts, but did not, however, mention the smell, which wasn't good.

She handed over her photo ID and watched as Matt passed his service revolver and shoulder holster to the guard, who locked both in a metal box.

"Everything all set?" Matt asked another guard who was currently propping up the wall near a large metal door, the man's name tag printed with *Infirmary*.

"Just the way you wanted it, Lieutenant, yeah. Except that the prisoner says he's changed his mind and doesn't want to talk to you now," the guard told them as they followed him through a series of locked doors and sliding bars that made Jessica feel smaller, less confident and almost guilty (of something— everybody's guilty of *something*). "But we figured you've come all this way, so you might as well give it your best shot. Not a regular interrogation room, not in the Infirmary wing, but we make do. He's behind Plexiglas."

"Why?" Matt asked, looking to Jessica. "He's that dangerous?"

"You could say that. He spits. He's got full-blown AIDS and figures himself a lethal weapon. Mostly he's just a pain in the ass—sorry, ma'am."

Jessica's eyes widened, and her heartbeat went into overdrive. She slipped her hand into Matt's as one more door opened, and without warning, they walked into a room to see a man in a white jumpsuit with Prison Hospital stenciled on it, and wrist and ankle chains that were bolted to a large iron ring in the floor. He was sitting behind a glass partition that had been set up on the top of a heavy oak table.

The Plexiglas was like the sneeze shield at a salad buffet—except that it wasn't.

"Oh, God…not like the movies, is it?" she whispered as she looked at the man. He was about fifty, maybe eighty. He was so thin she was surprised the manacles didn't slide off his hands. His skin was deathly white and he had ugly open sores on his bald head. He had a smile like a shark, except that a shark had better teeth.

"You can wait outside," Matt told the guard.

"I could, but I'm not supposed to," the guard answered. "Knock if you need me. I'll be right on the other side of the door." He raised his voice. "Herman? Herman, you behave yourself now, you hear me? Tapioca pudding tonight, your favorite, and you don't get any if you don't play nice, understand?" Then he winked at Jessica. "Got to hit them where they live, you know? With Herman, that's dessert. Okay, Lieutenant, he's all yours. Good luck."

"Thanks. Jess? You don't have to sit down. You can stay back here."

Jessica looked at the pair of folding chairs on their side of the table. "No. I'm okay. Let's just do this."

"Hello, pretty girl, ain't you a sight for sore eyes," Herman Longstreet crooned as Jessica sat down, glad she'd decided to wear slacks and not a skirt. Even so, she felt as if Herman's gaze was passing right through her clothing. "And it ain't even m'birthday."

Matt flashed his shield as he introduced himself. "You wanted to talk."

"Don't anymore," Herman said, still leering at Jessica. "But you can stay, sweetheart. I can show you a real good time."

Matt slid back his chair and got to his feet. "Okay, that's it, we're out of here. Herman, I heard you're dying. We sure don't want to waste any more of your valuable time."

"Oh, sit down," Herman said, slicing a look at Matt with his unnaturally light gray eyes, red-rimmed and bloodshot, before shifting his gaze to Jessica yet again. "You're one of 'em, right? The Sunshine sisters? I don't get out much. You the movie star?"

Jessica shook her head. "No, that's Jolie. I'm Jessica, the one you asked for. The one with the cable show."

"Just checking. I think I seen one of your sister's flicks. Too skinny for me. You're more my type. I seen you a time or two on the TV. Guys in here jerk off to gals like you all the time. Think about that next time you smile at the camera, huh? Like you're performing a real public service, you know?"

Jessica was pretty sure Matt growled, but she ignored him. "And you heard about my sisters and me because of the Fishtown Strangler case being in the news again, right? You asked for us to come here because of the Fishtown Strangler case. Because you know something about it."

Herman leaned back in his chair as far as his chains would allow. "Not so fast. There's no rush. Can't we just…*chat* a bit? And you could, you know, maybe open a couple of buttons for me while we're talking, hmm? Been a damn long time since I've seen a good set of—"

"Shut it, Longstreet."

"No," Jessica said, swallowing hard. "No, it's all right, Matt. But fair's fair, Mr. Longstreet. I give you something, you give us something." She raised her hands to the top button of her blouse. She normally wore this blouse with the collar open, but today she'd felt the need to cover up. "Do we have a deal?"

Herman grinned at Matt. "Dumb bitch bought it. Yeah, like I could get it up anymore, even if I wanted to. You guys want what I know real bad, don't you? But I told you—I changed my mind. Ain't nothin' in it for me, you know? Nothin' you can give me. You can't get me outta here, and you can't get me outta dying."

Jessica felt her cheeks flush hot with shame. She had actually been willing to open her blouse for this monster. Where was her brain? No wonder Matt got so mad at her.

"I can give you chocolate-chip cookies," she heard herself say, remembering what the guard had told them, and desperate enough to give anything a shot. "Homemade, with extra chips. How about brownies?

You like them with nuts or without, Mr. Longstreet? And prison tapioca? Do they give you maple-nut syrup to drizzle on it? Maybe warmed honey? I'll bet they don't. I bet they don't even use real tapioca."

She had his full attention now. "You can't do that," he said, but some of the glee had left his voice.

"Sure, she can," Matt said. "She's a hell of a cook, Herman. She can make spinach taste good. And I can arrange to get the food to you."

"Caramel-fudge-ripple cake," Jessica said, licking her lips. "Three layers—it's my specialty. Apple tarts. *Fudge.* Once a week for as long as…for the rest of your life, I promise. Pinky-swear, Mr. Longstreet. Just tell us what you called us here to tell us."

Herman began blinking furiously. "For the rest of my life. Right. All three or four weeks of it, if I'm lucky. You know how long I've been in here?"

"Twelve years, five months, two days," Matt said, pulling an envelope from his inside jacket pocket. "These last six months in the prison infirmary, circling the porcelain bowl. You're going to die in here, Herman. You're going to be buried in here in a pine box. Herman Longstreet, petty thief and three-time loser. Nobody's going to remember you were ever alive, are they? Nobody can change that. Except you. Right, Herman?"

"I don't like you," Herman said, glaring at Matt.

"Ah, Herman, now you hurt my feelings." Matt

pulled a tape recorder from his pocket, spoke the day, place, time and who was present into it, and then set it down on the table. "I'm going to read your rights now, Herman." He pointed to a camera mounted at the ceiling in a corner of the room. "It's showtime, Herman. Smile pretty for the videotape."

The convict looked at Jessica again, his eyes narrowed. "Caramel-fudge ripple?"

Jessica, mindful now of the tape recorder and camera, just nodded, hoping nobody would ever see that she had volunteered to open a few buttons for this monster. Matt could have warned her that everything that happened in this room would be taped. Hell, she should have figured that out for herself!

After Matt had read the man his rights and Herman had waived them, Matt said, "You say you want to confess, Mr. Longstreet. Here's your chance. Say the right words, and everybody remembers your name."

Herman nodded. "I know. Blondie here can do a show on me. The newspapers will be all over it, just like they were back then, when it was happening. I'd be a part of history. That's what I figured when I saw that crap about the Fishtown Strangler being back, killing that guy's wife." He tried to lift his bound hands, to point a thumb at his chest. "That was *me*. Nobody else. *Me*. And I got away with it. Petty thief, your lily-white ass, pig. Those are *my* kills, damn it. People should *know*. A man should be *remembered*."

For a moment Jessica feared she might throw up. They'd wanted answers, and Herman Longstreet was about to give them answers. She looked to Matt, whose expression hadn't changed. He opened the envelope, reached inside and then, one by one, dealt out six photographs. Autopsy photos of the six victims.

"Tell me about these women, Herman," Matt said, touching the photographs, aligning them on the tabletop. "And you're speaking now of your own free will. You asked us to come here to hear your confession, and when we're done here, you'll also sign a printout of our conversation. You have not been coerced, correct? Say it, Herman, or the party stops now. Are you making these statements of your own free will?"

"Yeah, yeah, my idea. All of it." Herman leaned forward, grinning at the photographs. "That them? Hard to tell, you know? All of them whores look just like the other one, once their faces are turning purple and their eyes are popping out."

Jessica put a hand to her mouth, had to look away from the table.

Matt shoved the photos together. "Just what I thought. Dying man wants to pull the cop's chain one more time. You saw the story and figured you could use it to get yourself a little attention. You're not the Fishtown Strangler. You no more killed these women than I did."

"No! They're mine! I did it! Put those pictures back. Yeah, like that, spread 'em out. Oh, yeah, I do love the dark meat. Okay, her," he said, motioning with his chin, "that second one. She was the first. I didn't mean it, didn't plan it or nothin', you know? She said something…laughed at me, called me Limp Dick. *Bitch!* I paid good money for her. She had no call to call me names. So I showed her. I showed her good."

Matt said, "Let the record show that Mr. Longstreet has just indicated one Yasmin Overlook, first victim of the Fishtown Strangler. Go on, Herman."

Herman raised his head to smile at Jessica. "Killing. Watching the light go out in their eyes. God, it was good! The first one's always the best, you know? The next one, not so good as the first. But practice makes perfect, right?"

"Okay, that's enough reminiscing. Who was next?" Matt asked him, drawing Herman's attention back to the photo array.

Again Herman pointed with his chin. "That one. Buckteeth, I called her. She was the second. And then that last one on the left. She was no good, didn't even fight worth a damn. Just kept crying and begging me. Better when they fight, you know? More fun for me. That one, third from the right?"

"Kayla Morrison," Jessica whispered before Matt,

for the record, recited the names of the victims Herman had identified.

"Yeah? That her name? Nice name for a hooker. She was my last. Next damn day I got picked up for breaking my parole and got sent here."

He looked at Matt. "Which one was it? Which one of these whores gave me AIDS? Which one of them bitches killed me?"

Matt shook his head. "None of them, Herman. None of them was HIV-positive or had AIDS. We know where you got it—you got it right here. You really have to be more careful when you're bending over in the shower, Herman. Or maybe you really loved the guy."

At last Herman Longstreet looked like the dying man he was. "No…no. You're wrong. It had to be one of them. I'm no queer. I'm a killer, sure, I'm telling you that. Clearing my conscience and all that shit. But I ain't no queer."

"That's not what your former cell mate said. Before he died, that is. He gave the doctors here a list of all his jailhouse lovers. From what I remember, you were number three on his list. His long list. And you did it for cigarettes. We already know all that. It's true, Herman, cigarettes kill. One way or another."

Jessica didn't know where to look, what to do. How did Matt do this every day? It was all too real for her. But she couldn't resist asking the convict a question. "Mr. Longstreet? You didn't tell us about the other two victims."

Herman shook his head, a totally defeated man. "Only one more. Not two. Only one more. I...I want to go back to my cell."

Matt and Jessica exchanged quick looks. He removed four of the photographs, leaving only two.

"Herman. Herman! Have your pity party later. We're not finished here. Pay attention. I've got two more photographs here, both of them your work."

Sighing, Herman leaned forward once more. "I told you, man, only one more. That one, on the left. Picked her up near the river. Played with her for a long time and then dumped her behind some bar. They all look pretty much the same, like I said. Except for the buckteeth and maybe the eyes. But not that one. She's real pretty, even laid out like that. Young. I *paid* those whores. I couldn't have afforded a pretty one. I don't know nothin' about that one. She ain't one of mine. You just put her in the pile to trip me up, but it ain't happening. She's not mine."

"Let the record show that the prisoner has identified Tarin White," Matt said as he picked up the first autopsy photo and showed it to Jessica. Joshua Brainard had been returned to the top of the class in Suspects 101.

She got to her feet. "I need to leave here. Right now," she told Matt, longing to get outside, breath air that hadn't been polluted by Herman Longstreet's casual evil. She wanted to call Jade and Jolie, tell them what she'd learned. More than anything in this world, she wanted a shower. A long, hot, cleansing shower…

"Someone will be in touch real soon, Herman, so you can sign your statement," Matt said, sliding the envelope back into his jacket pocket after recording the other victim's name for the record and signaling the end of the interview. "Unless you die first, which wouldn't bother me too much."

"Yeah…right. Okay. Hey! About the cookies? I like white chocolate chips."

"Don't hold your breath," Jessica said, tight-lipped.

"Fuck that! You said you'd send me all that stuff. You promised. You know what you are, bitch? You're nothin' but a damn *liar!*"

Jessica hesitated in the doorway as the guard held the door open for her and Matt. "And you're nothing but a damn *murderer*. I wouldn't throw you a marshmallow if you were standing in the middle of a burning room. Which you will be, the minute you get to hell."

The guard threw back his head and laughed, even as two more guards entered the room to take Herman Longstreet back to the prison infirmary. He handed Matt a boxed videotape. "Here's Herman's screen test, Lieutenant. You can sign it out up front, at the desk."

"Thanks. Now let's get the lady out of here, okay?" Matt slipped his arm around Jessica's shoulders as they followed the guard back through the maze of locked doors and rolling metal gates. "How are you doing, kiddo?"

"Not too good," she admitted. "It's hard to believe Herman Longstreet is actually human, isn't it?"

"Jess, he left *human* behind a long time ago. I'm just sorry you had to see that, and if he hadn't demanded you show up as a prerequisite for him to talk, you wouldn't have been here. Now all I want to do is get you out of here. Just let me pick up my weapon."

Jessica stood to one side in the small office, her arms wrapped about herself, as Matt walked up to the window, where an overweight gray-haired man in a rumpled brown suit was signing his name on a form. Two younger men, both carrying heavy briefcases, waited nearby, clearly junior associates of the man at the counter.

The man turned around and smiled when he saw Matt. "Hey, the people you meet at this resort, huh?" he said, putting out his hand. "How's it going, Matt?" He looked past him, to see Jessica. "You *are* going to introduce us, aren't you?"

Without waiting for Matt's answer, the man crossed the short distance, his right hand out, so that Jessica automatically took it in hers. "Jessica Sunshine, right? My wife and I watch you every Sunday night. Well, unless the ball game runs late. I'm Jeff Walingford, by the way, Chief Deputy Assistant DA."

"How very nice to meet you, Mr. Walingford," Jessica said as Matt joined them, still strapping on his shoulder holster.

"What are you doing out here, Matt?" the assistant DA asked as a guard and his minions waited for him. "We're here to go a few rounds with a slimy defense attorney who wants to cut a deal for one of his clients. Real bottom-feeders, defense lawyers. Which reminds me—how are you doing with those classes?"

Matt shot Jessica a quick look. "Uh, fine. Fine. I'm all done, actually. All that's ahead of me now is the bar exam, which is the end of next month."

"You'll have no problem with that," Walingford said, patting Matt on the back. "Come see me once you're official, all right?"

"Well, sir, I would, but I'm afraid I plan to go over to the dark side, with the rest of the bottom-feeders."

"A *defense* lawyer? You're kidding! Matt, son, where did we go wrong?"

Matt grinned. "Oh, it isn't you, sir. I'm probably just flawed."

"Well, it is where the money is, isn't it? All right then. Good luck. Ms. Sunshine? A pleasure to meet you."

Jessica only nodded, incapable of saying anything else. She did, however, recover her voice by the time they were outside the prison gates and on their way back to Philadelphia. "Telling me I can't take hunches to court. All that business about rules of evidence, needing probable cause, no taping someone without their knowledge. All of it. You were talking like a lawyer, not a cop. All my fears that what we were doing could cost you your job. All those big thick books piled in the back of your Jeep. When were you going to tell me, Matt? Were you *ever* going to tell me?"

"I'm sorry, Jess."

"You're sorry," she parroted. "Well, good for you. And when I was all worried that you'd end up like Teddy, old before your time, burned out? Alone and still living in some rattrap? You could have told me then."

"I can't argue with that. You're absolutely right. I should have told you then."

"Damn straight you should have told me then! We were going to bed with each other!"

And then she stopped.

They were going to bed together. Big deal. People went to bed with each other all the time. She was the one who wanted more.

"Jessica, I said I was sorry. I should have told you. I definitely should have told you. I've been going to school at night for a long time. Yes, I'm about to sit for the bar exam. Yes, I'm going to be a defense attorney. At damn near forty, I'm about to start over, start from scratch. It's what I want, what I've wanted for a long time, but it's not going to be easy. I'm going to really have to tighten my belt until the cases start coming in. This is no time for me to get involved with… Damn it, this isn't coming out right."

"Right man at the wrong time," Jessica whispered, knitting her fingers together in her lap. A lawyer. The reason he'd gone to college in the first place, most probably. Until Mary had died, and he'd switched to the Police Academy.

Matt was merging the Jeep with the traffic. "What did you say?"

"Nothing," she said, pasting a smile on her face. "I'm sorry, Matt. You don't owe me anything. No reasons, no explanations. So, you're going to be a lawyer soon. That's really exciting. And it couldn't have been easy, working all day, going to school at night. Weekends, too, probably? They do that now, have weekend classes. I'm…I'm very proud of you."

"Jess…"

She put a hand to her mouth, pretending to yawn even as she prayed he'd take the hint. "Boy, I think our late night is catching up to me, big time, and we still have to play Twenty Questions with Jade and Court, and then I'm guessing you have to go back to the station house with what you've got, and then wade through a bunch of that paperwork you hate, huh? Me? I have to run to the studio to see what the heck I'm going to be covering on Sunday night's show. Kevin's been covering for me, but I have to show my face at some point. Do you mind if I try to sleep until we're back at Sam's place?"

"No, you go ahead," Matt said, his fingers white-knuckled around the steering wheel. "It shouldn't take more than an hour to get back. I'll wake you when we get there."

CHAPTER SIXTEEN

IT WAS SUNDAY morning.

"He's *packing?* You're really going to let him go?"

Jessica dampened her fingertip on her tongue and used it to pick up a few sugar sprinkles that had fallen off her glazed doughnut, onto her knit top. Then she sucked on her finger. "Correction. He's *packed,* and already gone. It was my suggestion, Jade," she told her sister. "He needs some space."

"He needs a good hit upside his head! He's a grown man, for crying out loud. What's the matter with him?"

"Jade, don't," Court warned quietly before returning to his copy of the *New York Times*.

They were sitting in the living room of Sam Becket's mansion. They'd spent most of the previous day running scenarios yet again, trying to figure out exactly how deep the connection between Tarin White and Joshua Brainard had gone, and what else Teddy might have discovered that led to his murder. Matt had been at the station nearly nonstop, still ankle-deep in paperwork that would wrap up the

Fishtown Strangler case. His captain had bought him a case of beer. Imported beer.

There'd barely been time to celebrate the fact that, in just two weeks—mostly due to dumb luck, but that wasn't important—they'd managed to solve two of Teddy's cold cases, the Vanishing Bride and the Fishtown Strangler.

Teddy would have been so proud of them. For five minutes. Then he would have said, "So? What are you going to do now—sit here on your hands? Go get the rest of them!"

They'd at last agreed it was time to back off for a few days, to recharge their own batteries and to wait until Clifford Brainard and his son returned from "a short vacation at their summer home in Colorado, where the elder Brainard will continue his recuperation after a medical scare this past week."

"How do you feel about this, Jess?" Jade asked, clearly not ready to abandon the conversation on Court's say-so. "Are you okay with it? Or is letting Matt leave, even pushing him out the door, part of some grand plan?"

"Jade! As if I'd do something like that," Jessica said, her eyes twinkling. "Me? Besides, remember that saying? If you love something—someone—let them go. If they come back, you're aces. And if they don't? Well, then it, him, whatever, was never yours in the first place. Something like that, anyway. So, hey, Matt—fly! Be free!"

Jade sat back against the pillows, sighing in relief. "Oh, good. You do have a plan."

Jessica got to her feet. "Of course I have a plan. The man loves me."

Court folded his newspaper and also got to his feet. "I don't think I want to hear this. We men like to hold tight to the illusion that we're the stronger sex. We already know we're not the smarter one."

After Court retreated to Sam's den, Jade smiled at Jessica. "Morgan Eastwood called this morning. Another, I believe, pretty strong-minded woman, which is why I'm thinking about her now. Court was in the shower, so I spoke to her—lovely accent."

"Jade. She's English. *We're* the ones with the accents."

"Okay, I guess you're right. Anyway, she's arranged to fly through Philly in the next couple of days, on her way back to England. It's only a two-hour layover, but she made it clear she expects Court to come to the airport to see her, and she also invited me. She won't rest until we agree go to Romney Marsh and join her in this treasure-hunt idea of hers."

"I'm with her. Let me know when to book my flight," Jessica said, thinking for a moment of the priceless uncut emerald the Becket pirates had called the Empress. "Matt's, too."

"Bringing us full circle," Jade pointed out happily. "Tell me what you're planning."

"Nope. I don't want to jinx it. Let me just say that Ernesto is helping me."

"Ernesto? He's still here? I thought he'd go with Matt, not that I mind. He's probably better off here until he leaves for Penn State on Tuesday."

"That's what Matt said. But Ernesto wants to go back to his mother's apartment to pack his books and the rest of his clothes. Naturally, I volunteered to drive him over there."

"Naturally. And the rest is what you're not going to tell me? Are you sure about this, Jessica? Maybe what you two do need is some space between you."

"You want Court to go back to Virginia?"

"We're not talking about Court and me."

"No, we certainly aren't. You and Court are tops on the Don't Ask, Don't Tell charts, as always. Please tell me you both see it—that you're still in love with each other."

"Oh, we see it, Jess," Jade said, sighing. "We just don't know what to do about it. Maybe what we need is a *plan*."

Jessica grinned. "You can't use mine. You already have Rockne."

"Excuse me? *Rockne?*" Jade turned on the couch cushions as Jessica all but skipped out of the room to find Ernesto. "Jessica Marie, *what* are you talking about?"

"Later, sis," Jessica said, heading for the stairs. Then she stopped, snapped her fingers as she remembered something, and backtracked to the kitchen to hunt for some plastic wrap.

MATT STOOD in the middle of his living room, looking at it through Jessica's eyes. Cold, sterile. Dingy metal blinds on the windows, but no curtains. No carpets scattered on the wood floor, so that his footsteps echoed when he walked. No plants—not even fake ones—no pictures on the walls.

How long had he been living here? Two, three years? *Five?*

And so what? He slept here, that was about it. What with being on the job and his law classes, his internship six months ago that had cost him income for six months, he didn't have the time or the money to call in Martha Stewart.

He and Mary hadn't had much. Still, she'd managed to find a way to hang curtains and to save enough of their grocery money to buy that ivy plant she'd tried to train to grow in a wire circle stuck in the pot. She'd been crazy about that plant.

He'd forgotten to water it in the weeks after she died, and the damn thing had shriveled and gone all brown.

He wasn't real good with plants. Or fish. Or people.

Matt kicked his duffel bag to one side and walked over to his desk. He pulled out the chair and sat down. Took a deep breath and let it out slowly. Opened the bottom drawer and lifted out the wedding album.

He closed his eyes as he opened the cover, and then opened them again, to see that first photograph of the two of them smiling into the camera. Full of hopes and dreams and love for each other.

It had all been such a long time ago.

He turned the page.

Tracing a finger alongside a close-up of Mary's face, he thought for a moment that he could hear her clear joyful laugh again. The way she'd called him *Mattie*.

They'd been such kids.

What would she say if she could see him now? How and where he lived, what he'd done with his life, the hard solitary man he'd become?

Maybe…maybe…

Maybe it was at last time to turn another page. Time to turn to a new page.

Sliding the album back into the desk drawer, he retrieved his duffel bag and went to unpack and take a shower. Wearing another new pair of jeans and a dark blue T-shirt, he grabbed his keys and headed out to the local corner store to restock his refrigerator. An hour after that, he was sitting in front of the television set, a half-eaten baloney sandwich on the table beside him, catching the end of the Phillies' game, talking to the set when the third baseman blew a routine ground ball that cost the Phils a run…because there was nobody else to talk to.

Space. Jessica said she was giving him space. And he'd grabbed at the suggestion.

"You're out of your freaking mind, Denby," he said into the room, his voice echoing back at him. "You don't need space. You need *her*. So what in hell are you doing *here?*"

He was already halfway out of the chair when there was a knock on the door and he heard Jessica call out, "It's the police. Open up!"

"What the…?" Matt said, grinning as he went to the door and opened it, to see her standing there, Mortimer's plastic wrap–covered bowl in her hands.

"Hi. Don't be mad. I've always wanted to say that. You forgot poor old Mortimer again. I could be wrong, but I think the poor thing's developing a complex."

She pushed the bowl into his hands almost before he was ready to receive it, and then dug in the pocket of her slacks. "And here's his food. Here—take it."

God, she was infuriating. God, how he loved her. "Jess—"

"Ernesto? Come on, you're lagging behind. The steps are too much for him—pick him up."

Matt deposited the fish bowl on the table next to

the door and leaned his head out into the hallway. "Pick who up? Jess, what's—a *dog?* You bought Ernesto a *dog?*"

"Nope," Jessica said, taking a small fat bundle of dark red fur out of Ernesto's arms and turning the puppy so that she could grasp its chin and point it toward Matt. "I bought you a dog. Well, a puppy. Isn't he gorgeous? Look at those eyes. Ernesto, give him the puddle pads and the puppy kibble. Sorry, Matt, he's not trained yet, but the guy said he's almost there. Of course, he's a setter, like Rockne, and we all know what a brain trust Rockne is, so...well, so good luck with that, huh? Look at that face, Matt. Seriously, just look at it. Isn't he *wonderful?*"

Matt dutifully looked at that face. Okay, it was a cute face, a cute dog. "Yeah. Wonderful. Jess, I can't have a dog. I forgot Mortimer, remember? I forgot Ernesto, for crying out loud."

"And Ernesto will never let you forget that one, *amigo,*" Ernesto said, grinning.

"Shut up, Ernesto. How am I supposed to take care of a puppy?"

"Not my problem, Matt. Okay, sweetheart, go to Daddy," Jessica said, pushing the puppy into his arms. "I'm the giver, not the receiver. But here's the thing, Matt. You're damn near forty years old. You've got to learn to commit at some point. You started small, with Mortimer. You moved up to Ernesto, sort of."

"He *forgot* Ernesto," Ernesto said again, and then backed up two quick paces when Matt growled at him.

"Stuff happens," Jessica said, shrugging. "Again, here's the thing, Matt. I figured you're ready to take the next step. Ergo, one cute fat puppy. Dogs are very loving and very forgiving. You can practice on him, build your confidence, and who knows, one day you might be ready to take the next step."

Matt rubbed at his face, now wet with puppy slobber. "Any suggestions on where to go in that next step?"

"Up to you," Jessica said brightly.

"Like, okay, I could maybe take that step toward you, Jess?"

"Toward *someone,* Matt," she said, her smile gone now. "And hell, yes, toward me. Take your time. Start with the dog. I'll be there when you're ready for something more."

And then, before he could put down the damn dog and take Jessica in his arms, tell her that she was right and he was wrong and that he loved her in a way that made his life a living hell when she wasn't there to drive him crazy, she was gone, running lightly down the flights of stairs to the street.

"Poor *pequeño perrito,* your daddy is a schmuck," Ernesto said, rubbing behind the puppy's ears before shaking his head at Matt. "And I came to *you* for advice about women? Look who I'm calling a schmuck, huh?" He stepped into the apartment. "Got any soda? Oh, and in case you're wondering, she's on her way to her studio to do her show. Not that you care, right? *Amigo?* Where'ya going? You going to go do the right thing? All *right!*"

"Just take care of the damn dog, genius," Matt told him as he picked up the keys to his Jeep. "And throw down some of those puppy-pad things!"

It took a while to pick out just the right bouquet— yellow roses, because he had a feeling Jessica would like yellow roses, and some of those little white flowers the girl at the flower shop called baby's breath.

Then he had to call the station to ask the name of the jewelry shop that gave discounts to city employees before he could drive to the mall and max out his credit card on a diamond he wished could be larger than it was.

By the time he got to the station, Jessica's live show was just about over, and by the time he convinced the guard that, yes, he really was a cop, and no, the flowers weren't hiding a microphone or some damn thing and was allowed on the set, she was into her wrap-up.

"…and that's it from me tonight. You can go to our Web site to read more about any of our stories, and we hope you will," Jessica said, looking straight into the camera. "So, until next week—" she began turning her head to one side in her characteristic sign-off "—this is Jessica Sunshine saying good…"

She saw Matt walking across the set toward her as Kevin at first tried to wave him off, but then quickly ordered a camera to be put on him. She saw Matt, and the yellow roses, and the open ring box he was holding out to her, and the silly grin on his face…

CHIEF DEPUTY DA Jeffrey Walingford, sitting in his brick colonial in West Chester with his wife, the television tuned to *The Sunshine Report* as it always was on Sunday nights, nearly dropped his bowl of cholesterol-lowering oat cereal as Jessica Sunshine's patented solemn sign-off suddenly turned into a wide smile that lit up the small screen.

"Louise? I think…I think that's the lieutenant I told you about the other day," he said as Matt, his face in profile, went down on one knee. "My God, he's proposing! On live television!"

"Shut up, Jeff," his wife told him. "She said yes. Did you see that? She said yes. And now they're kissing. Oh, isn't that *romantic?*"

* * * * *

Watch for Jade and Court's story in
MISCHIEF 24/7,
coming from HQN in April 2009,
as the MISCHIEF *series from bestselling*
author Kasey Michaels continues.

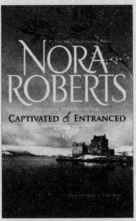

REQUEST YOUR FREE BOOKS!

2 FREE NOVELS
FROM THE ROMANCE/SUSPENSE
COLLECTION PLUS 2 FREE GIFTS!

YES! Please send me 2 FREE novels from the Romance/Suspense Collection and my 2 FREE gifts (gifts are worth about $10). After receiving them, if I don't wish to receive any more books, I can return the shipping statement marked "cancel." If I don't cancel, I will receive 4 brand-new novels every month and be billed just $5.49 per book in the U.S. or $5.99 per book in Canada, plus 25¢ shipping and handling per book plus applicable taxes, if any*. That's a savings of at least 20% off the cover price! I understand that accepting the 2 free books and gifts places me under no obligation to buy anything. I can always return a shipment and cancel at any time. Even if I never buy another book from the Reader Service, the two free books and gifts are mine to keep forever.

185 MDN EF5Y   385 MDN EF6C

Name	(PLEASE PRINT)

Address	Apt. #

City	State/Prov.	Zip/Postal Code

Signature (if under 18, a parent or guardian must sign)

Mail to **The Reader Service:**
IN U.S.A.: P.O. Box 1867, Buffalo, NY 14240-1867
IN CANADA: P.O. Box 609, Fort Erie, Ontario L2A 5X3

Not valid to current subscribers to the Romance Collection,
the Suspense Collection or the Romance/Suspense Collection.

Want to try two free books from another line?
Call 1-800-873-8635 or visit www.morefreebooks.com.

* Terms and prices subject to change without notice. N.Y. residents add applicable sales tax. Canadian residents will be charged applicable provincial taxes and GST. Offer not valid in Quebec. This offer is limited to one order per household. All orders subject to approval. Credit or debit balances in a customer's account(s) may be offset by any other outstanding balance owed by or to the customer. Please allow 4 to 6 weeks for delivery. Offer available while quantities last.

Your Privacy: Harlequin is committed to protecting your privacy. Our Privacy Policy is available online at www.eHarlequin.com or upon request from the Reader Service. From time to time we make our lists of customers available to reputable third parties who may have a product or service of interest to you. If you would prefer we not share your name and address, please check here. ☐

BOB08R

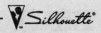

SPECIAL EDITION

FROM *NEW YORK TIMES*
BESTSELLING AUTHOR

LINDA LAEL MILLER

A Stone Creek
Christmas

Veterinarian Olivia O'Ballivan
finds the animals in Stone Creek
playing Cupid between her and
Tanner Quinn. With the whole
town helping to plan this love
connection and the holiday
season fast approaching, Tanner
and Olivia may just get everything
they want for Christmas after all!

**Available December 2008
wherever books are sold.**

KASEY MICHAELS

USA TODAY bestselling author Kasey Michaels is the author of more than ninety books. She has earned three starred reviews from *Publishers Weekly,* and has won a RITA® Award from Romance Writers of America, a *Romantic Times BOOKreviews* Career Achievement Award, Waldenbooks and Bookrak awards, and several other commendations for her writing excellence in both contemporary and historical novels. Kasey resides in Pennsylvania with her family, where she is always at work on her next book.

Readers may contact Kasey via her
Web site at KaseyMichaels.com.

We *are* romance™

www.HQNBooks.com   PHKMBIO07